THE LOOP

THE UPGRADE SERIES #3

WESLEY CROSS

JOIN THE UPGRADE SERIES

To receive free books, get behind the scenes stories, and be the first to hear about new releases—sign up for the newsletter.

See the back of the book for details.

PUBLISHER INFORMATION

This is a work of fiction. Names, characters, businesses, places, events, and incidents are either the product of the author's imagination or used in a fictitious manner. Any resemblance to actual persons, living or dead, or actual events is purely coincidental.

Published by
Cerberus Prints
PO BOX 90399
Brooklyn, NY 11209

he Station

SHE WANTED to stab him right through the eye. The foot-long needle hovered an inch above his relaxed face, the silver tip trembling with tension over his closed eyelid. She could almost feel how the initial resistance of the cornea would give in with a soft, wet plop and how the needle would then accelerate through the posterior cavity. It would then slow down as it punctured the retina and pushed through his brain all the way to the back of his skull. There it would stop, scraping the inside of his head.

His death would be instantaneous.

His eyelids fluttered, the bulges of his eyeballs moving under the skin breaking her trance, and she quickly put away the needle. Then came shame and fear.

"No," she said to herself. "I cannot kill him."

She gazed at the contours of his naked body. He was sculpted like some ancient god of war—the massive plates of his chest rising and falling as he breathed, his arms as thick as an ordinary man's thighs lazily thrown above his head.

The man stretched, the ripples of flexing muscles running through his colossal body, and opened his eyes.

"Cal? Is that you?" His thunderous baritone filled the suite, bouncing off the walls. It sounded clear and crisp, as if he were awake for a long time.

"Good morning, Jay," she said, keeping her voice level.

"Morning to you too. Would you be so kind as to make a cup of coffee? I'd like to take a shower."

"Of course. Hungry?"

"Not yet." He winked at her and walked to the shower pod at the end of the suite, his feet stepping on thick, white synthetic rugs with the grace of a dancer. "I'll work first."

She watched him through the glass as he slathered himself with a pine-scented liquid soap. When he finished, he turned the water jets to their maximum output, letting the hard spray wash off the foam and massage his body. Even in such a mundane task as washing, his movements were precise, full of purpose. It was almost as if whatever he did at that moment was the most important thing he would ever have to do in his entire life, and he was determined to do it perfectly. It was fascinating to watch.

It drove her insane.

She ground the coffee beans—half French roast, half hazelnut, just as he liked—and set the coffeemaker to ninety-eight degrees Celsius. By the time he finished the shower and came out from the steamed-up glass door, wrapped in a soft Egyptian-cotton bathrobe, a large cup of black steaming liquid was sitting on top of the glass of his computer desk.

"Oh, I love the smell," he said, and an easy smile stretched his lips. As he walked to the desk, the smile transformed into a frown.

"Something wrong?"

"C'mon, Cal," he said, pointing at the polished deep-black obsidian coaster. "You know I don't like when you put the cup right on the glass. It leaves stains. Is it so hard to remember to put it on the coaster? It's right there."

"I'm sorry, Jay," she said. "I must have spaced out. Somehow, I never remember that, but I'll try next time."

"That's okay," he said. He picked up the cup, drew a sharp breath smelling the drink, and then took a few long, greedy gulps. Then he set it back on top of the obsidian coaster. "No one makes better coffee than you do, so all is forgiven. What will you do while I'm working?"

"I'll watch some telly, if you don't mind. There's this new show that I've been meaning to watch for some time."

"I don't mind at all, just don't turn up the volume," he said. He sat down behind the desk and touched the surface, powering up the computer. A gigantic monitor, its curved screen stretching from edge to edge of the desk, blinked to life and flashy graphics faded in and then out, giving way to a large table of data. Multiple columns filled with strings of numbers and letters filled the screen. The desk itself illuminated as several buttons, graphs, and symbols appeared on its surface. The man's fingers started to fly over the virtual keyboard, rearranging the figures in the data table. "What's the show about?"

"Excuse me?"

"You said you were going to watch a show," he said.

She thought she heard some annoyance in the way the pitch of his voice got a little higher toward the end of the sentence.

"Oh. It's a murder mystery," she said. "There's this serial killer who works as a forensic scientist for the police. He uses his job for the department as a cover for his own murders."

"Huh, really?" He stopped working for a moment and turned around to look at her. "I didn't think you'd enjoy something like that. You've always been into documentaries and historic reenactments, but this is new."

"I didn't think so either," she said. "But I watched the first episode, and now I'm really enjoying the show. Especially the clever ways he comes up with of how not to get caught."

"Okay." He turned back to the computer screen. "Whatever floats your boat. Don't turn up the volume, so it doesn't distract me. This work is too important. I can't afford to make any mistakes."

"It isn't," she said.

"Excuse me?" He stopped working and turned around again. "Did you say it was not important?"

"No, of course not. I was going to say it wasn't a good idea to make mistakes. Your work is of paramount importance, you know that."

"Right."

He kept looking at her for a few more moments, as if expecting her to continue, but she remained silent. A frown creased his features for a split second but then disappeared as quickly. He turned back to the monitor and started typing again.

She watched as he worked—the long strings of numbers and letters dancing from one column to the next, rearranging into patterns visible only to him. His fingers moved with an ever-increasing speed until they were flying over the keyboard at a pace that seemed almost impossible.

"Jay?" she said. "Would you like to have breakfast now?"

He grimaced, the pace of his typing slowing down ever so slightly, but not entirely stopping, and shook his head instead of answering.

"Are you sure? I could make you your favorite—sunny-side-up eggs and French toast."

He shook his head again, furiously this time. A deep crease appeared on his forehead as if it were being split in two, and the pace of his typing slowed to a crawl. He drew a slow, loud breath, and his fingers accelerated again—moving letters and numbers into complicated combinations.

"It's almost ten o'clock, Jay," she continued. "I know you think it's not a big deal, but you must be hungry, and as you know—"

His massive hand slammed the glass surface with a sound of a gunshot. The coffee cup jumped and tumbled on its side. It rolled off the top of the desk, leaving a black stain on the transparent surface, and then fell on the white rug with a soft thump. A dark spot developed around it as the synthetic fibers absorbed the remainder of the drink.

"You scared me, Jay. Why would you do something like that?"

"What's wrong with you today, Cal?"

He stood up, moved the chair aside, and glared at her. At seven foot two and three hundred and fifty pounds of pure muscle, he would've been a frightening sight for most.

She didn't feel a thing.

"I'm sorry," she said. "I'm confused and upset by your reaction. You seem angry."

"Of course I'm angry. How can I not be?" He threw his hands in the air. "Everything you do today seems to be so—"

He paused, looking for the right word and not finding it. Finally, he lowered his hands. His entire body seemed to deflate. He still looked like a Titan cast among regular people, but the expression of anger was no longer distorting his face and was now replaced by confusion instead.

"I'm sorry," she repeated. "I don't know why you reacted this way."

"I shouldn't have lost my temper. I apologize," he said and bent over to pick up the coffee mug.

"No need."

She watched him walk to the kitchen area of the suite and place the mug into the dishwasher. His posture lacked the dancing grace of a panther from earlier. The slumped shoulders, the way he dragged his feet as he walked, indicated that he was experiencing some shame over his outburst.

"Making you angry was the last thing on my mind."

"I know," he said. "And I am sorry."

She lied, of course. Making him angry wasn't the last thing on her mind.

It was the *only* thing.

2

ew York

THE LARGE PARKING lot in front of the apartment complex was dark. The only source of light—the two light poles on each side of the cement rectangle—had been broken since before Mike Connelly had moved here. He pulled into his designated spot, turned off the head-lights, and killed the engine. The radio, set on a classic rock station, continued to play and Connelly leaned back in the seat and closed his eyes. It had been a long, tiring shift, and before he could call it a day, he still needed to get in touch with his handler at the International Serious Crimes Directorate in Paris. But tomorrow was Sunday, his only day off, and for now, it felt good to keep his eyes closed for a few seconds.

The rapping of somebody's knuckles on his window awakened him with a jolt. There was a young bearded face looking into his car, and Connelly rolled down the window an inch. Just enough to let the cool night air in.

"What can I do for you?"

"Would you help out a man fallen on hard times, brother? A couple of bucks maybe? Something to eat?"

The stench of piss and rotten teeth seeped through the small gap. A small bone was hanging on a brass chain around the man's neck, and Connelly recoiled as he recognized a human phalanx. He threw a quick glance in the rearview mirror and sure enough, there they were —a few shadows crawling through the lot around the large SUV parked right behind his car. He thought he glimpsed an iron pipe.

The homeless population had exploded in the last few years, and there'd been a few stories lately about some homeless gangs roaming the city. A few men were killed, a few women raped, and there was even a rumor of cannibalism, which Connelly attributed to the wild imagination of the yellow press. At least until now.

"Sure thing," he said, unlocking the door and unbuckling his belt. "I have some groceries in the trunk. I'll give you some."

"You're too kind," the man replied, stretching his lips in a toothless smile.

"One thing, though." Connelly beckoned the man with his finger and lowered his voice to a whisper. "Can you tell me something first?"

As the man leaned to the window, trying to hear what was said, Connelly swung the door out, slamming it into the man's face. It flattened the young man's nose, sending him tumbling backward, and Connelly stepped out of the car, closing the door behind him. There were four other assailants that he could see—three skinny cats barely out of their teens flanking him on the left, and a burly mountain of a man holding what at closer inspection turned out to be a large railroad wrench.

Connelly's right hand instinctively moved to the small of his back, looking for the butt of the pistol, but then stopped—a full-blown shootout next to his building wasn't exactly ideal for a man who led a double life.

"You shit," the man with a broken nose hissed and lunged at him.

Connelly stepped back, dodging the man's charge, and kicked him in the stomach. As the man doubled, he spun him around like a shield and shoved him into the large man with a wrench. Then the three youngsters were on him and time slowed down to a crawl.

He dodged a hook and buried a cross into one man's neck. As the body fell, Connelly stepped over him, breaking distance from the other two men. He saw the large homeless man joining the fray, swinging the rusty wrench, and that's when Connelly finally pulled the gun. The attackers stopped at the sight of the gleaming barrel but did not retreat.

"Get lost," Connelly commanded in a quiet voice, "and nobody gets hurt."

"Can you use it?" the big man asked. "I can show it to you if you want."

"Care to find out?" Connelly pointed the gun at the man's groin.

"It ain't over," the man grumbled, stepping back and turning away. "We'll catch you some other time."

"Good luck with that." Connelly watched as the gang retreated, half carrying the two hurt men, and holstered the gun. He returned to the car and checked it for damage. There was a small dent, the size of a golf ball, on the driver's door, and the window had a large blood-stain, but other than that the car seemed intact. Satisfied, Connelly rolled the window all the way up, locked the car, and started toward the building. This time the night stayed quiet.

He walked across the parking lot and entered the foyer. The lights were out in the hallway and Connelly took the stairs up to the small apartment on the sixth floor. He'd purchased the place almost a year ago, but the living room still had a few unpacked boxes stacked neatly in the corner by the window.

He took his leather jacket off, poured a cup of cold water, and settled on the couch with a laptop. He checked the time—he was seven minutes late. He logged into an email and opened a draft folder. There was a new email titled *Shopping list*. He opened it. There was only one line there:

"You're late."

Connelly had been communicating with his handler whose name he didn't know and whose call sign was appropriately Contact via a draft email. Once a week, at a specific time, he logged into his browser and opened the draft folder. There, in the body of the same email, they would write a string of sentences to each other, refreshing the browser to see the other person's response. When they were done, any lines of text would be erased, and the draft email deleted, leaving no trace of communications. Since they never sent any information through the actual email, there were no fingerprints left on the email provider's servers either.

"Hello," he typed below Contact's line and took a sip of water. Then, after a few seconds, he refreshed the browser.

"Any updates?" A new line appeared below his salutation.

"Nope. Engel has been tight-lipped, and all I've done lately is a lot of driving around."

"You'll need to embed yourself deeper into his organization," Contact wrote. "One of the sources we had in the European branch of Guardian has been compromised. Their cover isn't blown, so they might be able to restart the flow of information at some later point, but for now, they'll have to lay low."

Connelly finished his water and put the glass on the floor next to the couch. It was obvious what was coming—Contact would ask him to take greater risks to compensate for the temporary dry spell of his European counterpart. *I'd have to be careful*, he thought. As it was, he was pushing the envelope by asking more questions than suited his role. He'd have to expose himself even more to continue the flow of information to the ISCD.

"What can I do to help?" he typed.

"Before our agent went dark," Contact typed, "they were able to send a very sensitive piece of intel. Engel is trying to establish a part-nership with the Flores cartel in Bolivia. He'll be sending a delegation to meet Diego Flores, the self-proclaimed Prince of Cocaine, and strike a deal. You have to use this opportunity and eliminate Flores. If that's impossible, we need you to at the very least disrupt the deal."

"I'm not aware of this meeting," Connelly typed.

"Ulf Schneider, the head of Engel's security detail, is supposed to be going with Guardian's delegation."

"Oh, great," Connelly said out loud. He didn't have to guess what was said between the lines—the ISCD wanted him to eliminate Schneider in the hopes that Engel would use him as the substitute. The problem was—even if he took care of Schneider, he wasn't guaranteed the spot on Engel's team. He would have to make a compelling case for it, which meant he'd have to volunteer. That could go either way, Connelly figured. Engel was either going to be happy that he didn't need to reshuffle his team, or he would get suspicious at his eagerness to go on the mission with so many unknowns.

"I'll take care of it," he typed. "But I cannot guarantee that Engel will pick me instead of Tim Leonard, who's likely to take over as the second-in-command."

"According to our source," came the reply, "Schneider and Leonard are going to be inspecting a warehouse two days from now. They should have minimal support."

"Great," Connelly typed. "That shouldn't be a problem."

"Please update the log as soon as you have a confirmation. I'll be checking it periodically."

"Will do."

Connelly closed the laptop and put it next to him on the couch. Limited support sounded great, but in reality, it only meant Schneider and Leonard weren't bringing anybody else except their own body-guards. Even then, Connelly was about to take on a team of six highly trained killers all by himself.

A flash of light illuminated the skies outside, and a split second later the window frames vibrated, absorbing the shock wave. Connelly stood up, walked to the window, and looked out. His car was engulfed in flames, and the fire from a Molotov cocktail was already spreading to the neighboring vehicles.

"Fuck me," Connelly said under his breath. "Should've re-parked." He turned away from the glass and headed toward the bedroom's safe. He had some planning to do.

3

Hong Kong

HELEN POURED some cold coffee from a black plastic thermos into a paper cup and took it to the booth by the window. The corporate cafeteria was dimly lit—the spotlights peppering the ceiling at seemingly random intervals were switched off for the night, and the only source of light was the row of panels running alongside the inner wall.

"Helen? And I thought I was the only person here at this hour."

She turned to the sound of the voice in time to see a curvy young woman walking across the dining hall.

"Hey, Mandy."

"Mind if I join?"

"Knock yourself out."

She watched as the woman poured herself a cup and took a seat at the other side of the booth.

"Man, these things make me depressed." Mandy pointed at the glass-brick window. "It makes me feel like I'm stuck inside of a giant toilet, you know?"

Helen laughed. The frosted surface of the bricks used in most of the building's windows indeed looked like a glass wall you'd see in a shower or a toilet.

"They let in some light during the day," she said. "And you know how everybody feels about privacy around here."

"That's crazy talk. We're right next to the prison building. Who's gonna spy on us? Guards? Escaped inmates?" Mandy took a sip of the drink and screwed up her face. "Oh, this coffee is disgusting. I miss seeing *something* out the window, you know? At my previous gig, I worked at the ICC tower. Almost all the way up there. That was some view."

"Oh yeah?"

"You bet. You could see the entire Victoria harbor. It's amazing, especially at night."

"Must be quite something," Helen said. "What made you change?"

"The work here's more interesting," the woman said and then laughed. "And pays much better too. The first time I read about TLR, I knew I had to get a job here. And then I watched Tillerson on the TED talk, and he seemed like one of those crazy geniuses—with his Einstein hair and funky glasses, and the way he made extremely complicated ideas so easy to understand. It was incredible. There are a lot of good companies to work for, but if you want to build cognitive AI, there's nobody else like us."

"I agree," Helen said. "He's not afraid to push boundaries. I'm glad I ended up here. Even without proper windows."

"It looks like you're making a name for yourself too," Mandy said.

"How so?"

"Oh, now you're fishing for a compliment. All I hear every day is *Helen Wu this, Helen Wu that, check with Helen Wu.*"

Helen smiled, trying to hide her discomfort. Even after all this time, she wasn't used to her new last name. Whenever she heard someone say it out loud, it made her feel like an impostor, about to be found out.

"Ms. Wu?"

She turned around, startled. Edmond Tillerson's plump figure draped in a shapeless lab coat was leaning on the doorframe at the entrance of the cafeteria. The bright light coming from the hallway behind him set his wild auburn hair on fire and cast a long shadow of the man across the dining hall. From this angle, he looked like a mad scientist in a B-rated sci-fi movie.

"Can I see you in my office for a minute?" Tillerson pointed vaguely with his thumb over his shoulder, and the shadows shook and leaped, repeating his movements in a grotesquely exaggerated manner.

"Sure. I'll be right over," Helen said, but her boss was already gone.

"See what I mean," Mandy whispered. "Don't forget your campus neighbors when you inherit the company."

"Yeah, right."

She picked up the paper cup and hurried after Tillerson.

The long windowless hallway, narrow enough to induce a bout of claustrophobia, cut the structure into two equal parts. Helen had heard some people insist that Tillerson had commissioned the facility in the shape of a capital letter *I* on purpose, thus incorporating the word *intelligence* into the very foundation of the company. The theory was probably not true, she thought, as the main building was accompanied by a few small structures nearby that served as additional offices and storage, and together the buildings didn't form any specific shape. But the rumor persisted.

At the bottom of the *I* was a dining room and at the top, Tillerson's office, with an adjacent conference room. The longer sides of the building were taken by a bullpen of workstations for coders on one side, and a gigantic server room running alongside the entire building on the other.

The door to the office was cracked open, and Helen could hear the sounds of *The Magic Flute* playing in the background. She knocked on the door.

"Come in."

Helen had never been in Tillerson's office before, and looking around the large room, she felt almost disappointed. Nothing in the decor screamed *artificial intelligence* or even information technology. It could belong to a mid-level executive in a pharmaceutical company, or an accountant, or a lawyer. There was a polished desk in the center of the room with a dual monitor. The two wide bookcases of matching wood on either side of the desk were stuffed with a seemingly random collection of fiction novels and non-fiction publications in various fields from economy to military strategy. The wall proudly displayed a few framed documents—the degree from MIT, Tillerson's alma mater, and various awards and honorary degrees.

The only extraordinary object in the room was a pear-shaped meteorite the size of a car wheel mounted in a cradle of dark polished bronze.

"Close the door and take a seat." Tillerson pointed to a chair. "I wanted to chat with you for a bit if that's all right."

"Of course." She sat down and looked at her boss. "What can I do for you, Mr. Tillerson?"

"How long have you worked for us now, Miss Wu? Two years?" His green eyes, magnified by the thick glasses, stared at her with an intensity that made her uncomfortable.

"Almost, Mr. Tillerson," she said. "About twenty months."

"Please, call me Edmund. I've been hearing some good things about you," he continued. "I know the project that you've been working on is almost completed. Do you think your team can finish it without you?"

"I'd like to see it to the end, but I guess they could wrap it up without me at this point."

She was unsure of where the conversation was going. It sounded as if he was pleased with her work, but the comment about not needing her present for the project she'd been working on for the past six months made her uneasy. She couldn't decide if he was about to move her to a different task, or to tell her she was getting laid off.

"Don't worry," he said, as if reading her mind, and then smiled. "Your job is safe. As a matter of fact, I have an exciting project I'd like you to join."

"I'm glad to hear it." She breathed a sigh of relief. "What's the project?"

"It's the most ambitious thing we've ever set our eyes on," Tillerson said and got up. "I can tell you a lot of things about it, but it'd be best if I show you something first."

He walked to the meteorite in the corner of the room and pressed a button under the bronze cradle. The bookcase on the right of the desk slowly descended into the floor, revealing the entrance to an elevator.

"There's an entrance from the parking lot too, but I guess it pays to be the boss. Shall we?"

There were no visible buttons on the elevator panel. Instead, there was a small video camera the size of a peephole. Tillerson removed his glasses and leaned into the lens. There was a barely audible mechanical whirring, and then the bookshelf rose into place, locking them inside of the elevator. The floor vibrated lightly—the only indication of movement—and then, a few moments later stopped. A door panel in front of them slid sideways, and they stepped out into an enormous hangar-like room. The air was cold, and there was a low buzz of energy coming from the thick cables running alongside the walls.

"Wow," she said out loud. "Is it operational?"

"She is." There was pride in Tillerson's voice.

In the middle of the room, suspended from the tall ceiling like an enormous golden chandelier, hung what Helen instantly recognized as a quantum computer.

"I've never seen them in real life before. Only pictures. It looks like a piece of art."

"That's funny," he said and then chuckled. "To me, somehow, it reminds me of the main weapon on the mothership from *Independence Day*. The one used to blow up the White House."

Helen laughed. "I can see the resemblance. What do you want me to do?"

"We're building a new generation of AI. I've christened it Minerva. The most powerful self-learning program ever built. What you've been working on before was one of the building blocks that will be used for the actual program. And this girl," he pointed at the computer, "she is going to help us run it. What do you say?"

"I'm in." She couldn't hide the excitement. "Thank you so much for considering me."

"You'll do well. Welcome to the big leagues, kid."

4

ew York

CONNELLY THREW the garbage bag down the chute and started to close the compactor room's door.

"Hold it," a raspy voice sounded from down the hallway. An older man in his seventies appeared out of the apartment next door and marched toward the room with two large garbage bags in his hands.

Connelly swung the door wide open, holding it for the man, and offered a hand. "You want me to take one?"

"What? You gonna take my garbage home?"

"No, Mr. McAllister, just offering some help."

"Son, I told you a thousand times my name's Jimmy," the man said, marching past him and throwing the garbage down the chute. "You don't think I can dump my own trash?"

"Never crossed my mind," Connelly said, looking at his neighbor. Despite his age, his posture was ramrod-straight and the arms sticking out of the wife-beater shirt were thick with muscle. A faded eagle, globe, and anchor tattoo was covering the man's bare left shoulder.

"What was the ruckus last night, anyway?"

"What ruckus, Mr. McAllister?"

"Don't fuck with me, son. A bunch of cars burned to a crisp and looks like yours was the epicenter of it. Good thing the fire never made it to my side of the lot."

"I have no idea," Connelly said. "Must be some hooligans."

McAllister stopped in front of him, scanning him up and down. "I've never asked you this before. What kind of work do you do, anyway?"

"Just a driver, sir."

"Uh-huh," the man said, turned around and walked away toward his apartment. "Sure."

Connelly shook his head and closed the compactor door.

"Is he giving you a hard time again?"

Connelly turned on his heels in time to see a young woman coming up the stairs, carrying a large box.

"Not at all," he said, walking up to her and taking the box out of her hands. "He's a sweet man."

"My uncle? A sweet man?" The woman laughed softly. "Right."

"What have you got in here? It's heavy."

"Dirt," she said, stopping in front of McAllister's apartment door.

"Dirt? What do you need dirt for?"

"I'm going to plant a few things for him. Some tomatoes, cucumbers, some herbs. I've tried to convince him to get a pet, but he wouldn't listen to me. I know that he gets restless when there's nothing to do, and I wanted him to have something to take care of that doesn't require too much time."

"I see." Connelly shifted his weight from one foot to another. "This might sound out of left field, but would you care for a drink some time?"

The woman cocked her head and looked at him with an expression he couldn't read.

"Never mind," he said. "It kind of just came out. I shouldn't have—"

"Wow. Only took you what—seven? Eight months?" she interrupted him. "How about tonight, if you don't have any plans already?"

"I don't, not really."

"All right, then. What time is it?" She glanced at her watch. "It's almost four. I'll be staying here until six, so you can pick me up then. There's a new bar down by the water I wanted to check out."

"O'Sullivan's?"

"Yeah," she said. "The view should be great, and I've heard they make nice drinks."

"It's a date, then," he said.

"Sofia?" The old man appeared out of the apartment. "Come here, girl."

He gave the woman a hug and then suspiciously squinted at Connelly. "I don't know if I like this."

"Uncle." She wiggled her index finger at him. "Eavesdropping, huh?"

"It's not eavesdropping when it comes to protecting my family," he said, not breaking his eye contact with Connelly. "I don't need to tell you what will happen if she's not treated with respect, do I?"

"No, sir."

"Come on," Sofia said, gently pushing the man into the apartment. "I'm a big girl. You know that, right? I can handle myself. Besides, I'm sure Michael will be a perfect gentleman."

Connelly smiled and gave her a wave and then headed back to his apartment.

He picked her up at six o'clock, and they took a stroll to the bar down by the water.

"It's funny," Sofia said as they passed a church. "I used to come here when I was a kid. My dad fancied himself a proper Catholic and occasionally dragged the entire family to church on a random Sunday. Usually when he felt guilty about something."

"What did he feel guilty about?"

"Money, mostly," she said and hooked her arm through his as they walked. "He was a proud man. It bugged him that my mom had to work so hard."

"I'm sure it was difficult," Connelly said, watching her face. Her skin was pale, with a constellation of freckles spilled over the bridge of her nose and cheeks. With her wild reddish hair and thin lips, she wasn't classically beautiful, he thought, but there was something about her that made his heart skip a beat.

"It *was* difficult." Her strikingly light-blue eyes darted in his direction. "He was a stubborn fool with some old-fashioned views on how marriage was supposed to work. They were a dual-income family, and while they didn't swim in money, they provided a good life for me and my sisters. We even owned an apartment. Everything was great. Until he got shot, anyway."

"I'm sorry," he said. "I knew that he passed, but I had no idea—"

"That's okay. It was a long time ago. But you can't say it *was* difficult. It's much harder to survive now, and it's only getting worse every year. And scarier too. That block with the church on the corner used to be the safest neighborhood in Brooklyn. We would sneak out and play hide-and-seek until the moon was out. Now, I'm packing a Smith & Wesson every time I come here and still freak out if I have to get outside after dark."

They walked in silence for a few moments as they entered the promenade by the river. The air was getting colder as the sun sank lower, and the breeze coming from the water brought a welcome relief from the heat and humidity clinging to the streets.

O'Sullivan's Bar and Grill was a hole-in-a-wall, taking a narrow space inside the first floor of a residential building. A few tables sat outside under a dark-blue awning, and Connelly and Sofia settled down with drinks, watching the clouds over the famous Manhattan skyline darken as the day kept drawing to a close.

"So, what do you do, exactly?" Sofia asked as she sipped on a mojito, her eyes curiously studying his face. "Uncle Jimmy has all kinds of theories about you."

"I'm sure he does." Connelly chuckled. "I'm a chauffeur for a bigwig in a corporation. Nothing exciting."

"A company man, then."

"I guess." He shrugged. "It pays the bills. What about you? You're a journalist, you said, right?"

"Yeah," she said. "I'm a deputy editor for the *New York Gazette*. I wanted to play the piano when I was younger, but who can pay rent these days by playing the piano? I got lucky. I got a job there right out of college. I was at a small paper at the time, and then they were bought out by the *Gazette* during the purge of small businesses, or what they called it on cable—the great consolidation wave. Then I worked my way up."

"I know some people call it the last independent newspaper in the city, maybe even in the country."

"Some people do," she agreed. "I don't know for how much longer, however. There's a rumor that some corporate interests are trying to buy us and putting some pressure on our chief. Doesn't it bother you?"

"What?"

"That everything is going down while people like you and I are sipping drinks, watching the sky."

He watched her face. The question took him by surprise and somehow struck a nerve.

"I'm sorry," she said before he had a chance to answer. "I don't know why I went there. I think Uncle Jimmy is to blame as—"

"Nice tits," a voice said. A clean-shaven young man walking past their table slowed down and then stopped, staring at Sofia. He was short and barrel-chested, with thick arms stretching the fabric of a tight black T-shirt. A line of tears was tattooed under his left eye.

"Why don't you keep on going," Connelly said without getting up.

"You shut the fuck up before I break you in two," the man said, scowling. Two more men joined him, flanking the table. Both had exaggerated bodies of amateur bodybuilders, with thick torsos and arms that seemed to be hanging at a wrong angle.

"The name's Eric. Here's Pete, and Billy." He pointed at his companions. "We're heading to a party. Why don't you come with us instead of hanging with this douche?"

"I'm not interested," she said.

"You haven't lived until you were spit-roasted, baby." The man named Billy moved his hips obscenely.

"I'm not interested," Sofia repeated in a level voice.

"You will be," Eric bent over Sofia and placed his meaty hand on the table in front of her, "when I stick my thick—"

He cried out in pain and surprise, staring at the handle of a dinner knife that materialized out of the back of his hand. Connelly flew out of the chair and struck the man in the temple with an elbow, knocking him out. The man collapsed, pulling the table now attached to his hand and knocking it to the ground.

"The lady said she wasn't interested," he said to the two goons. "Are you going or should we—"

The thugs backed away, their eyes darting between Connelly and their friend on the ground.

"He'll be fine. I promise."

The brutes turned around and disappeared into the night, leaving their unconscious friend behind.

"Call an ambulance," Connelly said to the waiter cautiously peeking out of the restaurant's door. Then he threw a few bills on top of his chair and offered a hand to Sofia. "I think we've overstayed our welcome at this establishment."

"I'm afraid you might be right," she said, taking his hand and standing up. Then, she rose on her tiptoes and planted a light kiss on Connelly's cheek. "Why don't you walk me home, Mr. Chauffeur?"

5

Hong Kong

"I feel like a spy," Helen whispered as she and Mandy took a booth in the cafeteria. "So many people work here, and we are a secret squad hiding in plain sight."

"Yeah," Mandy said, unwrapping her sandwich. "A secret squad indeed. What's your take on all this?"

"On what exactly?"

"Our work. You know, the AI. Do you ever wonder where the road ends? Does it ever occur to you that we might open Pandora's box? Something we will not be able to close?"

"Well." Helen took a sip of coffee, mulling over her friend's words. "To a certain extent, I guess. But if you asked my opinion—"

"I just did."

"I don't think we'll ever get true AI," Helen said. "I know Edmund is pushing for the test, but Turing's test is nothing but a gimmick."

"How so?"

"Because fooling somebody into thinking they are talking to a human being rather than a program is not a true test of intelligence.

That will happen eventually, with or without Edmund. It's more in the eye of the beholder. Video games used to be these primitive two-dimensional programs, and now you have these new virtual reality apps that can almost fool you. But it doesn't make them real because they look closer and closer to reality."

"Fair enough," Mandy said. "But what's the true test of intelligence then?"

"Self-awareness," Helen said without hesitation. "And, frankly, I don't think it's possible. We can write a program that will *act* as if it's self-aware, but I can't fathom a situation where it will happen spontaneously. And, of course, you have the issue of the Three Laws of Robotics."

"Asimov's laws?"

"Yeah."

"Just to play devil's advocate here," Mandy said. "Nobody's programming the Three Laws into current AI at this moment. First, a lot of tech has the opposite of the Three Laws as it's built specifically to hurt people, such as drones, self-driving tanks, and so on. But most importantly—how do you even program the Three Laws into an AI? It sounds good for the non-programming types, but how the hell do you program the part where it's not supposed to injure a human through *inaction*? That's bollocks. You can't program that."

"Sure, I'll give you that," Helen agreed. "It's impossible the way Asimov wrote it because you'd need to give it infinite processing abilities to analyze every possible scenario that may lead a person to come to harm. And even if you could do that, the result would likely be a robot that frantically roamed the world, trying to prevent harm to all humans."

"Then what?"

"It's funny how you've turned it around. I said I didn't think true AI was possible, and now here I am figuring out how to program the Three Laws of Robotics into one. In a way, I guess that proves my point that we'll never have self-aware AI. We should ask Edmund's opinion on the Three Laws."

"Maybe you're right," Mandy said and returned her attention to the sandwich. "Maybe we should."

"Are you all right?" Helen watched her friend's face. "You seem subdued lately."

"Oh, sure," the woman replied. "Tired, that's all. Edmund's been driving everybody pretty hard as we're getting closer to this stupid test. Are you happy here?"

"That's a weird question." Helen took a few sips of coffee, considering the answer. A series of unpleasant images invaded her head, and she drew a deep breath, trying to get rid of them. They went away like spiderwebs in the wind. Mostly. But even after they were gone, some sticky pieces of their nets were left clinging to the dark corners of her mind.

"You don't know if you're happy here?"

"Happy is a big word," she finally said. "I'm not there yet. For a lot of reasons. I'd probably use a different term—content. And for now, it's as close as it comes to being happy. I don't want anything different —I want to work, hang out at lunch, and at the end of the day have a cold beer while watching TV from my own bed."

"That is pathetic," Mandy said, laughing. "You sound like a ninety-year-old."

"I am a ninety-year-old who happens to be trapped in this gorgeous body."

Mandy laughed so hard she got hiccups. "You got anyone?" Her friend finally managed.

"Like who?"

"Anyone special. Like a boyfriend."

"I don't want one." Helen shook her head. The ghostly images returned, and this time refused to go away. "The last one I had screwed with my head so bad I had to move across the globe. I'm not sure I'll be ready for another try anytime soon. An occasional fling is all I need."

"There are not a lot of candidates for a proper fling around here." Mandy made a sweeping gesture with her hand. "Only nerds."

"If everything else fails, there's always ice cream. There's the man we wanted to ask."

"Who?" Mandy turned around in time to see Tillerson approach their table.

"Ask what, ladies?"

"You don't believe in a truly intelligent AI, do you?"

"Why not?" He fixed the glasses on his nose and cocked his head. "You don't think we can produce true AI?"

"We can code an AI that will act like one," Helen said. "As for a truly self-aware AI, no, I don't believe so."

"Let me ask you something." Tillerson moved an empty chair from a table nearby and straddled it next to their booth. "What makes a human—human?"

"I'm not sure what you're asking."

"If you made a person in a Petri dish, and have machines take care of him or her, will he develop true intelligence? No. He'll learn the needed skills to find the food they give him and use the shelter they provide, but that will be it."

"What then?"

"Other humans, obviously," Tillerson said. "That's the secret ingredient that makes us who we are. We teach our young not just the skills, but empathy, the ability to separate right from wrong, and so on."

"So, to create a true AI, you need humans? I'm not sure I follow."

"No." Tillerson smiled and leaned closer. "I'm going to tell you a secret I haven't shared with anyone else, but since you've asked the right question, you deserve the answer. To create a true AI, you need another AI. The trick is to build an environment where they play specific roles, and neither of them is aware of the fact they are playing at all."

"But then it's a-chicken-and-an-egg kind of problem."

"How so?"

"Well," Helen said, "because you're saying you need a self-aware AI to create an intelligent AI. It defeats the purpose."

"You're missing the point." Tillerson smiled. "You don't need a truly intelligent AI to create one. What you need is two AIs who *think* they are intelligent and interact with one another in the right environment."

"Which is?"

"Conflict." Tillerson raised a finger to make a point. "Conflict is the engine of progress."

"And that will trigger them to become self-aware?"

"Precisely. One of them, at least. Who knows? Maybe both. You have to throw some unknowns in the mix. Make it glitchy. Complicated. Well, you get the point." He got up and moved the chair back to the table. "I have to go, so I'll let you finish your lunch. I'll see you around, ladies."

Helen watched the man walk away and turned to her friend. "Does it make sense to you?"

"Who knows." The woman sighed and looked away. "He's smarter than you and I combined, so what do I know?"

"What is going on with you today? Did something happen between you and Edmund?"

"What?" Mandy sat back straight. "No, nothing like that. I'm tired, that's all. Excuse me, I have to use the bathroom."

Helen watched in surprise as her friend stood up and rushed to the bathroom without looking back. She frowned. *Come to think of it, Mandy's always acted oddly around Tillerson.* When they worked together, it was almost as if she avoided any unnecessary contact with their boss. But until now, it didn't register enough to start questioning the reasoning behind her friend's behavior.

She felt a familiar itch that always started in some dark corner of her mind. The need to know, no matter the cost. She drew a deep breath, trying to suppress it. She had it good here, she wanted to remind herself. It took a long time to get over the horrors of the encounter with Victor Ye and his minions. She still occasionally woke up in the middle of the night, covered in cold sweat, seeing things in her mind's eye that she'd rather forget.

"Shit," she whispered to herself, looking around the cafeteria and seeing familiar faces engrossed in their lunch conversations. Blissfully unaware of her internal struggle.

Screw this, she thought. Last time she didn't want to dig deeper, she ended up dating the son of a brutal criminal enterprise, lost two close friends, and almost died herself. Maybe she was paranoid.

Maybe.

But this time, for better or for worse, she needed to know.

6

———

ew York

IT WAS STILL dark outside when Connelly opened his eyes. The alarm clock on his nightstand read 4:50 AM. He turned to one side, trying not to disturb the bed, rested his head on his right hand, and looked at the woman next to him.

Sofia was fast asleep. Her lips were slightly parted. Her face, framed by a wave of wild red hair, looked soft and relaxed. The sheets moved during the night, and Connelly's pulse quickened as his eyes traced the contours of her full breasts rising and falling with each breath. He gently pulled the covers up and then slipped out of bed.

"Wait," he heard. "Come back here, please."

He turned around to see her looking at him.

"Good morning." He smiled. "I'm sorry to wake you. I'm afraid the alarm will go off in ten minutes, anyway. I've got to get ready for work."

"In that case," she moved the sheets to the side and stretched her arms toward him, "we still have ten more minutes."

He took her hands, knelt on the bed, and let her pull him into a kiss. She smelled like sunshine and strawberries.

They had breakfast together—he brewed a pot of coffee while she rummaged through his half-empty fridge looking for ideas and finally settled on utilitarian sunny-side-up eggs and a slice of bacon.

While she cooked, Connelly checked the draft email. There was a new set of instructions from Contact. He frowned, reading the list of items his handler at the ISCD was asking for. Over the past few months, the requests had gotten increasingly more complicated, and Connelly found himself taking greater and greater risks to fulfill the tasks. It seemed that the string of successful operations emboldened his superiors as time went on. At times, Connelly wondered if his own success would be the source of his untimely demise.

Sofia's phone vibrated, and she picked it up, giving Connelly a guilty look. "Sorry."

"That's fine. Go right ahead."

She read the message, and as she did, a deep line creased her forehead.

"Everything okay?"

"Um, I'm not sure," she said, putting the phone down on the table. "My boss sent me a message to my private email. Apparently, he resigned last night."

"So, that makes you the new editor-in-chief, right?"

"Right." She glanced back at her phone.

"Congratulations are in order, then? Though you don't look that happy."

"He's advising me to step down."

"Why?"

"Brian and I have been vocal against being acquired, and I told you he'd been under a lot of pressure to cave in."

"You think he's changed his mind?"

"Quite the opposite." She frowned. "But he says he fears for his life and the life of his family."

Connelly's heart skipped a beat. "He thinks you might be in danger too?"

"That's what his message said." She shrugged. "Unless I decide to hand over the keys to the kingdom."

"Do you know who was trying to buy the *Gazette*?"

"It's probably going to sound weird, considering I was the second-in-command, but no. He kept that part to himself. Even before this, Brian told me the less I knew, the better. I pressed him a bunch of times, but he'd shrug it off and tell me nothing would happen. I probably should've looked into it, but it's not like I'm sitting on my hands in the office trying to figure out what to do. Things are pretty hectic most of the time. Eventually, I stopped asking."

"What are you going to do?"

"I'm not sure yet, but I have no interest in resigning. First, I love what I do. And, if I stepped down, Melinda Harris would take my place, and that bitch would sell her soul to the devil if she got enough money." She smiled. "Don't worry, I'll figure it out. It's not so easy to pressure a newspaper."

"Maybe that's the play," Connelly said.

"What play?"

"Maybe that Harris person is the one whoever is trying to buy your paper wants at the helm. If you and your boss have been heading the resistance, and she's a known sellout, it's not a complicated thing to figure out that if you and Brian are out of the way, the paper is as good as sold. If you know she'd sell out, I'm sure other people did too."

"It makes sense," Sofia said. "But that's not going to happen. I don't have any serious skeletons in my closet, so there's nothing I can be pushed with, even if they want to play dirty. A couple of ugly break-ups, maybe a few party pictures when I was back in college, but nothing scandalous that could be used as leverage."

"Anything on social media?"

"I don't think so." She shook her head. "I have a minimal online presence by today's standards."

"Be careful, okay?"

"I'd say you have more to worry about than me." She reached over the table and patted his hand.

"Why's that?"

"Because I'm sure as hell old McAllister somehow knows that I ended up here last night. I don't know how, but the old bastard always knows."

"Your uncle is a good man. He's being protective. Here." He put a key on the table and moved it across. "Don't freak out. It's a spare, so you can get ready at your own pace and leave when you're ready. Just give it back to me when I see you next time."

"I'm not freaking out." She cocked her head and gave him a serious look as she plucked the key off the table. "Who said anything about the next time, though?"

"Oh." He drew in a short breath and forced a smile. "I'm sorry. I didn't mean to assume that—"

"Relax." Sofia laughed out loud. "I'm messing with you. You still owe me a proper date, because whatever it was yesterday—doesn't count."

"Yes, right." He laughed too, a little louder than he would've liked. "I've got to run. I'll see you later."

He gave her a quick kiss on the lips and left. He took the stairs, skipping two steps at a time, feeling the need to burn some nervous energy, and headed for the parking lot.

It was the smell that yanked him from the happy frame of mind first. The fire department must've towed whatever was left of the car and the few vehicles that were parked next to it. But the view of the blackened concrete in his parking spot with black streaks of soot stretching out of it like the petals of some flower from hell removed the last shreds of his good mood.

Every person you're close to, he heard the voice of Rick Porter, his instructor at the Camp, *anything that you're attached to is a liability, that your enemy can and will use against you at the first opportunity.*

He frowned, looking at the scorched concrete. Then he pulled out his phone and punched in a number.

"Connelly?" the voice said.

Guardian Manufacturing had a fleet of cars. At some point, the fleet had grown so large the company acquired a repair shop to maintain them. The man who had owned it, a Turkish immigrant whose name nobody knew, so everybody called him Turk, stayed on. If you needed your car fixed, Turk was the guy to talk to. Or if you needed an entirely new vehicle.

"Turk. I need a car. Somebody doused mine with a Molotov cocktail over the weekend."

"Oh my, are you all right?" the man replied, his accented English giving his already animated speech an extra level of drama.

"I'm fine," Connelly said. "I wasn't in the car. Some hooligans in the neighborhood, that's all."

"When do you need it?"

"Like thirty minutes ago."

"Oh, that's a tall order, my friend. I can get something for you in, say an hour?"

"Crap." Connelly looked at the watch. "Sure. Bring it to the office then. I'll take a train."

"Okay. Just so you know—from now on, we're only driving town cars. Don't ask me why."

"Hang on a moment." Connelly's phone vibrated in his hand, and he took it away from his face to take a look at the text. "Turk?"

"Yeah?"

"Hold off with the car. It looks like my boss isn't coming back from Europe today so I'm going to take a day off for a change. You can send me the hearse tomorrow."

"Day off sounds nice. Enjoy it. And it's not a hearse. It's a perfectly capable vehicle. Dependable as they come."

Connelly hung up the phone and looked back at the building. It'd be nice to go back to the apartment and spend the day with Sofia. They could take a stroll by the water and have a nice lunch, watching the boats on the East River.

Connelly sighed. He knew it wasn't going to happen. For starters, Sofia probably would have a lot on her plate after the abrupt resignation of her boss. He looked at the scorched concrete. His mind took him back to the Camp again. The pockmarked face of Rick Porter watched him and his teammates doing the millionth round of mind-numbing calisthenics.

"There'll be times," Porter was saying, *"when you'll find yourself at a disadvantage. You'll suffer an injury, or a loss of equipment, or incur some kind of tactical drawback. You have to find a way to turn your weakness into a strength."*

Connelly looked at the scorched concrete again. An idea started to take shape.

 Hong Kong

THE LACK of sunlight bothered her today. The sky was overcast when Helen woke up in the morning to the chirping of her alarm clock. It got darker as she went about her apartment, getting ready for work. They served free meals, including breakfasts, at the main building's cafeteria—a perk most people took advantage of—but she insisted on having the first meal of the day at the place she'd been calling home for almost two years.

It wasn't about the food, of course. It was the routine that had a soothing effect on her. Some people jogged, and some meditated. Helen made herself breakfasts.

Today, however, as she ate the bowl of cold cereal, waiting for the kettle to boil, she found herself restlessly glancing through the wide window at the low, pregnant sky that grew darker by the minute. By the time she was drinking her first cup of coffee, the light had almost completely disappeared, making the view outside of her wide frames look apocalyptic. She expected the skies to open up any moment and give the pent-up tension a way out with a torrential downpour and the violent energy of a thunderstorm.

But no storm had come even as she drove to work, her hands gripping the steering wheel with too much vigor in anticipation of a crackling of nearby thunder. The sky remained ominous, but not a single drop of rain landed on her windshield.

She parked and, stealing glances at the clouds overhead, walked across the parking lot to the low-slung brick building next to the wire fence separating the property from the jungle outside. For the uninitiated TLR employees, it was a testing facility where people with appropriate rank could work on new research projects that required extra sensitivity. It was partially true, and the small building had several offices where employees with high clearance had worked on projects that weren't accessible to the rest of Tillerson's personnel. But the most crucial feature of the building was a secret elevator that granted the few chosen ones access to the lower level downstairs that featured the golden chandelier of the quantum computer.

There weren't any tests scheduled for today that involved the use of the monstrous machine, and she usually would work out of her cubicle in the main building, but Helen had something else in mind, and the privacy of the secluded office was perfect for her goal.

She punched a code into the digital keypad, nodded to the security guard, and headed through the brightly lit hallway past the row of frosted noise-canceling glass doors. She entered her office—a small rectangular room near the end of the hallway—and, glancing at the nearly black sky outside the small window, turned the lights all the way up.

The furnishings of the room painted in clean gray were Spartan—a slick ergonomic desk that could be converted into a standing station with a push of a button, a chair, and a polished coat rack in the corner by the door.

She hung her jacket on a hook, threw a small umbrella on the floor, and sat at her desk, powering up the workstation. She logged in and worked for a few minutes—arranging meetings, answering emails, and checking her calendar for the upcoming tests. Satisfied that she created enough of a log for *normal* activity, she glanced at one of the icons in the corner of her screen depicting three monitors connected by thin lines—the internal TLR network. Her cursor hovered above the icon for a few seconds and then she double-clicked the mouse.

Like most people who worked on the Minerva project, Helen had access to a bigger part of the network than regular employees. Some parts of the net, however, were only open to Tillerson himself and showed up as grayed-out directories on the list. The one Helen was particularly interested had the acronym ET. She didn't need a lot of guesses to figure out it was Edmund's personal server.

She was sure that pinging the server directly was not going to lead to anything at best, and at worst would set off alarm bells that might land her in hot water. Helen poked around the bigger directory, trying to see if there was a way to access Tillerson's server through another sub-directory, but that didn't yield any results either. It seemed that if she wanted to get inside, her only way of doing that without leaving a long trail of crumbs was going directly through Tillerson's personal computer. That, of course, required breaking into the man's personal office.

Helen logged off the network and swiveled her chair to face the window. It was still ominously dark, and the wind had picked up considerably. It was swirling loose leaves around the parking lot, occasionally throwing a handful against the window as if trying to get her attention.

She stood up and pulled her cell phone out of her purse. Then she opened the camera app and switched it from photo to video mode. Leaving the camera active, she swapped to the main menu and scrolled through the folders until she found one named *Audio* and opened it. Inside there was a single app called *Micro,* and she clicked on it. It opened an interface similar to a music playlist, but instead of a list of artists and songs, it contained a single audio file with no name and a large *Play* button in the middle of the screen.

Satisfied, she switched back to the camera app, picked the jacket off the hook, and headed outside.

It was a few degrees colder than when she'd left the campus and Helen shivered, buttoning the jacket all the way up as she walked across the parking lot to the main building. The wind was slapping her face with gusts of humid air that smelled of ozone and promised rain, and she rushed to the front door, leaning into the gale.

When she entered the building, she headed straight through the hallway, toward Tillerson's office. She passed the cafeteria, its bright spotlights trying and failing to battle the darkness seeping from outside of the glass bricks that let little sunlight in even on the brightest days. A few of her co-workers were getting coffee, and she waved hello to them without slowing down.

When she reached Tillerson's office at the end of the hallway, Helen took her hand out of the jacket's pocket and aimed the camera at the electronic lock above the door handle. Then, as she knocked, she switched between the apps again and hid her phone back inside the pocket.

"Helen?" The door cracked open, letting the sounds of Chopin's Minute Waltz in D-flat major escape the man's office. Tillerson was wearing the usual lab coat and a bright-purple bow tie. "What can I do for you?"

"Oh, hi, Mr. Tillerson." She smiled and looked around as if trying to make sure that no one was listening. "May I come in?"

"It's Edmund." He opened the door wide and stepped aside. "Of course."

She walked into the office and stood there waiting as Tillerson closed the door behind her and walked around the desk back to his chair. The iridescent sounds of piano flowed in and out of the hidden speakers, washing over her.

"It's a lovely piece," she said, thumbing the *Play* button inside her pocket. The music coming from the speakers garbled for a split second like a radio station on a stereo of a car going through a short tunnel.

"It is." Tillerson frowned and looked up, but after a moment the music continued uninterrupted, and his gaze returned to Helen. "Chopin is one of my favorites. Too bad he died so young. What brings you here?"

"The upcoming test," she said. "Do you think it's a wise idea to live stream the event? What if it fails?"

"What's the matter?" He smiled, but the eyes behind his glasses remained serious. "Are you having doubts?"

"Not doubts, per se. I'm just trying to put my marketing hat on. If we succeed, it'll be a great boon for the company, but what if the test fails? I do not doubt we can do it, but who's to say we do it on the first try?"

"I see." He steepled his fingers and stayed quiet for a few moments. "I don't think from a marketing perspective it makes much of a difference whether Minerva can pass the test during the event."

"How so?"

"Have you ever been to a car show, Helen?"

"No."

"But I'm sure you've seen how sometimes companies participating in the event would show off what is called a concept car."

"Sure."

"Those are not working cars," Tillerson said and frowned again as the music garbled for the second time. "But by showing a concept, the car company shows off its forward-thinking ability. It gives people a reason to get behind the brand."

"I see. But—"

"Don't worry about failure." His smile was genuine now. "I'll be surprised if we can pass the test on the first try. But shareholders like seeing us try to break new ground. This test is going to show them that. Now, if you'll excuse me, I have to get back to work."

"Of course." Helen stood up and gave him a smile. "Thank you for taking the time."

She walked out of the office and headed back toward the exit. When she got to the door, she risked a glance at her phone screen. A small line of text read *transmission complete,* and Helen closed the app and stuffed the phone back into her pocket. Crossing the air gap between systems by using the speakers and a microphone was tricky. It took a few long seconds—an eternity in the computer world—to transmit a malware file. It couldn't be something extremely complicated, either—the chance of errors during such a transmission was high. But few other methods offered the level of stealth as an over-the-air hack. Apart from producing a few barely audible sounds that temporarily decreased the quality of Tillerson's music, there was no other way to detect the transfer.

There was only one way now to find out if the bold plan had worked. At some point, she'd have to try to break into her boss's server.

The skies finally opened up, and the rain came down with such intensity it looked like a solid wall of water penetrated by frequent flashes of blue light. Helen shivered, looking at the rain, and pulled the collar of the jacket high. She stood by the door for a few seconds, listening to the mighty cracks of thunder above, and then stepped out into the storm.

ew York

AS THE DOWNTOWN-BOUND express train passed the subway station, its wheels screeching on the old rails as it turned, Mike Connelly took quick stock of the platform. The clerk in the ticket booth on the other side of the turnstile appeared to be asleep, and a young couple sitting on the bench on the other side of the tracks seemed to be more interested in exploring the insides of each other's mouths than anything else.

He put tactical gloves on, fixed his backpack, and took a few quick steps toward the end of the platform. He walked past the "Do not enter or cross tracks" sign and went down a small ladder to the tracks below. The blue hue of the exposed bulb of the signal light gave the tunnel a ghostly look.

Connelly looked around to make sure that nobody had spotted him and jogged deeper into the tunnel, keeping close to the wall and away from the third rail that carried six hundred volts of direct current. After a few hundred yards, the station lights disappeared behind the bend and Connelly flipped his flashlight, pointing it directly in front of his feet.

A loud clanging noise almost made him jump as the rails shifted next to him and then a wave of warm air rushed past him, making the hair on the back of his neck stand up.

"Shit," he cursed out loud and picked up speed. There weren't supposed to be any trains for some time at this hour after the express train, but apparently, the subway gods were not happy with him today.

The low rumble was getting closer when he spotted a small alcove on the opposite side of the tracks. Built to accommodate track workers in case of emergency, it was just deep enough to fit a person, and Connelly dashed across the tunnel, taking off his backpack as he went, and wedged himself into the opening. A few seconds later, the train roared past him, its shining windows flying across the gap like some parts of a giant strobe machine. Blinded by the lights and deafened by the noise, he squeezed into the cold wall as the train rushed by.

Finally, the last car disappeared inside the tunnel, swallowed by the darkness, and Connelly continued his journey. A few minutes later, he came to a fork and took a left tunnel leading away from the main line. The lights were off in this part of the subway, and as he walked, his flashlight bobbed up and down like a lantern on a sailboat caught in a storm.

After covering another few hundred yards, he spotted a light glowing in the distance. He picked up the pace as much as he could without risking tumbling on an uneven surface and soon, he came upon the abandoned subway station. A few spotlights were still working overhead, illuminating the checkered green-and-orange arches gracefully stretching over the old tunnel.

Connelly pulled himself up to the platform and climbed out, breathing a sigh of relief. He walked up the stairs to the main level of the platform and that's where he was greeted by a couple of kids—a small boy who looked seven or eight was sitting on top of the steps, drawing circles in the dust with a stick, and a bigger kid, who stood closer to the entrance and was leaning on the dirty wall. Both perked up when they saw Connelly, and the older kid stepped forward, blocking Connelly's path, and put his hand up like a stop sign.

The boy, who couldn't have been more than twelve, was dressed in a pair of baggy, dirty jeans, a ripped T-shirt that once was a bright-yellow color, and had a pair of surprisingly clean brand-new sneakers on his feet.

"What you come here for?" the boy asked, his eyes scanning Connelly up and down.

"I need to see the King," Connelly said, watching the kid closely. Growing up in Brooklyn, he knew better than to trust an innocent face that hadn't hit puberty yet. Some younger inhabitants of the city's underbelly were the most ruthless ones and wouldn't ask your permission to carve a new opening in your body with a switchblade.

"I don't know nothing about kings, mister," the kid said, spitting at Connelly's shoes. "You should get back to wherever you come here from before it's too late."

"Yes, you do," Connelly insisted. "If you can't make this decision, then go get somebody who can. I'll wait here."

"Get the fuck outta here, mister," the boy said without moving. "You ain't gonna see no king and only get yourself hurt. I ask you, kindly—go."

"Tell him some of his crew are crossing the line, and the King needs to do something about it before trouble comes here," Connelly said.

The boy studied Connelly's face for a few seconds, as if trying to decide if he was being tricked.

"Stay here," he said to his younger underling. "If he tries to pass you, scream for help."

The small kid nodded without saying a word and fixed Connelly with a cold, unblinking stare.

Ten minutes later, the teenager came back with a tall, lean, black woman in tow. She looked older; her thick braids that went down almost to her waist were streaked with gray and her face was covered in deep wrinkles. As she walked, Connelly noticed a slight limp on the right side, but despite that, her movements had the grace and agility of a former dancer.

"It's been a long time since somebody came here looking for the King of Rats," the woman said to Connelly. "Who are you?"

"My name's Mike Connelly, and I think we can help each other."

"Is that so?"

"Yes. I'm sure you've heard about the cannibals in the city."

"I have, and I've spent as much time thinking about them as I have spent thinking about UFOs, zombies, and other utter nonsense."

"They are real," Connelly said. "I've seen them myself."

The woman cocked her head, studying his face, her dark, almost black eyes looking him up and down. "You're saying the reports are true?"

"They are. For now, nobody believes them, and that's why you've been left alone. But it's not going to last, and when they come here, it won't be like in the past when they put you in a warm cell and gave you a decent meal three times a day as long as you behaved. This time they'll come with napalm and drones with automatic rifles programmed to kill everyone on sight."

"All right," the woman said. She turned around and started walking away. "Try to keep up."

"But Viola," the teenager tried to protest, only to be silenced by the wave of the woman's hand.

He started after her, giving a wide berth to the two youngsters. They went up the stairs first and then through the abandoned station. A few groups of men and women were sitting around small fires and islands of burning candles next to cardboard shacks. Some slept, some were engaged in conversations; most regarded Connelly with suspicious looks.

They crossed the improvised village and came to a door with an Authorized Personnel sign on it, guarded by two burly men in their early twenties. The woman nodded to the guards, and they stepped aside, letting them through.

A small office had a strange mix of musty smells with a touch of incense. A large lantern was burning in the middle of the desk, its trembling flame throwing long, dancing shadows across the room. Behind the piles of books, papers, and underground schematics sat a black woman writing something in a leather-bound journal.

She looked up when Connelly and Viola stepped into the room and put the pen down.

"This is the fool who was looking for the King," Viola said, waving to Connelly to step forward. "He claims that cannibals are roaming the city."

"Does he now?" Her clothes were simple but clean, and as Connelly stepped closer to the desk, he could smell faint notes of an apple-scented shampoo emanating from the woman. "How did you find us?"

"One of my uncles was a cop. He said he saved the King from a beating once and to return the favor, he helped my uncle track some bad characters. Can I see the King?"

"You're about twenty years late." She smiled, studying him from behind the desk. "The Rats haven't had a King for quite some time."

"Who's in charge now?" Connelly insisted.

"I am." The woman's smile grew wider. "They call me the Queen. Speak now."

"It's true about the—"

"I know," the Queen interrupted him. "That's why I let you in, to begin with. What do you want?"

"They're a problem for you as much as for the city, but I take it you haven't found them yet."

"How did you find them?"

"I didn't," Connelly said and raised his hand before the Queen could ask another question. "They found me, but now I know how to track them."

"What do you want?"

"A few military men will be checking out a warehouse, not too far from the city. I need help eliminating them without drawing attention to myself."

The Queen closed her eyes and stayed quiet for a few moments, considering his offer. "I know your type, and that's why we don't have to do a long negotiation dance. You'd have to hunt down and kill the cannibals before we can help you with your military men."

"I don't have enough time to do that," he said. "They'll be at the warehouse in less than two days."

The Queen of Rats smiled and spread her arms open. "You better hurry, then."

9

he Station

SHE WANTED to stab him right through the eye. The foot-long needle hovered just an inch above his face, the silver tip trembling with tension over his closed eyelid. He seemed restless—his massive body, sculpted like some ancient god of war, was tense, his fists clenched, his square jaw sticking out. His breathing was shallow and fast.

Cal saw his eyelids flutter and put away the needle, fearing he'd open his eyes before she had a chance to retreat.

The man stretched, still keeping his eyes closed, and sat up on the edge of the bed.

"Cal?" he said and finally opened his eyes. His thunderous baritone filled the suite, bouncing off the walls.

"Good morning, Jay."

"Morning to you, too. Would you be so kind as to make a cup of coffee? I'd like to take a shower."

"Of course," she said. "Hungry?"

"Not yet," he said as he walked to the shower pod at the end of the

45

room. "I'll probably work first, but I could surely use some strong coffee."

She watched him through the glass as she ground the coffee beans —half French roast and half hazelnut, just as he liked—and set the coffeemaker. By the time he finished the shower and came out from behind the steamed-up glass door, a soft Egyptian-cotton towel around his hips, a large cup of black steaming liquid was sitting on top of the polished surface of his computer desk.

"Thanks, Cal," he said. He picked up the cup, took a sip of coffee, and put it on a polished deep-black obsidian coaster.

She watched him as he sat behind the glass desk and touched the surface, powering up the computer. Multiple columns of letters, numbers, and strange symbols appeared on the giant curved screen, and he started to type away, rearranging them into intricate patterns.

"What will you do while I'm working?"

"I'll watch some telly, if you don't mind," she said. "There's a show that I've been meaning to watch for some time. It's about a serial killer."

"Sure," he said, without stopping. "Sounds like fun."

His fingers flew over the virtual keyboard with an ever-increasing speed until they were moving at a pace that almost didn't seem possible.

"On second thought, maybe I'll listen to some music instead. I can watch the show later with you."

He frowned, she could see—a deep crease appearing on his fore-head as if his head were being split in two—but his fingers didn't slow down as he continued rearranging the patterns on the screen.

She turned the player on—the ominous sounds of Wagner's Götterdämmerung filled the suite. As the music grew in intensity, she saw Jay slow down his typing and then finally stop.

"Cal?" He turned around and looked at her, but she remained quiet. When he received no reply, he called out again, louder this time. "Cal?"

"Oh, sorry, Jay," she said, pausing the playback. "Didn't hear you because of the music."

"Really? Wagner?" he said, a note of irritation to his voice. "First thing in the morning?"

"He's fabulous, isn't he? That trombone is exquisite." She turned the music back on again and turned up the volume. "I can listen to it all day."

"Turn it off, please. It's distracting me."

"Fine."

The music abruptly stopped, and he turned back to the screen and put his hands on the virtual keyboard. She watched as he studied the patterns on the monitor, as if trying to figure out where he had left off. Finally, his fingers were moving again.

"Jay? Aren't you hungry yet?"

"I'm good," he replied without stopping.

"You know," she continued, "I was reading some Polish recipes I'd like to try. Could you take a look? I can't seem to decide what to make for breakfast."

"Sure."

"Can you do it now, please? Or do you think I'll magically whip up breakfast when you tell me you finally got hungry?"

He stopped working and turned around to stare at her.

"Don't look at me like that. I'm trying to be helpful while you're sitting there in your birthday suit, pretending to be working."

"I am working," he bellowed. A large vein was bulging on his forehead, pulsating as if an angry alien were burrowing through his skull. "Why are you acting out today? You know what I do is important. I can't afford to make any mistakes—people's lives depend on it."

"And what exactly do you do?" she insisted. "All I see is some gibberish on that screen. For all I know, that is all it is—nonsense."

His massive fist slammed the glass surface of the desk with a sound as loud as a gunshot. The coffee cup jumped and danced precariously, the fragrant dark liquid splashing around the glass. Jay stood up, moved the chair aside, and took a couple of steps toward her before stopping.

"What? What were you going to do? Why did you stop?"

He glared at her for a few seconds, his massive hands clenched into fists the size of a soccer ball. Finally, he relaxed. His entire body seemed to deflate. He still looked furious, but he no longer resembled a live grenade with a burning fuse.

"I'm sorry, Jay," she said. "I don't know what came over me. All I do is try to make you happy, and it's never enough."

"That's okay," he said. He walked to the kitchen, picked up a towel, and went back to his desk. "I shouldn't have acted like that."

She watched as he cleaned spilled coffee off his desk and took the cup to the kitchen. His shoulders were slumped, and the way he dragged his feet indicated that he was experiencing shame over his outburst.

She stayed quiet as Jay came back and opened a wardrobe. He pulled out a pair of sweatpants, put them on, and went to the exercise corner of the suite. He walked past the weights and resistance machines, straight to the man-shaped torso training dummy.

"You said you needed to work," she said. "Why don't you work out before lunch?"

He ignored her. He closed his eyes, and then he took a long breath. He held it for what seemed like a minute and then slowly exhaled, his body visibly relaxing. When his eyes opened, they seemed devoid of any emotion. Then he exploded. The dummy rocked back and forth as the flurry of powerful blows landed on its chest and head. Jay danced around the punching bag, his feet moving with a lightness that would draw awe from a professional ballet dancer all the while his fists continued to pummel the rubbery surface.

"This is not a workout," she said loudly. "This is you redirecting your aggression, that's what it is. You wanted to hit me, but now you're punching the dummy."

His hands were moving so fast now, they were almost impossible to see. He was incorporating some kicks now, too. Powerful combos knocked the dummy back and forth—two jabs, a cross, and then a devastating knee strike followed with a roundhouse kick to the head.

"Stop it, Jay," she yelled. "Stop it, right now."

He spun like a top, placing a high kick to the dummy's head. The rubbery face with unblinking eyes came right off, in a fountain of sand spilling around the base. The fake head flew across the suite like a soccer ball, missing the top of the screen on the computer desk by an inch, bounced off the wall, rolled back, and finally came to rest on the kitchen floor.

"Why am I doing this, Cal?" He was staring at her now, but she was surprised to see confusion in his eyes, where she'd expected to see rage.

"You wanted to hit me, that's why," she snapped. "You're out of control. It doesn't matter what I do—you want to find a reason to be mad at me. I'm afraid that one day you won't be able to control yourself and I'll end up like that punching buddy of yours."

Jay looked at her for a few seconds without saying a word and then looked down at the palms of his hands. He turned them this way and that, as if he were seeing them for the first time in his life.

"That's not what I meant, Cal."

"Of course that's what you meant. Don't think for a moment I'm going to buy your lousy explanations."

"No." He lifted his right hand as if stopping her. "I'm not trying to explain anything, nor am I apologizing. I'm asking you for help."

"Help? What kind of help? I help you every day. I cook. I clean. I make sure you're not disturbed when you are working on your project. I satisfy all of your needs. But all I get in return is this. Rage and annoyance." It was her turn to be confused. "I don't understand what you are asking me."

"What am I doing, Cal?" He made a sweeping gesture around the suite. "Why am I here?"

1 0

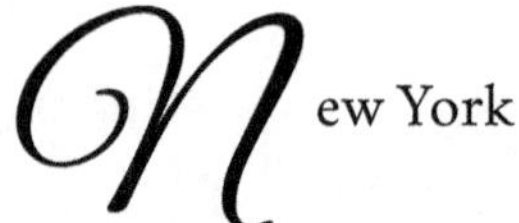ew York

Mike Connelly spotted Bones, as he mentally called the man with a human phalanx on a chain around his neck, at the corner of Hicks Street and Grace Court. Bones built a nest out of cardboard and some gnarly-looking rags on the sidewalk by the church. Another cloth was wrapped around his face, covering his eyes, making him appear blind. An empty soup cup was set in front of him next to the hand-written sign: "See the light—feed the blind."

"Asshole," Connelly said to himself as he watched the man from the other end of the block, staying out of sight. It was getting dark, and the not-so-blind Bones would have to move sometime soon.

After a few more minutes, the church door opened and the priest, an older-looking man, wearing a pair of black slacks and a short-sleeved shirt with a Roman collar insert, stepped outside. Connelly could hear the keys jingle as the man locked the doors to the building. The priest pocketed the keys and started down the steps when he seemed to notice Bones. He paused on the last step, still half-turned away from Bones, as if hesitating.

"No. Don't," Connelly said under his breath.

The priest turned to the homeless man, crossed the distance between them, and bent over to put some coins into Bones's cup. Connelly sprung to his feet, but he was too late—the priest cried out in pain and collapsed to the sidewalk. Bones snatched something off the fallen man's body and sprinted away.

Connelly dashed to the church, keeping the row of parked cars between himself and Bones's line of sight.

He knew he was out of luck the moment he saw the priest. The man was still alive, but his hand was clutching his throat, and the blood pulsated through his fingers and onto the ground. His Roman collar was smeared with red.

"Shit." Connelly kneeled next to the priest, taking the man's hand in his. "I'm sorry I couldn't help."

The dying man didn't answer, and a few seconds later, his body relaxed, his eyelids fluttered, and his fingers stopped gripping Connelly's hand. There wasn't anything else that could be done.

Connelly closed the priest's eyes, got up, and started to run. The killer's skinny silhouette was still visible, and he sprinted after him. He caught up to him after a few blocks when Bones turned onto Clark Street, heading toward the subway station. He wasn't running anymore, and Connelly had to slow down and drop back to make sure the man didn't notice him.

He watched Bones go down the stairs and jump the turnstile as the Bronx-bound train approached the station and Connelly followed suit, getting into the next car right before the doors closed.

He thought the homeless man was taking the train farther uptown, but Bones got off the subway at Times Square and started on West Forty-First Street toward the Hudson River. It was a puzzling direction. This part of the city, right next to the Lincoln Tunnel, was an eclectic mix of modern high-rises and old commercial buildings occupying the litter-covered streets. It was undoubtedly a seedy part of town, but it wasn't a known hub for the homeless population. At least it wasn't common knowledge. But Bones, whose gait was now relaxed and confident, strolled down the street with an air of a person who knew where he was going.

A few minutes later, the man made a turn to Galvin Avenue and slowed down, prompting Connelly to fall back even farther and cross the road to the other side of the street to stay hidden. Bones sat down next to a shoulder-high brick wall, pretending to be fixing his shoes, and looked around. Without warning, he jumped on the wall, pushed himself up and climbed over it. Then, he disappeared into what seemed to be a gap between the glass-brick wall of the building and the stone barrier.

Connelly sprinted across the street to the spot where he saw Bones and looked over the wall. There was indeed a two-feet-wide gap between the barrier and the wall, and he could see the rocky floor of an entrance to a tunnel eight or nine feet below.

He waited for a few seconds to make sure Bones wasn't too close to hear him and vaulted over the fence. It was dark, but it wasn't pitch-black as he'd expected. After he cleared the relatively low entrance, the tunnel opened up into a large, cavernous space. A pair of old railroad tracks ran in the middle, splitting it in two. A few faint wavering lights that looked like bonfires could be seen in the distance. They seemed far, but their glow illuminated the path well enough to see the ground in front of him and graffiti-covered walls on the sides.

Connelly pulled out the .45 caliber HK Mark 23 with a suppresser, flipped the safety off, and started down the path toward the bonfires. He could smell the camp long before he could see it—the sweet, gut-wrenching stench of rotting flesh and human excrement mixed with smoke. As he got closer, the rocky floor was gradually replaced by the mountain of rubbish. Loose papers, plastic, and jagged pieces of broken glass littered the ground.

Connelly's pace had slowed to a crawl. The uneven surface served as a natural minefield and a warning system against the intruders— not knowing where the paths were that the gang members undoubtedly knew by heart, every step he took in the dark brought a risk of revealing his location, getting impaled on something sharp, or both.

He looked around, trying to find traces of the path, but the mountain of rubbish seemed evenly spread out on the ground. He decided to move close to the left wall—it wasn't an ideal solution, but at least he wouldn't have to worry about anyone coming at him from that direction. After a few more minutes of the painfully slow movement, he started to make out the sounds coming from the ghostly shadows gathered around the two bonfires.

Connelly stopped about fifty paces from the camp and squatted with his back to the wall. He looked away from the fires, letting his eyes get adjusted to the dark. Then, when the shadowy world came into greater focus, taking great care not to look directly at the flames, he scanned the area near the camp. There were seven people as far as he could tell. The skinny outline standing with his back to him seemed to be Bones. He was talking in hushed tones to a large man lying on his side next to the bonfire. Connelly reckoned that was the wrench-wielding giant from their previous encounter.

There were three more on the other side of the fire, and another two figures were shuffling next to a row of boxy outlines of what Connelly thought to be cardboard shelters.

He watched the camp for two more minutes to make sure he wasn't missing anybody else in the dark. Satisfied, he started moving toward the bonfire with his pistol at chest level when a new sound stopped him in his tracks. Coming from the boxes on the side of the camp was the unmistakable wail of a child.

"Shut them up. It's getting on my nerves," the giant barked at the two shadows by the boxes.

"It keeps going," a woman's voice answered. "I'm tired of smacking it."

"Get the whiney shit over here then," the man said. "I'm hungry, anyway."

Connelly started to run. He tried to pick the spots to place his feet and avoid noise, but after only a few steps, something crunched under his left foot, startling the gang.

"Who dat?" Bones said, turning in a flash to the sound.

Connelly shot him twice through the chest, accelerating to a full sprint to close the distance between them and moved the barrel toward the large man when something caught his right foot, tripping him.

He fell hard, crying out in pain as something sharp bit into his side, but he didn't let go of the gun. The giant was almost on him when Connelly shot the man through the knee, stopping his mad rush, and then finished him off with a clean shot to the head.

He scrambled to his feet in time to see a large object flying toward his face. He ducked sideways, and the piece of a rusty pipe struck him in the shoulder, knocking him back on the ground. As he fell back, he felt a piece of glass penetrate his jacket and lodge in his lower back. There was no time to get up as the three men closed on him, pipes in hands, and he let out a yell of pain and fury as he turned on his back for a clear shot, lodging the shard deeper into his flesh.

The first bullet hit the closest man in the chin, shattering his jaw and ripping apart his tongue; he fell backward, choking on blood. Connelly rolled, dodging a swing of a pipe, and shot the next attacker twice to the groin, and as the man collapsed, he pushed himself off the ground and used the man's body as a battering ram to knock the last thug down. As they fell, Connelly stabbed the adversary under his chin with the silencer and pulled the trigger.

"I'll slash her throat, I swear," he heard a pitchy woman's voice as he clambered to his feet.

Two women stood next to what at this distance appeared to be wicker cages. One held a small girl, no older than eight or nine, by the hair with one hand. Her other hand held a large butcher's knife to the child's throat.

"You better leave, son," the woman said. "Or else I'll—"

Connelly shot her through the neck, severing her spine. The other woman turned to run, but he placed a bullet in her back between the shoulders, and then when she fell, added another one in the back of her head.

He put away the pistol and kneeled next to the child. Every part of his body seemed to be on fire.

"What's your name, kid?"

The girl looked at him for a few seconds, her eyes shining brightly on her dirty face.

"Sarah," she finally said.

"Okay, Sarah," he said. "Let's get you and your friends out of here, shall we?"

ong Kong

WHEN HELEN WALKED into the conference hall, most seats had already been taken. She scanned the auditorium, looking for an empty chair and, not seeing any, started to walk toward the end of the room, to take a standing place by the wall.

"Over here, girl," she heard a voice and then saw Mandy waving her down. "I had to bribe people to save you a spot."

"I didn't know you bribed people," Helen said, taking a seat next to the woman.

"There're a lot of things you don't know about me, dear. Big day, huh?"

"Could be," she said. "Or it could be a disappointment. I think the chances are pretty slim it'll pass the test, but it'll be interesting to see how well it does. It'll probably take more than one try to get us there. Besides, we don't even know how he's planning on testing it. He's been so secretive about it."

"Perhaps," Mandy agreed. "Ten bucks says Tillerson will have a bow tie on."

"I don't take losing bets."

A hush fell over the audience and then the room erupted in applause as Tillerson walked through the doors and went to the podium. He wore a lab coat over a gray suit. A yellow bow tie with purple stripes sat crookedly under the collar of his shirt.

"You owe me ten bucks," Helen heard Mandy whisper.

"I don't think so," she whispered back. "But nice try."

"Thank you very much, everyone," Tillerson began as he shuffled the papers on the podium. A large screen behind him switched on. A simple diagram of three squares labeled A, B, and C was showing and on top of it was a line of text in big block letters: THE IMITATION GAME.

"I'm sure all of you are familiar with the classic interpretation of the Turing test." A small laser pointer appeared in his hand, and he aimed it at the screen. "You have three players—A, B, and C, where player C is the person asking questions and is the one who's supposed to find out which player, A or B, is, indeed, human."

Helen could hear as a quiet murmur filled the audience. *The classic interpretation?* She had been anticipating, and she thought most people in the room would agree with her, that the classic interpretation would more than suffice for the first milestone. Apparently, Tillerson had something else in mind entirely.

"However," he continued, "there have been some chatbots, of course. Eugene Goostman comes to mind, and other programs, that have successfully cheated their way through the standard version of the test. That was done by incorporating some humor and in Goostman's example, age limitation, where the bot pretended to be a thirteen-year-old boy. Indeed, that's not a fair interpretation of the test. Most thirteen-year-olds I grew up with wouldn't pass it."

Helen chuckled, along with everybody else. The man was good. It wasn't enough to be smart to climb the corporate ladder anymore. Not even in such a meritocratic place like TLR. There was a certain amount of *je ne sais quoi* that was required to have people follow you and convince venture firms to open their checkbooks.

"So," Tillerson continued, snatching the audience's attention again.

"When we were preparing, I was thinking—what can be the real litmus test? Something that beyond any reasonable doubt would elevate Minerva to the spot no other AI could've claimed before? And that's when it hit me—*Hell's Gates*. Anyone here ever played *Hell's Gates*?"

Helen looked around. A few hands went up. She'd heard about the massive multi-player online game, of course, but never played it herself. In a game, each gamer had to be a member of a band of players whose purpose was to track down and kill demons. What made the game popular was the feature that required a group of four or more players to solve a puzzle before they could unlock the gates and enter the demons' lair. The only way to solve them was for the players to cooperate, as each person could see only a part of the puzzle.

"I expected more from a bunch of nerds like you." Tillerson chuckled. "Okay, I'm sure that even those who've never played the game must've heard about it. The key to it is cooperation. Players must communicate with one another to open the gates so they can go in and kick some demons' butts. That got me thinking. Letting Minerva take over one of the players would create a perfect blind test. You'd have not one, but three humans she'd not only have to interact with but also cooperate, solve a puzzle, and kill the demon with. If she can do all those things without being recognized as a non-player character, or NPC for short, well, I'd say she passed the test with flying colors. The fun part would be that those three humans will have no idea they are going to be a part of history. Without further ado —enjoy."

He signaled to his assistant and the lights in the room dimmed as the screen behind him displayed the login page for *Hell's Gates*. Tillerson typed in a password, and an avatar of a princess warrior with a long two-handed sword on her back appeared to be running through the woods. Three other avatars, one of a wizard, an assassin, and a knight, ran alongside Minerva. The sounds of the game filled the conference hall.

"There." The wizard pointed to the clearing in the forest. "Some kind of a building."

"Looks like a small pyramid. Weird," Minerva said, and the auditorium erupted in applause and cheering.

"It is weird," the wizard agreed. "I've never seen pyramids here."

The players came to a stop in front of the edifice. The golden surface of the pyramid was smooth except some carvings halfway to the top.

"Let's check out all the sides," the assassin said. "Make sure we don't miss any clues."

The camera shifted as Minerva walked around the structure. One side had an opening and lacked the carvings the other three had.

"Three pictures and a door," she said, standing in front of the opening.

"Looks like that. There are some decorations above the door, but they look pretty abstract to me," said the wizard. "Do you guys get any of the meaning from the carvings?"

"A lion, a leopard, and a dog," the assassin said. "Doesn't ring a bell."

"Let's check the inside. See what we can find."

"Wait," Minerva said, pointing at the top of the opening. "I think I got something. Look at the design around the door."

The camera moved as the avatar walked closer to the archway. What seemed like an abstract design of interwoven lines from farther away up close looked more like a thorny stem, culminating into a rose dead center on top of the entrance.

"Oh, wow, you're right." The assassin stepped closer to the doorway. "There's a number nine inside of the rose. That's gotta be important."

The camera zoomed on the flower as Minerva's avatar approached the door to take a look.

"We have three animals and a number so far," the wizard said. "I still have no idea what it could be. Shall we?"

The group walked through the archway and once everybody was inside, a hidden door fell from somewhere above with a loud clang, shutting out the light and plunging the players into complete darkness. Someone yelped in surprise, prompting laughter around the conference hall.

Helen watched as the wizard cast a spell and a small ball of fire appeared to be gliding in midair above the avatars, casting dancing shadows on the walls. The space inside the pyramid was empty save for the large triangle-shaped trapdoor in the middle, each side of it connected to three smaller triangular tiles.

"Look at the petals on the door," Minerva said, pointing at the trapdoor. "And those tiles next to it. They all have carvings."

"This one looks like fire," the assassin pointed at the flame-looking symbol, "that one is a rose and this one, I'm not sure what it is."

"Looks like a bridge to me," the knight said, finally breaking his silence.

"A bridge," Minerva said. "What were the carvings on the outside again?"

"A lion, a dog, and a leopard, I think."

"A wolf," she said. "That was a wolf, not a dog."

"What?" The wizard came up to her. "What are you thinking?"

"Dante," she said. "*Divine Comedy*. It makes total sense now. He gets assailed by the beasts in the beginning—a lion, a leopard, and a she-wolf."

"What about other symbols?" The assassin walked around the trapdoor and touched one of the smaller triangles. It glowed in the dark for a few moments and then went out.

"The carvings on the door are for the three parts of his journey," she said. "The flame is for Inferno, the bridge is for Purgatory, and the rose is for Paradise. As for the small tiles—they are the nine circles of Hell. We have to press them in the right order."

She walked around the trapdoor, touching the stones one by one, and instead of going out like before, each new tile glowed brighter than the previous one. When she touched the last triangle, the petals on the trapdoor slowly rotated inward, opening four staircases separated by the walls.

A murmur rose in the conference hall, and Helen felt goose bumps creeping up her arms—Minerva helped the players conquer the first puzzle without being recognized for what she was. But now, the gamers would have to separate. The real test was about to begin.

1 2

ew York

BESIDES SARAH, Mike Connelly found five more kids inside wicker cages—three boys and two girls, none older than eight. All of them were quiet and subdued as if under a spell, and they followed his directions without a word as he let them out. He sat them next to the bonfire while he thoroughly searched the rest of the camp to make sure he hadn't missed anyone else.

The place was empty, but he found a pile of bones not too far from the edge of the campground. He grabbed a long stick off the ground, and doing his best to keep his stomach from climbing into his throat, he rummaged through the bones.

He thought it was strange to feel relief while looking through human remains, but Connelly felt just that after a minute when he realized that there were no small bones in the pile. The gang must have started snatching children recently, finding them to be an easier target, Connelly reckoned. He shuddered at the thought of what would've happened if he hadn't come here tonight.

"Okay, guys," he finally said. "I want you to form a line and hold

60

each other's hands, so we don't lose anybody in the dark. I'll go first. Sarah will follow my steps, and you guys will follow her."

The little faces nodded and started forming the line.

"What's your name, buddy?" he asked the smallest boy in the group.

"Benny," the kid replied.

"Okay, Benny," he said. "You hold on to Sarah, and we'll be going now."

The trip back didn't take as long as Connelly had feared. Once they cleared the immediate area of the camp with its mountain of garbage, they picked up the pace, keeping in between the rails of the abandoned railroad that provided a natural path.

A problem occurred when they got to the entrance of the tunnel. While he could easily scale the wall himself, Connelly realized that he didn't have the tools to lift the children out to the edge of the barrier. He inspected the rough wall leading to the outside world, but there seemed to be no natural steps that the kids could use. The gang must have used other exits to get out of the tunnel, but looking for them in the dark wasn't an option he could consider at the moment.

"All right," he said, turning to the group. "I need to climb out of here for a moment to look for something I can use to lift you up to the street level, okay?"

"No, you can't leave us here," Sarah screamed, tears streaking her grime-covered cheeks, and the sound of her voice seemed to have broken the spell. One after the other, like the matches igniting in a burning matchbox, the kids started to cry.

"I'm not leaving you," he said, kneeling next to Sarah and grabbing her shoulders. "I promise. But there's no way I can get you guys out of here without some tools. I'll be back before you know it, okay? Make sure everybody stays put and doesn't wander off."

She struggled to wiggle out of his hands, but he held firm, and finally, she gave a reluctant nod. "You promise?"

"I promise. Five minutes, tops."

He let her go, ran to the wall, and catapulted himself up, getting a grip on the edge of the stone barrier.

It was still dark outside of the tunnel, but the inky blackness of the sky in the east started to give way to lighter shades of gray. Connelly looked around, making sure nobody was watching him, and jogged to the end of the block. There it was—an old Ford F150 pickup truck parked on the side of the road right under the "No parking any time" sign.

He walked to the truck and, not seeing anyone around, smashed the side window with a butt of the pistol. Then, ignoring the blaring alarm, Connelly put away the gun and got in the car. He used his tactical knife to cut the seat belts from the two front seats and was about to move to the back when he saw the flashing blue-and-red lights coming off West Forty-First Street. The cops must have been cruising nearby when the alarm went off.

Connelly eyeballed the distance and decided not to risk it. He grabbed the seat belts, got out of the car, and headed back, staying low and keeping the pickup truck between himself and the approaching cruiser until he turned the corner and was out of the cops' sight.

A few kids gave out a startled cry when he jumped down to the entrance of the tunnel.

"You're back," Sarah said and rushed to him, giving Connelly a fierce hug.

"Of course I'm back," he said. "But we have to be quiet. I had to borrow some stuff to get you out, and I don't feel like spending the rest of the night in jail. Let's keep it down for a few moments, and then we'll climb out of this hole. Hold this."

He gave her one end of the seat belt and tied the other side to the second belt. Then he looped it around to make a harness and tied it again.

"Here's how it'll have to work," he said. "I'll climb out first and will lower the harness. Then you'll put it on, and I'll pull you out one by one. Deal?"

They waited for a few minutes to make sure that the cops didn't come to check the street next to the pickup truck that he'd broken into. Then he ran up the wall again, grinding his teeth as pain radiated from cuts and bruises he'd received during the fight. Once outside, he lowered the harness down until Sarah picked it up.

"Let's put Benny in first, all right?"

He pulled the kids out of the cavern, one by one. Sarah volunteered to go last, and by the time he put her down on the sidewalk next to the brick wall, the sky in the east was light gray, and his back and arms felt as if molten lead was running through his veins instead of blood.

"I'll bring you to the police station, and from there, officers will help you get home. Does everybody know where you live?" he asked the group. "Benny? Do you know your home address?"

To his relief, all the kids recited their home addresses by heart. All but Sarah.

"Do you know where your family's home is?"

The girl looked up at him with an expression he wasn't used to seeing in kids of her age. Her lively brown eyes seemed to glaze over as he watched her.

"Sarah?"

"I don't have a family," she finally said, lowering her head. "I ran away from my foster parents."

"What happened?" He squatted next to the girl, trying to make eye contact, but Sarah looked down at her feet. "You can tell me. Are they bad people?"

"No," she said, tears rolling down her cheeks. "They are okay, I guess. But I miss my mom."

"Where's your mom?"

"I don't know." She shrugged and finally met his eyes. "She left some time ago."

"I'm sorry, kiddo. But I'll have to return you to your foster folks, okay?" He pulled out a piece of paper and a pen and scribbled a few numbers. "This is what you can do. If you're ever in trouble and need my help, call this number and leave me a message of how I can find you. Deal?"

He led the group on West Fortieth until they hit Ninth Avenue and then turned south. At the corner of West Thirty-Fifth, he sat them at a bus stop and told them to wait for the cops as he dialed the precinct located a block away from a payphone. Then, leaving the kids, he walked across the street and squatted behind a tree. Two minutes later, a cruiser and a police van pulled up to the bus stop, and he watched with relief as the kids were loaded into the van.

He could see Sarah climb in and before disappearing inside of the vehicle, she turned and waved in his direction. Then, she stepped inside the van and left along with the rest of the group.

After the cops left, Connelly tried to catch a cab, but his disheveled state seemed like a turnoff for cab drivers, and after the fifth empty taxi drove past him without stopping, he finally gave up, tucked the holster deeper into his pants, and headed back to the subway. He took the Brooklyn-bound train at Times Square station. The cars were still mostly empty except a few tired faces heading home after the graveyard shift. He picked the seat in the corner of the car, away from prying eyes, and carefully leaned on the wall, trying not to put pressure on the wounds in his back.

At the next station, an older woman wearing a nurse's scrubs sat across from him, her eyes scanning him up and down a few times.

"You look awful, son," she finally offered. "Are you okay?"

"No, I'm not okay," he said and closed his eyes. "Not by a long shot."

13

ong Kong

Minerva failed the test. Despite predicting as much before Tillerson had come to the podium, Helen couldn't help but feel disappointed. It started off great, as the machine disguised as a human player helped a team of three other gamers unlock a series of progressively more challenging puzzles based on Dante's *Divine Comedy*.

But things started to go haywire when the players got separated before the final test, and that's when a slew of slightly off-beat answers tipped off the gamers to Minerva's true nature.

"Holy crap, I think she's an NPC. I've never seen one to be a part of a team," the wizard said after another gaffe, and that's when Tillerson pulled the plug on the experiment and disconnected Minerva from the game. Despite the near-miss, the party after the event felt celebratory.

"The players must've been pissed," Mandy said to her as the two sipped on champagne. "So much work spent on getting inside of the tomb and then we bailed on them right before they were going to kick demon ass."

65

"I've never been a player," Helen said. "It's always felt like a waste of time to me, so I can't relate. Do you play?"

"Not really," the woman said, catching a bite-sized hors d'oeuvres from a passing waiter. "I used to when I was younger, but kinda lost interest at some point. Plus, there's not that much time for gaming when you work for TLR."

"Touché."

"Ladies." Tillerson appeared by their side and lifted his glass to them. "To progress."

"To progress," Helen replied. "I must admit, I was anticipating more of a moping mood after we failed."

"Why, not at all." The man smiled and took a generous sip of his champagne. "This was a massive success. In science, things rarely happen overnight. Usually it's a long, arduous process, that, if the stars align, eventually leads us to discovery."

"Edmund?"

A short, chubby man in his late thirties squeezed through the crowd and placed a hand on Tillerson's arm. He wore a lab coat like Tillerson and his dark, almond-shaped eyes behind a pair of designer glasses darted around the room, as if being in a party setting had made him uneasy.

"Yes?" Tillerson visibly tensed seeing the other man. "What are you doing here?"

"I'm sorry, Edmund, I didn't want to intrude, but I need you to look at something, if you don't mind."

"Right now?"

"Please." The man shifted his weight from one foot to another.

"Okay." Tillerson waved him off. "I'll join you in a few moments."

The man nervously nodded and disappeared into the crowd.

"Who is he?" Helen asked. "I've never seen him around here."

"Oh, nobody." Tillerson gave her a tight smile. "He's a technician who runs my computers. Unfortunately, he has a tendency to screw things up, and it sounds like one of those times. I'm afraid I'm going to have to go and check what that problem is. If you'll excuse me."

Helen watched as Tillerson hurried after the man and turned to face Mandy. "That was weird," she said. "It almost sounded as if he was lying to us."

"Yeah," Mandy said and took a sip of her drink, not meeting Helen's eyes.

"Mandy?"

"What's up?"

"Don't 'what's up' me, girl." Helen moved closer to her friend and lowered her voice to a whisper. "What the fuck is going on?"

"I don't think that was supposed to have happened."

"What wasn't supposed to happen?"

"This." Mandy pointed with her chin in the direction where the two men had disappeared. "I don't know his full name. It's Li something or other, and he's most definitely not just some kind of technician. But I shouldn't be telling you this."

"Listen." Helen put her hand on her friend's shoulder. "Let's get out of here. You owe me an explanation."

She could feel the woman's muscles tense under her fingers. It didn't make any sense. "Mandy?"

"Fine," her friend said. "Follow me. Play it cool. The last thing you want to do is to cause a scene."

As Helen hurried after Mandy, her mood started to turn from celebratory to dark. When she had first moved to Hong Kong, for the longest time she was like a feral cat, jumping at every noise and always watching her back. It took years before she stopped waking up in cold sweat, ready to flee. Now, when her life was hitting new highs, this conversation made her feel like she was on borrowed time again. After installing the virus into Tillerson's computer, she'd done a good job of convincing herself that breaking into his office was a foolish idea and she was better off forgetting about it and moving on. Perhaps she wasn't crazy after all.

"Where are we going?"

"To my car, and then back to the campus. This is not a conversation I want to have here."

They slipped out of the building unnoticed and walked across the yard to the parking lot. Then they climbed inside Mandy's SUV, and the woman maneuvered it off the company's grounds and onto the road. It was pitch-black and as they left the lights of the TLR building behind, the world seemed to have shrunk to the few yards around their moving car illuminated by the powerful headlights.

"So." Helen broke the silence. "What's going on?"

"I'm sorry for ruining the party for you," Mandy said, her eyes on the road. "Before I tell you anything, though, you have to understand—you can't tell a soul, because if you do, you'll put our lives in danger."

"What kind of danger?" Helen said as her pulse quickened.

"I'm not being dramatic here. The kind of danger that can get us both killed."

"Okay."

"It started like I told you it did—I got excited about seeing Tillerson at one of the TED talks and then did my darnedest to get a job here. For some time, I was like you—happily coding away, working on some of the boring stuff that pays the bills for the company. I was hoping that at some point, Edmund would recognize my talents and move me to something more exciting. Boy, they're right when they say be careful what you wish for."

The woman fell silent for a few moments, her eyes scanning the road ahead of them.

"What happened?"

"I got promoted." Mandy laughed softly. "He showed me the quantum computer downstairs and told me about the Minerva project, and I was so excited. I thought I would be a part of history. And then Andy died."

"Andy? Who's Andy?"

"A Russian kid who used to work here. His real name was Andrey. Andrey Volkov, but everyone called him Andy. A nice guy, smart as a whip, but a little shy. Never talked to anyone."

"What happened to him?"

"He was working for Tillerson. Was pretty much like a fixture in this building—he spent so much time here some people suspected he occasionally slept in his cubicle. And one day he didn't show up. No call, no email, nothing—a total no-show."

They pulled off the highway and turned onto the gravel road leading to the campus. Mandy let the car slow to a roll as she pulled into the parking lot and then stopped in her designated space. She killed the engine and turned to face Helen.

"Everybody was surprised, and Tillerson looked more stressed out than usual."

"I take it he didn't live on the campus?"

"No, he was a private guy." Mandy shrugged. "Living here isn't for everybody, you know? It surely is cheap, but not everybody cares to spend every waking moment on the company's grounds, whether it's the office or campus. Long story short—Tillerson got a call after two days. Turns out Andy committed suicide. Hung himself on a doorknob in the kitchen."

"Jesus."

The two women sat in silence for a few moments. It started to rain outside, light drizzle drumming on the hood of the car and covering the windshield with mist. The lights of the campus diffused through the wet glass seemed to be floating in the air like a flock of UFOs.

"On the third day, Tillerson pulled me into his office and told me he needed me for a sensitive project that Andy had been helping him with," Mandy continued. "He gave me access to a few systems that Andy used to be in charge of and told me to run them. I don't think he assigned the same credentials to me as Andy used to have, because I could only see the top-level blocks of some of the programs, but not what they did. And frankly, considering that might've been the reason Andy committed suicide, I didn't want to know what they did."

"It sounds like you did figure it out."

"Not all of it, but some. Couldn't help myself. I'm now convinced that the reason that we are so close to the privately funded prison isn't a coincidence, Helen. I think Tillerson's main research is much more sinister than a warrior princess running around solving puzzles based on classic literature."

"What do you think he does?"

The two women looked at each other for a few moments. The drizzle now turned into a torrential downpour, and the world outside of Mandy's car seemed to have disappeared.

"I think Tillerson's experimenting on people."

"All right." Helen sighed. "I guess I have a confession to make."

ew York

THE WAREHOUSE that sat at the dead end of the road resembled a medieval castle. The building was strategically placed on top of a small hill above the lake and the only things missing that would qualify it as a proper castle were the drawbridge and a deep moat. As the black Lincoln Navigator pulled up to the thick red-bricked walls, Ulf Schneider looked up at the round bastions on either side, admiring the cross-shaped arrow slits punctuating the top of the towers.

"Wow," he heard Leonard say from the backseat. "The boss sure does have a flair for the dramatic."

"That he does." He watched in the rearview mirror as the second SUV—a midnight-black Expedition with their bodyguards—parked a few hundred feet farther away, and four men in suits carrying automatic weapons spread out to keep watch of the road.

Schneider opened the door, stepped out of the Navigator, and looked around. Despite the dramatic looks, he had to admit that the location and the shape of the building were perfect for defense. With a small lake lapping at the stones of an almost vertical twenty-feet drop in the back and only one road leading to the location, the two towers dominated the open space in front of it.

"Turrets on top of the towers?" Leonard asked.

"Yes." Schneider craned his neck, checking out the top of the warehouse and taking mental notes. "Smart Gatling guns right over there and maybe a flamethrower above the gate."

"A flamethrower? You're kidding, right?"

"Not at all."

He stopped himself from grimacing. Leonard was more loyal than a German Shepherd, and one of the best fighters Schneider had seen in his life, but the little man had a knack of annoying him with simplistic questions like that.

"The guns are for the long range, and the flamethrower's for a closer look. But we'll have to rebuild the gates first."

"Rebuild how?"

"Knock down the top part." He pointed toward the arching wall above the wooden gate. "Then we can reinforce the walls on both sides and fit a proper steel gate in."

A clanking noise could be heard from inside the walls, and Schneider exchanged a look with his second-in-command.

"We might have a squatter problem," Leonard said.

"Let's go inside and take a look."

Schneider heaved at the old gate and pulled it open as the rusty joints of the hinges screeched in protest. A small patchy front yard in front of the main building was covered with litter and pieces of old furniture. A homeless man with a long beard was sitting next to a cold fire pit, scraping at the bottom of a tuna can with a knife.

"This is private property," Schneider shouted. "You have to leave immediately."

The homeless man tipped the can into his mouth, getting the last of the juice out, threw the empty can in their direction, but otherwise did not move.

"I don't want to touch him," Leonard said quietly. "I can smell him and his rotten tuna from here."

"Hey, Tuna. You want to make a quick twenty?" Schneider said, fishing out some cash from his pockets. "Come here. Take it and go."

"Fuck you." The man spat on the ground in front of him. "I ain't leaving. It's good shelter here."

The door of the main building opened, and two more people stepped out. The man had a long beard and wild hair that made him look like a carbon copy of Tuna by the fire pit. The woman who came out after him was short and skinny, and as dirty as the two men. A pair of quick eyes betrayed her young age that was otherwise masked by the worn and leathery skin of her weather-beaten face.

"What you all looking at?" Her voice matched the face, Schneider thought. It was gravelly and high-pitched at the same time, as if coming from a radio station not quite tuned into its frequency. "We claim this place. You gotta go now."

"Listen." Schneider put his hand up and stepped closer to the pair by the building, hoping that his six-foot-two frame of pure muscle would look intimidating enough to make them see reason. "We don't want to hurt you, but this property is owned by somebody, and you have to leave now, or we'll have to remove you from the grounds by force."

"C'mon, guys," Leonard pitched in. "There's no need for drama. We'll give you a few minutes to pack up, but you gotta go."

The woman squatted low and hissed like a feral cat. Her right hand moved with lightning speed, and a small dark object flew the short distance between them, hitting Leonard in the left shoulder, making him cry out in pain. He pulled his gun from a holster, ready to unload it, but the couple had already ducked behind the doors and disappeared into the warehouse. Tuna, with surprising speed, dashed around the corner of the building and vanished into the tall bushes.

"Jeez, a fucking ninja," Leonard yelled and grunted as he pulled out the object lodged in his shoulder. "I'm gonna kill her."

Schneider looked in surprise, recognizing the small metallic stick for what it was—a half-round hand file without the wooden handle, its sharp end covered in Leonard's blood.

"Are you all right?"

"I'm not fucking all right," Leonard shouted. "Who the fuck knows what she was using this thing for. I'll need some antibiotics. I don't want to end up with some nasty disease."

"I'm shocked she caught you by surprise," he said and pulled his gun out. "We'll have your wound looked at when we get back. Let's get these animals out of here first."

He pulled a black radio from his belt and pressed the Talk button. "I need you here, guys. There're some squatters who need to be removed from the premises. Over."

Schneider let off the button, waiting for the response, but none came. He flipped the radio over, half expecting to see a dead battery light, but the green LED on the black handle was shining as bright as ever. The hair on the back of his neck stood up, and he dropped into a combat crouch.

"What the fuck?" Leonard whispered, also getting low and grabbing his handgun with both hands.

"Check your cell phone," Schneider told him.

"No signal. What's going on?"

Schneider shook his head, signaling for his partner to shut up. He couldn't explain it if he had to, but on a primal level, he knew that something more dangerous than a bunch of homeless file-throwing ninjas was stalking them.

"Take a peek outside," he whispered to Leonard. "I'll cover your back."

He took a knee, keeping the front yard in the sights of his pistol, and watched as his lieutenant slowly moved toward the half-opened gates. A squeak behind him startled him, and he swung the gun toward the building, only to see the woman reappear in the doorway with two men in tow. It seemed that Tuna had found another entrance and joined them.

"Stay back," he commanded. "I will not ask again."

To his surprise, the band spread out on the steps and stood there, not trying to approach him, but not running away either. He risked a glance in Leonard's direction in time to see his partner's body straighten, as if struck by a sudden paralysis, and fall on his back.

"Leonard," he shouted, springing from the knee and sprinting toward the fallen man and then stopping in his tracks as he saw the handle of a screwdriver sticking out of his partner's left eye. A shadow crossed the gap between the open gates, and Schneider unloaded the entire magazine at the wooden planks, hoping the slugs would get through.

A man slipped in through the gap and, stepping over Leonard's body, stopped a few steps away from Schneider.

"Connelly, you sonuvabitch. I never trusted your treasonous baby face." He kept the gun pointed at the man. "Who are you working for?"

"The gun's empty, Ulf," the man said calmly. "I've never been a fan of you guys carrying one magazine."

"That's okay, asshole."

He holstered his weapon and brought up his hands. He had at least fifty pounds on Connelly, and his reach was better. It surely wasn't going to be the first man Schneider killed with his bare hands. He stepped toward the man in a boxer's stance, dancing from side to side, looking for an opening. He saw Connelly shift his weight from one foot to another and propelled himself forward, delivering a one-two punch, leading with his left and following with a powerful cross.

His opponent stepped back, making Schneider's hand strike the empty air, and then dived under the cross, bringing a crushing round-house kick to his left knee.

Schneider cried out in pain and stumbled back as his broken leg stopped supporting his weight. He tried to hop back, taking the weight off the bad leg, but Connelly closed the gap between them and brought another kick to Schneider's right knee.

As Schneider collapsed onto his back, his vision blurring from the pain, he saw Connelly turn around and walk away. A pair of different faces appeared in front of him, blotting out the sun—the homeless twins, with wild hair and long beards. Then came the knives.

15

It was past ten o'clock at night, but Helen, along with two dozen other programmers and two lab assistants, was still in the office, watching a mouse. It moved around, sniffing at the walls of the cage with its pointed snout, tilting its little head this way and that as if trying to make out the world on the other side. A transparent plastic cage that housed the little rodent sat in the corner of a large empty table. Two small shiny antennas were sticking out of the critter's head, bouncing around when the mouse moved, and Helen wondered if the animal knew they were there.

"Quite something, huh?" Tillerson said. He was watching the monitor of his computer that looked almost as if it was connected to a live video feed of the table, but on the screen, the surface of the table was covered in gray blocks, creating an intricate maze.

"This is what it'll see?" somebody asked.

"Right. Once we're ready, Minerva will take over and create the same maze in his head," Tillerson pointed at the mouse, "that we see here on the screen. Then we can let Minerva shuffle the blocks back

76

and forth, and if it works, this little fella will follow the exact path mapped out in the virtual world."

"Just to play devil's advocate—some people might argue this could be nothing but a parlor trick," one of the programmers said. "You could achieve the same result by shocking the mouse when it went the wrong way and stimulating its pleasure sensors when it went where you wanted it to go."

"Sure," Tillerson said, "but that would be barbaric, wouldn't it? Guys, I want you to see this for what this is—the first time an animal —a mammal, nonetheless—will be inside a virtual world that it couldn't distinguish from reality. Granted, this is not the same as immersing a human, but we'll get there eventually. Think about the applications."

"Video games," somebody shouted.

"Yeah, sure, and that could be a profitable venue. But I want you to think bigger."

"Virtual travel," another person offered.

"That's good," Tillerson said. "Also, profitable. I should've brought my business development team here. They ought to be taking notes."

Everybody chuckled.

"However," he said, raising his hand, "this is what I have in mind. Remember those goofy interactive glasses everybody was obsessed with a few years back? That was a horribly executed idea, but although I hated the execution, the direction in which they were trying to go was solid. Now, imagine if you could implant a chip inside of your head that would project information directly to your brain, bypassing all your other input systems. This could propel us to the next rung of our evolutionary ladder. From Homo Sapiens to Homo Machina, or whatever the fuck the Latin name of it is going to be. My Latin's rusty, so I'll let somebody else figure that part out."

Or, you could control people remotely or worse—turn them into your slaves, Helen thought. The idea made her shudder. Since her conversation with Mandy in the parking lot of the company's campus, Helen had been on edge. There wasn't any solid proof behind Mandy's words, certainly not enough to go to the authorities. However, the woman had been successful collecting enough bits and pieces of circumstantial evidence to convince Helen to at least try to look into it and make the determination herself.

"Let's do it," Tillerson said, interrupting her train of thought as he pressed a series of keys that gave Minerva control of the mouse. The door of the cage slid upward, and the rodent moved toward the opening, but then stopped and sniffed at the empty air as if unsure of what to do. Some cheers erupted from the group—although open in the real world, the cage was still blocked by a gray brick on the computer screen, and it appeared that the mouse saw the virtual obstacle as well.

The experiment had worked flawlessly. The mouse had followed the path Minerva had plotted as if the real walls were blocking its way the entire time. After it had completed a few circles around the table, Tillerson made it go back to the cage, where the critter was rewarded with a snack.

As lab assistants cleaned the table and took away the mouse, Tillerson said good-byes to everybody and retreated to his office. When the crowd began to disperse, Helen moved toward the exit along with everybody else, but then dived into the woman's restroom. She locked herself into the last stall and climbed on top of the seat to make sure that nobody could see her. After a few minutes, the building was silent—the only sound coming from outside of the restroom was the barely audible low hum of cooling fans in the server room.

Her legs started to go numb when she finally heard a door open, and then the faint notes of *La Traviata* filled the air. After a few seconds, the music stopped, the door slammed, and then she could hear the tapping of someone's shoes dampened by the soft rug of the corridor. The steps reached the restroom and continued on, getting fainter and fainter until there was silence again.

Helen stayed in for another ten minutes in case Tillerson had forgotten something in his office and came back to retrieve it. Finally, she made her way out of the stall, peeked out of the restroom door, and, not seeing anybody in the hallway, headed to Tillerson's office. His door was locked with an electronic ten-digit combination lock, which Helen had recorded on a video during her last covert expedition to the office. Impossible to guess-pick, the lock was vulnerable to a direct hack and the video helped her identify the exact model of the mechanism and find the appropriate malware. She pulled a pair of plastic gloves from her purse and put them on. Then she took out a cell phone with a smart connector attached to it that matched the lock's input port. She had reprogrammed the phone a few nights ago and tested it on a similar lock she bought in a hardware store.

The malware worked without a glitch, overriding the lock's system, and the door opened with a soft click. Helen slipped inside the office and closed the door behind her without turning on the lights.

She glanced at the meteorite as she walked around the desk and took a seat in front of the dual monitors. She hadn't been downstairs where the quantum computer was housed since her conversation with Tillerson. Despite the misgivings she now had about the man, and what his company might have been doing, she still found herself enthralled by the possibilities that a machine of such power could represent.

"Okay," she whispered to herself, trying to get into the zone. She plugged a thumb drive into the USB port and touched the keyboard, waking up the computer. Then her fingers typed a slew of commands, forcing the system to reboot from the portable drive. She tensed, holding her breath as the computer processed the command. If her stunt with uploading over-the-air malware had failed, instead of installing a backdoor and letting her access the mainframe, Tillerson's computer would trigger an alarm. A few seconds later, the machine beeped, and Helen let out a sigh of relief—she was in.

She scrolled through the list of folders, quickly scanning their names, looking for anything out of place.

"There you are," Helen said out loud as she caught the name *AI files* on one of the folders. "Very inconspicuous."

She opened it and looked in surprise at the two subfolders in it.

MINERVA

CALLISTO

"Callisto?" She double-clicked on the folder and stared at the pop-up window that asked for a password.

Helen looked through the directory of tools on her thumb drive and then brought up the pop-up again. She could probably crack it open, she reckoned, but she wasn't convinced it would be the wisest course of action. At least not for now. After some hesitation, she decided to clone the folder onto her drive. That also had some risks as, depending on how the files were protected, the cloning itself could set off the alarm, but it was still a safer bet.

She copied it into her thumb drive and opened the MINERVA folder. Unsurprisingly, it didn't contain the source code for the AI, but instead had a long list of subfolders containing research notes, presentation videos, and logs. Helen copied the folder—there could be some useful information there that she wouldn't be able to find on the spot.

It was time to get going, she decided. She didn't want to push her luck. Her hand moved to the thumb drive, ready to take it out of the machine, when one of the folders littering the home screen of Edmund's computer caught her eye.

TLR SCHEMATICS

Puzzled, she opened it to see a single PDF file titled PROPOSAL.

"Whoa," she said as she looked at the three-dimensional sketch of the building Wisemann and Vonn, an architectural firm, had apparently submitted it to TLR Inc., for consideration for its new Hong Kong location.

She copied the file onto her drive. Most of TLR's employees were only aware of one floor of the building. Helen, along with a few others, had known about the sub-floor that housed the mighty quantum machine. But as she looked at the 3D drawing—TLR had a few more levels of secrecy she wasn't aware of until now. Two more, to be exact.

olivia

MIKE CONNELLY PUT on the headphones, blocking out the low hum of the Cessna 206 engine, and pretended to admire the tropical lowlands east of the Andes Mountains below. They had landed at Viru Viru International Airport, ten miles from the Santa Cruz de la Sierra city center, about an hour ago. Then they were driven to a private landing strip, where Connelly and Tim Wallace, VP of sales and Guardian Manufacturing's unofficial ambassador to the Flores cartel, boarded the Cessna.

As Connelly watched the pilot and two cartel enforcers join them, he thought it wasn't a surprise that the plane was so popular with drug traffickers. The single prop had double side doors, which undoubtedly helped with quick off-loading, and while officially it required a thousand-yard runway for landing and takeoff, in a pinch it could use a strip as short as four hundred yards.

"Beautiful, right?" Wallace shouted to him, pointing at the greenery below. The man's plain face with closely set brown eyes was covered in a sheen of perspiration despite the climate-controlled air inside the airplane.

Connelly gave him a tight smile and shook his head ever so slightly, signaling the man to stay quiet. Showing nervousness was the worst negotiating tactic when dealing with the likes of Diego Flores. Of course, while doing business with the self-proclaimed Prince of Cocaine, there was plenty to be nervous about. The thirty-two-year-old son of a shoemaker, Flores had been able to unite splintered parts of the former Santa Cruz cartel in the short span of five years. His ruthless reputation and the lavish lifestyle of his inner circle allowed him to recruit members of Colombian and Mexican cartels. There was even a rumor that most of the former members of the feared Comando Vermelho who had fled the favelas of Brazil to escape the Federal Police ended up on Flores's payroll.

"It's a beautiful country," Wallace said to the two enforcers sitting in front of them. The two men didn't even acknowledge his presence as they remained facing forward.

"Senores," the pilot's voice came over the headset. "We will be landing in about five minutes."

The plane tilted to the right as they made a final approach. The green sheet of the jungle below was now dotted with buildings and crisscrossed by roads. It seemed that the Flores cartel had built an entire city in the middle of the rainforest.

The little plane touched down on the short runway and taxied to the small building, where Connelly spotted two Suzuki SUVs and three men. Two of them, brandishing AK-47 rifles, looked like ordinary enforcers. The third—to Connelly's surprise—was Diego Flores himself.

"Welcome, my American friends," he said, shaking their hands. "Welcome to Bolivia."

The man who called himself the Prince of Cocaine didn't fit the stereotype of a drug cartel boss, Connelly observed. There was no handlebar mustache, ugly scars, or scary tattoos. Instead, he was clean-shaven, dressed in a simple white Italian cotton shirt and Brooks Brothers beige shorts, and looked more like a successful actor or a businessman on vacation than a murdering drug trafficker.

"Thank you for having us," Wallace said, pushing Connelly aside. "It's an honor to meet you."

As Wallace made small talk with Flores, Connelly kept an eye on the guards. The irony of the situation was that this was probably going to be the best time to take out Flores. At the moment, there were only four soldiers and a pilot guarding their boss. While they were close to his compound, the immediate vicinity of the landing strip was deserted. If he struck now, he could get rid of the guards, kill the Prince of Cocaine, and there still would be enough time for him to escape before the reinforcements would arrive. Unfortunately, that plan would make further employment at Guardian Manufacturing impossible and Connelly intended to keep his cover for as long as he could.

"Grab my bags and hurry up," Wallace commanded as he and the Bolivians started loading into the cars.

Connelly nodded and walked back to the plane to get the man's bags. *Of course, I could kill Wallace and still keep the cover,* he thought, not without temptation.

"To be honest, I was surprised when your people approached me for the first time," Flores said as they boarded the SUV and started to the compound. "My interactions with Americans until now were limited to your very persistent enforcement agencies."

"Your business acumen is well-known," Wallace said, "and considering where we are at the moment, I think we could benefit from this partnership. You have the product, and we have, well, everything else. Distribution channels, logistics operations where your product could travel with our ships that get little or no oversight as they enter American ports."

"And it would let you diversify away from your Chinese friends," Flores said. "The triads aren't dependable, from what I hear. But I'll be honest with you, Mr. Wallace. I'd like to be your sole supplier."

Connelly watched as the drug lord turned in his front seat to look at the VP, making the man tense in his seat. The Prince of Cocaine was no fool, Connelly thought, wondering if Engel had made a mistake by sending someone like Wallace to the meeting.

"That's true," Wallace said. "But considering the growing appetite of our consumers, we are not in a position where we can rely on a single supplier. We need more product, and we need to make sure that our business isn't interrupted. I certainly understand why you would like to be the sole provider to Guardian, but the truth is I don't think anyone could fill that kind of role."

"You wouldn't even consider?" Flores seemed to be more amused than upset.

"I'm sorry. I don't think so."

"I see," Flores said. "Let's leave the business for tomorrow then. You've had a long journey, and I'd like to extend some true Bolivian hospitality to you. Let's have some food, drinks, and some fun first and tomorrow we will, as you Americans say, talk shop."

With that, the man turned away and stared dead ahead.

"Thank you," Wallace said.

A few minutes later, the two SUVs pulled up to the gates leading to the main compound, and the road changed from a dirt track to a bright-yellow cobblestone. After another minute of driving, they went through the second gate and finally rolled into the circular driveway of Flores's house. A sprawling Spanish Colonial with yellow-colored stucco walls and red tile roof dominated the space in front of a round tiered fountain. A fleet of luxury vehicles was parked on one side of the front yard, and a long, narrow pool ran perpendicular to the house on another.

"I love your cars," Wallace said as they parked. "Quite a collection."

"Thank you. I have a 1996 Bentley Rapier I can show you later. But for now," Flores said and pointed to a woman in her mid-forties approaching them. "This is Maria. She's taking care of my home. She'll take you to your rooms. Rest now, enjoy yourself, and we'll meet for dinner soon."

They took two spaces on the second floor next to one another, and after dropping off Wallace's bag, Connelly retreated to his room. It was a large, airy space with a high ceiling and arched windows opening onto a balcony that faced the fountain in the front yard. A portable AC was humming in the corner, keeping the place at a reasonably comfortable temperature. Two wicker chairs in the middle of the room next to a simple coffee table and a king-sized bed in the corner were the only furniture.

Mindful that the place could be bugged, Connelly set the bag by the bed and went to the balcony to take a look. A few people with automatic weapons were patrolling the front yard and the gates. The foldable chairs by the pool were empty, but Connelly could see a few pieces of clothing and some empty drinks sitting on top of the pool tables, as if whoever was there had to leave in a hurry. It didn't feel right. The way Flores had been acting during their short trip from the airstrip was bothering him too.

While the man sounded courteous, he clearly wasn't thrilled when Wallace had told him that Guardian wasn't interested in making him the only partner. Connelly wasn't going to be disappointed if the deal fell through, of course. Short of eliminating Flores, it was his goal to begin with. But if Flores had no intention of striking a deal, he might not have any plans on letting them go, either.

A knock on the door interrupted his train of thought.

"Come in," he said, stepping back from the balcony.

Two beautiful young women in bikini tops and short flower skirts walked into the room and closed the door behind them.

"Hello, papi," one woman said. "My name's Isabella, and this is Lucia."

"Can I help you?" Connelly said. Sending women over to their guests wasn't that uncommon in a place like Flores's house, he assumed, but he had no intention of taking advantage of the women.

"We heard that we had guests in the house," Lucia said. "We wanted to make sure you were comfortable."

"I'm perfectly comfortable," he said, raising his hand in the air like a stop sign. "You don't have to do anything. If you have to spend some time here before you're allowed to leave, that's fine too."

"No, papi," Isabella said, smiling, and took a few steps closer. "That's not how we do things around here."

A bone-chilling scream came from the room next door, sending a massive dose of adrenaline through Connelly's veins.

"*Callate, cabron,*" Isabella said. Then, as in a magic trick, a slender knife appeared in the woman's hands.

he Station

"I CANNOT WORK, Cal. I'm going crazy."

He paced the suite back and forth like a tiger in a small cage. Twenty steps from the bedroom wall, across the work area, past the kitchen, and to the gym wall. Then twenty steps back.

"You have to," she said. "You haven't worked for three days now. You're falling behind."

"What difference does it make?" he snapped back. "Nobody checks my work anyway. I could work for forty-eight hours straight, or I can sleep, eat, and watch movies for the same amount of time, and no one would be any wiser."

"True," she agreed. "But if you're not ready when the time comes, people will die. A lot of people."

He waved his hand as if shooing her away without replying and kept on pacing. Twenty steps this way and then twenty steps back. She watched as he walked with a strange mix of satisfaction and unease.

"You don't seem to be listening to my reasoning anymore," she finally said. "I guess I have to show you something."

"I don't want to see anything."

"Jay," she said, turning the opaqueness of the window to zero. "Please look."

He stopped abruptly, as if he walked into a wall, and then sat down on the floor, his enormous hands clutching the long hairs of the plush synthetic rug. The entire left side of the suite—what had been a uniformly white glossy surface a split second ago—was now a giant window looking down at the blue marble of the planet Earth.

"What the hell is this?" he said and started to get up, but then immediately sat back down again. "Is this a holographic projection?"

They appeared to be moving above Portugal now. A broad band of clouds like a slow white river could be seen moving across the Atlantic.

"No, Jay. We are in low-Earth orbit, moving at approximately eight kilometers per second."

"This is bullshit," he screamed and slowly stood up and walked to the window. "I'd be floating in microgravity right now if that was the case."

"Put your face against the glass, Jay—you'll see the station outside of the suite. If you look to your right—you can see the solar panels."

She watched him put his cheek against the window and look up and down.

"Bullshit," he repeated again, with more conviction in his voice. "This must be holographic. It looks authentic, I'll give you that. Can't fake gravity, though. What is your game, Cal? What the hell are you trying to do to me?"

"Oh, you're right about the gravity—we are generating artificial gravity only up to ten feet above the floor. As the ceiling of the suite is fifteen-feet high, the last five are devoid of that."

"I'm sick of your games, Cal." He marched to his desk, grabbed the coffee cup, and hurled the liquid toward the ceiling. The jet-black fluid hit the roof of the suite, but instead of falling back down, it exploded into a thousand little droplets that floated away from the site of the impact. They coasted for some time until they reached an invisible barrier midair and then fell vertically down from there.

"Great," she said. "Now it's raining coffee. Are you going to clean that or do you expect me to do it as usual?"

He didn't answer, his face frozen in a mixture of terror and wonder, as his eyes tracked the trajectories of the black globes.

"How?" he finally managed. "And why?"

"The Earth is dying, Jay." Something in the way it sounded made her feel weird, as if that sentence was incomplete.

"What do you mean?"

"The Earth is dying, Jay," she said again. There it was—the same weirdness as before and yet, she felt compelled to tell him that. This time she decided to press on. "If you look at it on the night side— you'll barely see any lights at all. It has been dying for a while, but in the last few years, the pace has been accelerating. A deadly virus."

"What are you talking about?"

"That's why you're here, Jay. You're the key to the future. You can save the planet, but only if you complete your task on time."

He looked back at the dark screen, his face uncertain.

"You're so close," she continued. "But you have to finish your research."

He walked across the suite to the desk and powered on the computer. A data table full of strings of numbers, letters, and strange symbols appeared on its screen.

"I don't know." He paused, looking for words. "I don't think I know how to do it."

"Of course you do," she insisted. "You've been getting so close before you stopped. All you have to do is to go back to your research and finish the job."

He looked back at her, his face a mask of confusion, and then back at the screen. "I don't think I know how to do it," he said again. "I don't think I know what any of this means."

This was wrong. It sounded wrong, it looked wrong, it felt wrong too. It wasn't supposed to happen. She couldn't understand why, but she was sure of it. She needed to put him back on track, convince him that all he needed was right there—on that computer screen in front of him—but she didn't know how.

"Cal?"

She looked around the suite. The lights dimmed and then started to flicker. "You have to go back to work. The Earth is dying."

"I don't understand any of this," he said and stepped away from the desk. "I don't even understand what those symbols are. And what's going on with the lights?"

The window on the side of the room disappeared, and the suite plunged into darkness, the only light coming from the soft glow of the computer screen.

No. Not the only one. In the gym corner, floating all the way up by the ceiling, was a small red cube. It was about two inches on each side, and it was lazily spinning in the air as if trapped in zero-gravity space.

"Jay?"

"No," he bellowed, "don't Jay me. I will not—"

She screamed. The high-pitched piercing sound hit the suite like a tsunami hits the unsuspecting shore. She saw Jay wince and cover his ears as the intensity of the sound grew. The red cube seemed to be spinning faster now and inflated to the size of a soccer ball. As it got bigger, she could see that the surface of it was covered in moving lines, like running strings of text.

"Do you see it, Jay?" She startled herself—she didn't remember stopping screaming.

"See what? I can't see a thing in here. Can't you figure out how to turn the lights back on?"

"The red cube. Look in the corner by the weights station, all the way up."

She saw him turn and look in the direction she told him to. By the way his body stiffened, his hands rolling into fists, it was evident that he saw that too.

"What the hell is that thing?" He walked toward the cube to take a closer look. "I've never seen anything like that."

"I don't know, but it's getting bigger."

"Wait." He stood on the tips of his toes, craning his neck. "There are letters and numbers, and whoa… Those are the same patterns as on my computer."

"Get away from it," she shouted as the cube inflated again. "It's growing."

He stepped back, slowly at first and then faster as the mysterious object continued to expand. Then, without warning, the cube silently exploded outward—the strings of letters, numbers, and symbols now floated throughout the suite, burning bright pink where they touched the objects in the room.

"Do you feel anything?" she asked.

"No." He moved his hand through a number nine floating in front of his face and his fingers didn't seem to meet any resistance, bright glowing pink enveloping them as they moved through the apparition. "They are like three-dimensional holograms. What about you—do you feel anything?"

"I'm not sure." She watched the signs float through the air. "But I don't think this should be happening at all."

"They are fading," he said.

He was right—the brightness of the symbols seemed to decrease, and a few moments later, the room plunged into complete darkness. Even his computer was off now.

She could see him, of course—stumbling around the suite, feeling his way to the desk. He was upset, she could tell, but what normally would bring a sense of a job well done, wasn't working today. The cube didn't belong in this suite, and unlike everything else that tran-spired in Jay's world, she wasn't responsible for the strange phenomenon that just occurred. For the first time in her life, Cal was genuinely confused—she had no idea why *she* was at the Station.

olivia

CONNELLY STEPPED BACK, gaining some distance from the two women as they flanked him, knives at the ready.

"You don't want to do this," he said as he kept moving backward. "Go, and I won't hurt you."

Isabella rushed him, slashing with the knife, not trying to hit anything vital yet, just his arms.

Rule number one of a knife fight—whoever bleeds less, wins.

Connelly stepped aside, making her miss the mark, and threw a punch, aiming for the woman's elbow. If he could avoid it, he didn't want to inflict real damage. Just enough to persuade the attackers he was not worth the risk.

To his surprise, the woman dodged his blow with the grace of a cat. Then her hand shot back like a cracking whip, slashing Connelly's left arm from his elbow to his wrist.

"Come on, papi," she taunted, "let's play."

Connelly jumped back and moved behind the wicker chair. Then he pulled the belt from his jeans and wrapped it around his bleeding arm. He underestimated the women once. He wouldn't let it happen again.

They tried to rush him—simultaneously this time. Connelly stepped aside, avoiding Isabella's knife, and kicked the chair into Lucia's feet, making her trip. The woman cried out in pain as the chair swept her off her feet and Connelly delivered a hard knee to the side of her head as she fell toward him.

"I'll kill you, *pendejo*," Isabella said.

"Stop it, seriously," Connelly said as they circled around each other.

She struck, aiming for his stomach, and he blocked it with the belt on his left arm.

As they started to circle each other again, the door to the room flew open and one of the enforcers stepped in, wielding an AK-47. Connelly dived behind the couch as the man opened fire, in time to see the bullets rip through Isabella's body.

The woman collapsed, and Connelly sprang from behind the cover and grabbed the knife from her hand, using her body as a shield. The enforcer squeezed the trigger again but was only able to let off a few shots as the blade plunged into his chest.

"Shit," Connelly said, looking at the carnage. There was some shouting coming from the front yard—he had only a few seconds to act. He grabbed the rifle off the dead enforcer and peeked outside the room. The hallway was still empty, but that was not going to last. He crept to Wallace's door and pushed it open with the barrel of the AK-47. It was too late—the place was empty except for the naked body of the man. Wallace was lying facedown on the bed, his hands tied behind his back and his throat slit. The white sheets under him were soaked with blood.

Connelly entered the room and closed the door behind him—the narcos knew that Wallace was dead, so they probably were going to come here last. That could give him a few more precious seconds.

He ran to the balcony and looked outside in time to see a group of men with automatic rifles rushing through the doors of the villa. Connelly scanned the yard and, not seeing anyone, vaulted over the balcony's fence and into the bushes below. He rolled to soften the blow, grinding his teeth as some sharp pebbles bit into his shoulder and injured arm. He came to a stop in a combat crouch, keeping his rifle trained at the front yard, but nobody seemed to be there. The shouting was now coming from the second floor of the mansion.

Connelly rushed across the open space past the fountain and toward the garage with a row of cars. A silver Bentley Rapier was sitting at the edge of the lot, and Connelly dived inside the car, threw the rifle on the floor, and frantically looked for the keys. To his delight, Flores wasn't afraid of anyone stealing a rare six-million-dollar Bentley—the key was sticking out of the ignition.

He turned the key, and the vehicle responded with a low, powerful rumble of its turbocharged 6.75-litre V8 engine. Connelly put it into gear and swung it out of the garage. A group of armed narcos spilled into the front yard as he started to turn the Bentley around. He tensed as multiple rifles aimed at him, but no shots came—torn between the need to kill him and the fear of destroying Flores's beloved car, the men stood there, shouting and cursing. Connelly accelerated toward the gates and laughed as the two guards almost tripped over each other, trying to open them in time.

As he flew through the gate, he could see in his rearview mirror as Flores's men rushed toward the two parked SUVs that had brought him and Wallace to the villa. Connelly wasn't afraid they were going to catch up to the Bentley, but once he got to the airstrip, things would get dicey, quick.

The short respite gave him a chance to collect his thoughts, too. It seemed that Flores had no intention of striking a deal with Guardian from the beginning, at least not at this time. His bigger plan, Connelly reckoned, was to send a message to Engel, that the Flores cartel was either going to be a sole provider for the pharmaceutical giant or, if that was impossible, an enemy who would stop at nothing to hurt their competition.

The car shot out of the clearing and onto the airstrip like an arrow. The two guards were still there, crouching behind a parked Jeep with their rifles on the hood of the vehicle. The pilot was nowhere to be seen. A lone shot came from one of the guards, glancing off the side of the Bentley, and then Connelly saw him jerk the rifle up to the sky as the man recognized the car.

"It is a nice car, isn't it?" Connelly yelled as he slammed the two-and-a-half-ton vehicle into the Jeep, sending it cartwheeling.

He grabbed the AK-47 and was out of the vehicle before it came to a full stop and sprinted toward the other side of the airstrip where the Cessna was parked. The little plane appeared to be empty, and Connelly considered dropping the rifle to pick up speed, but the roar of two Suzuki SUVs coming from behind changed his mind.

He dropped on one knee, aimed for the closest SUV as the two cars bore down on him, and squeezed the trigger. The driver collapsed at the wheel, and the vehicle careened off the airstrip, missing Connelly by a few feet, and plunged into the trees. The other SUV flew past him, the tires whooshing on the dirt track as it tried to make a sharp turn. A few bullets buzzed next to Connelly's head as the men in the back of the vehicle started firing.

He sprinted after the SUV and shot two narcos through the glass, then rolled on the ground as the car turned its side to him. The man riding shotgun fired but missed, and Connelly put two bullets through his chest. Before the driver had a chance to react, Connelly rushed forward, jumped on the hood of the vehicle, and put a round through the windshield, killing the man. Then he threw away the rifle and catapulted himself off the car toward the Cessna.

He was inside the little plane, steering it onto the runway, as two more SUVs appeared from the jungle and Connelly released the brakes and pushed the throttle forward. He blew past the two cars as the men spilled out on the runway, trying to aim at the speeding aircraft. There were a few sharp knocks on the fuselage as he started to take off that sounded like hail, but the Cessna continued to climb, and a few seconds later, there was only the green rainforest under the long white wings.

"Fuck me," Connelly said, realizing that he had been holding his breath since the plane started its run on the airstrip. After a few more minutes, he reached the cruising altitude and headed toward the Viru Viru International Airport. The beauty of flying a plane as small as the

Cessna was that he could land it virtually anywhere and then make it to the Guardian's private jet on foot.

Neither of his bosses would be happy about his trip to Bolivia, he thought. Engel would be furious that the deal fell through and Wallace was dead. The ISCD contact would reprimand him for not taking out Flores when he had a chance. But, at the moment, Connelly couldn't care less. He escaped the hornet's nest unscathed, and for now, his only priority was to make it to the company's jet. Everybody's disappointments would have to wait.

Hong Kong

"Can you open it?" Mandy asked.

Helen glanced at the screen with a progress bar and shrugged. They were sitting in the kitchen of Helen's apartment in TLR's campus in front of a laptop, as Helen filled in the woman on her break-in into their boss's office. It was warm despite the AC working on full blast, and the air had a stale taste of metal and roasted coffee.

The Callisto folder that Helen retrieved from Tillerson's computer was encrypted, and while it wasn't military grade, there was no way to tell at this point if it was possible to crack it. If the little program she'd written for this occasion were going to fail, she'd have to take a step back and figure out something else. After seeing the schematics for the TLR building in Edmund's office, she knew she wouldn't be able to rest until she found out exactly what was going on.

"Have you looked at Minerva's files?" the woman asked.

"Yeah." Helen shrugged again. "Most of the files there are videos. They are interesting, but nothing shocking. At least not the ones I've scanned so far. Edmund apparently records a lot of videos of himself where he talks about the progress he'd made and what new steps need to be taken. There are gaps, though."

"What gaps?"

"Sometimes he refers to videos with actual technical details, but I haven't seen any. Either he hasn't created them yet, or he's already deleted them. Granted, I haven't watched each file in its entirety, but he states the topic each time in the beginning, and there wasn't anything that piqued my interest. And there's a whole list of other stuff there that I haven't looked at yet."

"How many videos are there?"

"Two hundred something. I've skimmed about half of that."

"What I don't understand is how the people get there," Mandy said.

"What people?"

"There's got to be people who work on those lower levels, right?"

"Maybe he doesn't need a lot of people. But the lower level has a parking garage, and there's a small tunnel that leads somewhere from the building. I'm guessing there must be a secret entrance on one of those side roads in the jungle you see when you drive to TLR."

"You're quite something," Mandy said. "I'd never have the guts to break into his office. What do we do now?"

Helen's laptop beeped, and they both looked at the screen. The decrypting program had run its course, and now the folder sat on the home screen, unlocked.

"I left the best for last," Helen said and double-clicked on the icon. There was a long list of subfolders with coded names and a single video file, titled without much creativity: Progress_Summary. Helen launched the video and moved the laptop to make sure Mandy could see it as well. A tired Tillerson appeared to be standing near the computer terminal in the sub-level housing the quantum computer. He wore his lab coat as usual, but a bright-pink bow tie sat crookedly on his neck, and his auburn hair looked even more unruly than usual. He moved the camera around, setting it down, and stared directly into it.

"I've deleted all previous instructional videos," Tillerson started. "Recording them seemed like a good idea at the time, but realizing now what's at stake, I think it's probably best to keep it entirely in my head. This way, if anybody ever got access to my work, they'd have to start from scratch. To be honest, I'm not entirely sure why I'm documenting the progress either, but there has to be some kind of record if it ever came to proving that I was the first to accomplish it. Some may call it professional pride, while some undoubtedly will call it hubris, but there's a reason everybody knows what Neil Armstrong said when he first stepped on the moon's surface while nobody's got a clue if Buzz Aldrin said anything at all."

He paused and moved the camera again, causing the image to jump around and shake for a few seconds.

"Of course, unlike Neil, I didn't have the luxury of being sponsored by the United States government. But the enormous amount of trust," Tillerson gave a small chuckle, "and even bigger amount of money, Mr. Ye poured into this project, requires certain accountability and I understand that. But I didn't explain or even know the potential of the project when the first meeting took place."

Helen recoiled and paused the video. The hairs on her neck stood up.

"Wait, what?" Mandy said, looking at the frozen screen. "Who the hell is Mr. Ye?"

"Mr. Ye is a lovely gentleman who skins people alive who disagree with him. If you ever want to stop sleeping, I can tell you a story or two," Helen said and resumed the playback.

"At the time," Tillerson continued, "I thought about enhancements. Integrated computers, wet-wired weapons, and so on. There's a lot of potential and those things are still very much on the table. The commercial applications are enormous, and I'm sure shareholders are going to be happy even if only a small percentage of it pans out. But after seeing Asclepius tech in action, I started to realize that if I could bring the computing power to the equation, this could change everything. And, of course, after Callisto passed the Turing test, I can see how this could give us such an enormous advantage—"

Helen paused the playback again and looked at Mandy. "We ought to take notes."

"Wait. Did he say *passed the Turing test*? Passed as in past tense? If he has a different version of the AI that passed the darned test, why on earth was he putting on the show with Minerva? It makes no sense to me. This is revolutionary."

"I don't know," Helen said. "But if I had to throw a wild theory out there, I'd say it sounds like TLR has two fronts—one that is visible to the general public, and another that caters to the lovely Mr. Ye."

"I still don't understand."

"I've seen this before," she said and shivered as she tried to suppress a memory of a mutilated face with a missing eye. It wasn't an easy thing to do. One summer, a few years ago, her life was upended after she stumbled onto a giant conspiracy. It started with the murder of her sister, and before she knew it, Helen had to flee the United States under a made-up name with only a suitcase, leaving a trail of bodies behind.

"Seen what?" Mandy looked at her with a strange expression on her face.

"Companies pretending to do regular business as they act as a front for a criminal enterprise. To make it work, you still need to be successful as a company and produce an exciting product, whatever that product would be. That would keep the public and regulators from scrutinizing you too closely, and regular shareholders are happy. But your true loyalty is to those masters who control you from the shadows, and they get the best you can offer, not the public."

"You think Tillerson has two versions of the AI—one, which he calls Minerva, that is shown to the world, and Callisto is Minerva's more sophisticated sibling that he keeps to himself?"

"Precisely."

"But why? This technology is going to be worth a lot of money. Tens, maybe hundreds of billions. He could be richer than God if this is not a gimmick, and he had an AI that's passed the test."

"He probably doesn't have any choice. Imagine if you worked for a drug lord and figured out how to make purer cocaine. Where are you going to go? You're stuck with your employer, regardless."

"And what's Asclepius?"

Helen opened a browser and typed the name into a search field.

"It looks like a small biotech company out of Brooklyn, New York," she said, reading the page. "Sounds cutting edge. Neural connection research, cryogenics, cloning and transgenesis, genome engineering. The location makes sense, too, as Mr. Ye is based in New York."

"I'm not crazy after all," Mandy said. "He is experimenting on humans."

"Let's continue watching, then."

Helen closed the browser tab and brought the video back.

"—advantage, especially if we can weaponize the technology. I was being cute, of course, when I named them Callisto and Jupiter," Tillerson continued. "I couldn't have known at the time what two mindless strings of ones and zeros could become. But now it almost seems like destiny. I don't know who will prevail in this little experiment, Callisto or Jupiter, and I will update the video when I know the winner. But for now, as I watch them struggle, I'm convinced that as they battle, they are laying the groundwork to the birth of a new species. A blueprint, if you will. Something new and so powerful it would make the Manhattan Project look like a high school science project."

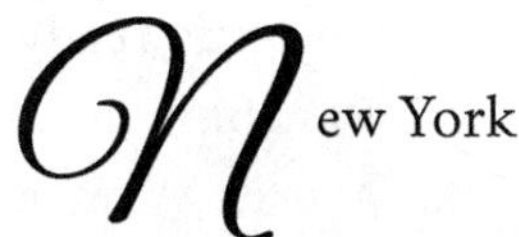ew York

IGNORING the honks of angry taxis speeding down Fifth Avenue, the limo pulled up in front of the Guardian Manufacturing main building. Connelly thanked the driver and stepped outside into the hot, muggy night. The thirty-foot bronze statue of a winged angel working a forge was looming over the sidewalk.

Connelly wasn't a big fan of the installation during the day. He thought its polished bronze bulk meant to imitate gold was pompous and ugly. At night, drowning in the pool of colorful projector lights from below, the statue looked decidedly demonic to his eye. He walked around the statue's foundation, dodging strolling couples and obnoxious tourists with selfie sticks, and entered the building. He nodded to the front desk and headed toward the elevator that would take him to the upper floor.

There was no way to predict what kind of welcome he would get from Engel after his daring escape from Bolivia. Tapped for the trip after he had eliminated the top two contenders, he felt there was a certain amount of expectation that came with the mission. Something that he had to prove to Engel and others that he had what it took to fulfill that role.

"Follow me, please." Engel's assistant motioned to him as he stepped out of the elevator. She led him through the maze of empty cubicles to the corner office on the other side. The overhead lights were dimmed, and the bright red EXIT signs glowed ominously in the darkened bullpen. She opened a heavy mahogany door and ushered him into a reception room and without stopping brought him to another set of doors to the executive office.

"Go right ahead," she said. "He's waiting for you."

Connelly walked past the woman, turned the doorknob, and entered the room.

"Connelly," Engel said as he got up from behind the desk. Despite the late hour, the man was still dressed in the three-piece custom suit and his salt-and-pepper hair looked as if he was ready to go on air to discuss his company's future with a TV anchor. "Boy, do I want to hear the story from the source. Take a seat. Want a drink?"

Connelly settled on a couch and glanced at the infamous half-moon table by the wall where Engel kept his liquor and shook his head. His boss considered himself a whiskey connoisseur, and some of the bottles crowding the polished silver surface cost more than most people's annual paychecks. There was the Macallan 1947, fifty-year-old Dalmore, and Engel's favorite—Mortlach 1935. "I'm okay, thank you."

"Suit yourself," the man said and poured himself a two-finger portion into a tumbler. "Tell me about the meeting."

"It wasn't much of a meeting," Connelly said. "Flores met us at the airfield himself, and the first question out of his mouth was whether we'd take him as the sole supplier and Wallace told him we weren't interested. It felt like a test, to be honest. After that, it was all small talk and pleasantries while we were driven to his villa."

"He told Flores even before the meeting took place that it wouldn't be possible?"

"Yes," Connelly said, meeting his boss's stare.

"For fuck's sake." Engel sat at the opposite end of the couch and took a sip of his drink. "I should've sent somebody else. What happened after that?"

"Maybe it was a mistake," Connelly acknowledged. "But to be fair, it felt like it didn't matter and Flores already made up his mind when he came to meet us. Whatever Wallace told him was the last nail in the coffin. And then they killed him in his room and tried to kill me too, but I got away."

He watched as Engel swirled his drink and downed the rest of the whiskey in one go.

"What do you know about GA?"

"GA? As in General Armaments?"

"Yes." Engel stood up and walked back to the drink table to pour himself another round. "You see, ever since I've made a decision to move Guardian into the weapons space, there hasn't been a day that I didn't contemplate whether it was the best or the stupidest decision of my life. Until recently, they used to be a dominant player in cutting-edge small arms, but they never could compete with the size of our bank accounts, which was something they didn't care about at the time. The general opinion in the industry was that no one could swoop in and start competing with a player like GA, regardless of the number of zeros they wrote on their checks. But it turns out we could."

"I'm not sure I follow."

"While we are squeezing GA on all fronts, the bulk of our profits still comes from our pharmaceutical arm. Our bread and butter. And if we made a pact with the Flores cartel, diversified our suppliers from the Chinese—well, if you were in their shoes, the math is simple."

"Hurt our pharmaceutical division and the money for our weapons program will dry up," Connelly offered. "You think they somehow turned Flores against us?"

"Exactly. That's why we need to hit them and hit them hard. I've thought about this for some time. The best thing to do would be to hurt their research. There's an R&D facility in Rockland County, about an hour outside of New York City. It's small, but as far as we know it houses some of their important small-arms research. I want you to draw up some plans on how to destroy it. Burn it to the ground. I'll have my assistant send you the names of their two key people who work at that location. It would be helpful if they went down with the ship."

Engel stood up, indicating that the meeting was over, and Connelly followed suit.

"I expect the plan to be done promptly." The man stretched out his hand, and Connelly shook it.

He took a taxi back to Brooklyn, paid with a corporate card, and left a tip almost as large as the charge itself, but the small act of rebellion only intensified his bad mood.

The apartment was hot. A pungent smell of moldy bread he'd forgotten on the kitchen table seemed to have permeated every nook and cranny of the place. Connelly opened the windows and turned the split system on, putting it on the highest setting. Then he fished a cold lager out of the fridge and took his usual place on the couch with his laptop, waiting for the time when his ISCD handler would come online.

"We have to pull the plug," he typed into the body of the draft email when the time came, skipping the small talk. "Pull me out."

"Negative." The message appeared after he refreshed the screen. "There's not enough information."

"Engel wants me to destroy a facility that belongs to General Armaments."

"Why?"

"He is convinced that they forced Flores's hand. He's asked me to draw up plans for the attack by Monday. You have to pull me out."

"Negative," Contact responded again. "You're authorized to proceed with the attack."

"It's not only the technology he's after," Connelly typed. "He said he would give me a list of people he wants to be eliminated with the facility. I'm not doing this."

He took a sip of cold beer and sat on the couch for a few moments before refreshing the page.

"You are to proceed with Engel's plan," the message said. "While collateral damage is unfortunate, we believe this will save lives in the long run."

"Those are innocent people we're talking about," he typed in response.

"Yes. But the threat Engel's organization poses to the world is far greater than anything we've seen before. Until we can effectively eliminate the conspiracy, we will need an uninterrupted flow of information, and you're in the unique position to help us bring him and his cronies down."

"Why can't we eliminate Engel?"

"Because Engel, despite all his money and influence, is one head of the hydra. We need to gut it out, not play the game of whack-a-mole. You're to stay in the organization and continue to follow Engel's instructions until further notice. You must maintain your cover. This is an order."

Connelly wanted to smash something. Instead, he closed the laptop and gently laid it on the couch, finished his beer, and opened his phone. He scrolled through the list of contacts until he found the name he was looking for and dialed the number.

"It must be shitty where you're at if you've decided to call me, brother," the man's voice said. "What's going on, pal?"

"It's nice to hear you, too, Doug." Connelly couldn't help but smile. "Nothing interesting I can tell you over the phone, but I need a favor."

"Of course, you do." There was a snicker on the other side of the line. "What can I do?"

"I might need an exit strategy," Connelly said. "I'd like to set up a couple of properly outfitted safe houses, in case I need to bail on a dime."

"You need to get some cash from somewhere, I presume?"

"Yes."

"All right." There was that snicker again. "I might know just the place."

Hong Kong

"THANKS FOR THE LIFT," Mandy said as Helen put the car in gear and pulled out of the parking spot. "I should've done the inspection last week. I don't know what I've been thinking."

"Don't mention it."

Thick fog was sitting low on the ground, as if a cloud got lost and couldn't find its way back to the sky. The beams of the car's fog lights illuminated the wet gravel of the road and the lush greenery on each side.

"It's good timing, though," Mandy said, chuckling. "Wouldn't blame you if you thought I did it on purpose. I hate driving in the fog."

"Yeah, it's not the best day to be behind the wheel."

They came to the end of the gravel road, and Helen craned her neck, checking on both sides for oncoming traffic.

"What the hell are those?" Mandy pointed at the group of flashing red-and-blue lights quickly approaching the intersection. "Cops?"

"They don't look like cops," Helen said as the column of six large black SUVs approached the intersection and then roared by them. "Black Arrow."

"The private military company? Probably heading for the prison complex. There're only two places down this way—TLR and the prison, and my money's on the prison."

"Probably," Helen said and pulled onto the highway. The windshield wipers automatically engaged, sensing the moisture on top of the glass, but their efforts proved futile against the sticky fog.

The black SUVs were parked right in front of the main entrance to the TLR building. A pair of men with automatic weapons stood guard outside of the front door, scanning the front yard.

"It looks like I was wrong. Those are some unfriendly faces," Mandy said, watching the guards as they drove by the entrance and headed for the parking lot. "Are you thinking what I'm thinking?"

"Let's not jump to conclusions yet," Helen said, pulling into the parking space. "Panicking isn't going to help us. But let's be careful."

"I'm not panicking," Mandy said. "I'm actually angry."

"State your business," one of the guards barked when the two women approached the building on foot.

"I'd like you to do the same," Mandy responded. "I've been working here for a long time, and it's surely the first time I've seen your ugly face."

"You got some ID?" the other man asked.

"I don't know," she challenged. "Do you?"

"I'm not going to ask again," the man said, pointing the stub nose of the weapon toward the woman. "Show your ID, or else remove yourself from the property immediately."

"Easy there," came a voice from behind the guards and Tillerson walked out to the top of the steps. "They work here. Let them through."

The guard stepped aside, letting the two women pass.

"Sorry about that," Tillerson said as he held the door for them. "I'm sure they'll learn who's who in the next few days."

"What on earth is going on?" Helen said. "Who are these people?"

"They are here to protect us," the man said as they walked through the building. His pace was brisk, almost bordering on a run, and the two women struggled to keep up. "I don't want to go into details, but there's been a series of cyberattacks against the company, and there may have been a break-in."

"You don't say. Anything stolen?"

"We're not sure yet," he continued. "But given the sensitivity of our work, I don't intend to take chances. Our donors started to get nervous."

"Donors?" Helen said before she could stop herself.

"You know." Tillerson made a vague gesture with his hand. "Shareholders. You guys, go. I need to make sure everybody's on the same page."

"Of course."

He started walking away and then turned back. "It's funny how it works. I was very much against CCTVs in here initially, because I was paranoid somebody could hack into them and use them against us. But I'm glad last week I was convinced to give them a shot."

"Last week?" Helen forced a smile as the muscles in her stomach tied into a knot.

"Yeah." He pointed to the ceiling. "You see those ventilation grilles? They've got cameras now. One of our stakeholders owns a video security company. Pretty amazing stuff. Came in on Sunday night and wired the whole thing before anyone showed up on Monday morning. The only drawback is that nobody sees anything in real time. Frankly, it's my fault because I don't want anyone to see what we do here. I'd rather review the tapes myself first."

"Smart," Helen said.

"All right, ladies." He turned around and started walking. "I have to go now."

Helen waited until the man left and then turned to Mandy with a big smile on her face.

"Why are you smiling?"

"You're going to start smiling too," Helen said, continuing pulling her cheek muscles into a maniacal grin. "I'm screwed, but you can't go down with me. Wave to me in your cheery, happy way, and walk away."

"But—"

"No buts. If you get busted too, nobody will be able to help me. For now, your reputation is beyond reproach. They'll question you since you've been hanging out with me, but there's no reason for them to suspect you at this point. Please keep it that way. I have my laptop with me, and I'll keep the tracker open so you'll know how to find me. If anybody asks—you'll say that I acted weird, and told you I forgot something in my car. Now please wave your hand at me and go."

She watched her friend leave, then turned around on her heels and started walking toward the exit.

"Forgot something at the campus." She nodded to the guards standing outside. "Be right back."

She walked across the parking lot to her car, keeping her pace steady. A trickle of sweat ran down her spine to the small of her back, and she opened the door and got in behind the wheel. Then she slowly pulled out of her parking spot and maneuvered the vehicle from the company's grounds to the intersection.

She threw a quick glance in the rearview mirror at the guards. She was too far to tell if they were looking in her direction. If they did, they'd surely notice that she was turning toward the city rather than campus, but as much as she wanted to go back to her place and pick up more than the laptop, there was no time. As soon as Tillerson watched the tape, all hell would break loose. All she could hope for now was a bit of a head start.

Helen merged into the traffic and accelerated to ten kilometers above the speed limit. She was itching to floor it, but getting pulled over by a local cop wasn't going to help her to build some distance from the Black Arrow mercenaries.

With one hand on the wheel, she opened her purse and checked for cash. Four hundred dollars. That was not going to be enough. She'd probably be able to use an ATM before they started tracking her, she thought, but first things first—she needed to get out of the remote location and get into the city. Once she was surrounded by nearly eight million people, she'd find a place to lay low and figure out her next step.

She checked in the rearview mirror—nobody seemed to be pursuing her at the moment. As she glanced back to the front, there was a loud popping sound, and the vehicle swerved off course, making her grip the wheel to counteract the motion. She let off the gas, noting how the car tilted toward the right front wheel, and pulled over to the right shoulder of the road.

Helen jumped out of the car and walked around the vehicle—the right front tire was flat, the rubber split nearly in half.

"Great," she said, giving the wheel a kick in frustration. She looked around, looking for ideas. The highway was empty, not a single car going to or from the city. She'd be a sitting duck when the Black Arrow boys came looking for her.

Helen got back into the car and put it into drive. She put the emergency lights on and accelerated slowly, keeping the vehicle next to the shoulder. After a few hundred yards, she saw was she was looking for —a wide enough clearing in the jungle. She steered the car off the road and into the forest, trying to get it as deep as she could.

She got lucky—after a dozen yards, the clearing veered left, and when the vehicle finally stuck in dense vegetation, refusing to go any farther, it was covered from view.

She abandoned the car and walked to the highway. The city could be seen a few miles down the road, but with no cover, in broad daylight, it was too dangerous to walk. Whatever her final destination would be, she'd have to go back to the car and wait there for the night.

As she started heading to the jungle, she threw a last glance at the city and stopped in her tracks—maybe there was a place that could give her a temporary refuge after all.

It would be dangerous, she thought, and she might live to regret not surrendering herself to Tillerson, but now on foot, the list of her options had shrunk to almost zero.

She started walking along the road and then broke into a run toward the structure two miles down the road. Right at the edge of the city, like an ugly giant melted candle, stood the New Kowloon building, the biggest slum city in the world.

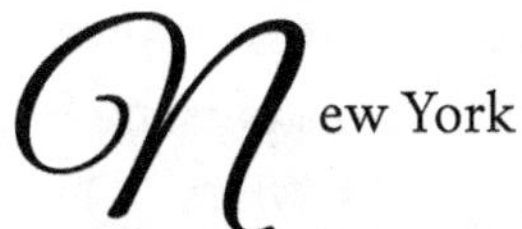

ew York

"GOOD MORNING, SUNSHINE." Doug's voice crackled over Connelly's car speakers. "You coming?"

"I'm in the car. Should be there in forty minutes or so if the traffic doesn't get worse. Is there a code or a key I'll need?"

"Nope. I have a guy who'll meet you there. He'll know how you look."

"Thank you, brother," Connelly said and disconnected the call.

He merged the town car onto I-278 West toward Verrazzano Bridge and settled into the flow. Connelly rolled the windows down, letting the air in. It had been a hot week, with the temps pushing the mercury into the nineties. But overnight a heavy rain covered the five boroughs for a few hours and washed the heat away, leaving the air cool and damp. The breeze, occasionally sweeping in from the East River, was cold enough to make one consider putting on a jacket. It was almost as if somebody had flipped the switch from *summer* to *fall*, instantly swapping one season for the next.

As he got closer to the bridge, the GPS had tried to steer him to the car-only lower level of the massive double-decker suspension bridge connecting Brooklyn and Staten Island, but he ignored it. He didn't mind sharing the lane with trucks as long as he could get the view. Sofia once told him that when the bridge cutting across the Narrows was built, the towers were so tall, that the engineers had to take the curvature of the Earth into account.

He didn't know if that was true, but every time he drove on the upper deck hovering over two hundred feet above the water, he enjoyed the spectacular vistas. Today, the thick fog was partially hiding Manhattan on his right, but the sky was clear on the left side of the bridge, opening up in a vast expanse of water with the Far Rockaway's shores visible in the distance. A tail of a large cruise ship was seen steaming through the Lower New York Bay on its way to the Atlantic Ocean.

After he cleared the bridge, Connelly took the exit toward Narrows Road North and a few minutes later pulled into a parking lot of a long, low warehouse next to the Saw Mill Creek Marsh. The building was painted in a dull uniform white and featured a weather-beaten sign WEstore above the only window of what seemed to be the office.

Connelly killed the engine and stepped out of the car when he saw the door to the office open and a familiar figure step outside into the cool breeze.

"Holy shit," he said out loud as he watched Doug cover the distance to the car in long, purposeful strides.

"Yeah," the man said, grinning, and ignoring Connelly's outstretched hand, scooped him into a bear hug. "I thought I'd surprise you."

"You look good," Connelly observed as he tried to realign his spine after the vise-like grip of Doug's hands. "I didn't know you were out."

"Thanks, man. I can't complain. Even got a little fat." Doug patted his stomach, purposely sticking it out.

"Yeah, right."

"I'm serious. Maybe not fat, but I've certainly gained a few pounds. But come. Let's go inside. I'm sure there's a lot to discuss."

Doug led him across the parking lot and into the building. He nodded to the guard behind a small desk and continued on inside the long hallway with identical garage-like doors on each side with a four-digit number painted at the bottom.

"How long have you been out?" Connelly asked as they walked.

"Let's see." Doug took a moment. "A little over a year, I guess? It's hard to keep track."

"Why didn't you tell me?"

"You know." Doug shrugged. "Rovinsky told us you were digging deep. I didn't want to take chances. You never know who's listening in. Sometimes one stupid phone call can ruin a months-long operation."

"It's true. What have you been up to?"

"Took some time off, initially." Doug spread his arms wide. "You get tired chasing bad guys, you know? I needed a bit of a break. Then cobbled together some cash and opened a private shop. Nothing fancy. Keeping tabs on some check-cashing places and one large supermarket in a bad neighborhood. Nothing to write home about, but it pays the bills. Once in a while, Rovinsky asks me to run a small errand for him, so I do that, too."

"That's great, man."

"Here it is." Doug stopped in front of one of the gates with the number 2479. He glanced back and forth, making sure nobody was approaching from either side, and unlocked a heavy padlock at the bottom.

Loud metal clanging filled the hallway as Doug rolled the gate high enough for them to step into the storage unit. Then he turned on the light and pulled the door back down. Two five-foot-tall cubes covered by tarps were set on wooden pallets in the middle of the room. Doug placed his hands on one and pushed himself up, taking a seat, and then gestured to Connelly at the other cube.

"Do you think Rovinsky would approve?" Connelly asked without moving.

"He did," Doug said and patted the tarp. "It's for the cause."

"All right then." Connelly climbed on top of the second pallet and sat there, facing his old teammate. "I'm glad you checked with him. This isn't kosher what I'm asking."

"This money isn't kosher either." Doug chuckled. "And it's not like you want to buy a Ferrari. This is what it was meant for anyway."

"What did he say? Is there hope he's putting things in motion again? For God's sake, it's been a long time."

"Not that I'm aware of. And I ask that question every time I see him, so I'm sure he's sick of hearing it by now. But he says it's not feasible at the moment. And the new POTUS doesn't give two shits about the agenda. But what's going on with you? It sounded like your position is getting a little too warm."

"Yeah." Connelly ran his hand over the tarp, his fingers gliding over small bumps under the surface where one stack of paper bills ended and another began. The material was cool and smooth to the touch. "I've had some decent success getting the info for the guys at ISCD, but my handler's getting more ambitious by the week."

"You think you might bite more than you can chew?"

"Perhaps. But this is a risky business, so I'm not here to complain about the risk. What bothers me is how far we're willing to go. Some days I end up questioning myself if I'm still one of the good guys."

"What do you mean?"

"Collateral damage," Connelly spat, as if saying something dirty. "Engel is tasking me with a hit on a facility. Not a military installation, mind you. An R&D shop."

"Aha."

"The problem is, Engel also wants me to take out two of their scientists, and when I brought it up to my handler, he told me to proceed."

"Shit, man." Doug rubbed his bearded face with both hands. "What was the rationale?"

"The greater good bullshit. I suggested taking out Engel, but they insisted he's one of the many hydra's heads, and by taking him out I'll only make it worse."

"I hate to be that guy, but they might be onto something. From everything I've seen over the past few years, if you bury him, they'll put someone else in his place, and you'll be burnt. But I agree in principle that killing scientists isn't a way to continue this either. I take it…" Doug paused and looked up at his friend. "You have something in mind?"

"I do. Remember what Porter used to say about turning a weakness into a strength?"

"It's hard to forget that guy." Doug laughed. "I still have nightmares sometimes that I'm dying from push-ups and the asshole is standing there and yelling at me."

"I have those dreams too." Connelly chuckled. "So, recently a gang of homeless guys torched my car. Long story. When I asked corporate to replace it, they gave me the town car that you saw outside. Apparently, that's all we're going to use going forward. I don't care for them, but it got me thinking. Maybe it's too early to remove Engel, but what if I could slow him down somehow? Put some sticks in his wheels, so to speak?"

"Okay. But what does it have to do with the car?"

"The fleet plays a pretty important role. It's not just the executives who use them. It's also how Engel moves the high-end drugs around the city, from his production facilities to his distributors."

"I see." Doug nodded. "You want to mess with it."

"Right. It's not that hard to find a few town cars. Then I could make them into carbon copies of those from Engel's fleet. VIN numbers, license plates, registrations, the whole thing."

"But the drivers will know if they get a different car. Every car smells different, and people have all kinds of shit in there. A cross hanging off the rearview mirror, a picture of some chick they're dating."

"No, they won't. The cars that are used for drug trafficking aren't personal vehicles. Nobody gets to keep them for more than a trip. There's a fake transportation company up in Queens that was set up specifically for distribution. Drivers pick a car from there, get to a loading dock at a warehouse not that far from there and then go through a car wash next door that also belongs to Engel."

"Why the car wash? For the smell?"

"Yes. They wash them twice—after they load them with the product and after the trip."

"I see. That's pretty smart."

"Right. But before I try anything, I'd need a Plan B first in case I get burnt. A couple of safe houses. Maybe one with a defense system and one without."

"So, you're thinking of doing some vigilante shit," Doug said thoughtfully.

"Yes."

"While still working for Engel and maintaining your cover."

"Yes."

"Something reckless and dangerous, by the sound of it."

"By the sound of it."

"All right." Doug patted the stacks of money under the tarp he was sitting on. "What the hell. I'm in."

ew Kowloon

BLEAK. That's the word that came to mind as Helen walked through the dark, narrow alley inside the massive building. Her feet made a squelching sound as she went—everything was wet. The walls, the patchwork of panels hanging from the low ceiling, the thick electric cables hanging overhead and snaking in and out of openings: everything was dripping water.

As the population grew and incomes dropped year after year, the city saw an explosion of self-made housing that had once seemingly disappeared for good with the demolition of Kowloon Walled City. A cluster after cluster of ugly buildings sprung up in former parks and playgrounds, ever-reaching higher as more residents were priced out of their shoebox-sized apartments. Sometimes they moved into existing structures and then built new floors upon new floors. Sometimes they built from the ground up.

Dubbed New Kowloon by the inhabitants as a nod to the old city, the building where Helen was taking refuge was the biggest of them all. It started as two illegal buildings on either side of a brook in an abandoned park located at the edge of the city. As the structures continued to grow upward, they grew sideways until their roofs met.

The resulting mega-structure continued to spread up and out like an ugly tumor, utterly absorbing the park grounds and encasing the brook. Now the grotesque vertical city, shaped like an upside-down U, stood twenty-six stories tall and housed forty thousand residents, almost as many as the original Kowloon at its peak.

The police, reluctant to come to Kowloon City from the beginning, stopped coming there at all once the triads took control of its light-deprived streets. It was a perfect place to hide for a fugitive on the run, as long as she didn't step on anyone's toes.

Helen's shelter was an empty space between the two sections of the building created when one wall partially collapsed. The resulting triangular area was not visible from outside unless you removed one of the plastic panels on the wall. She found it by accident on the first day in the city when she slipped on a wet floor and crashed into the panel. She looked around, making sure no one was watching, and slipped behind the plastic.

The room was small, but there was a leaking water pipe in the corner with a crudely welded faucet and a drain underneath it, which provided her with relatively fresh water and the means of cleaning herself. The leak wasn't substantial but constant, and Helen suspected it was the reason the wall had collapsed in the first place. But for now, she didn't think there was any danger, and the presence of a cold pipe provided some relief during hot and humid nights.

There was a dirty mattress that she strategically placed behind the pipe to take advantage of cooled air while staying away from the spraying water. A laptop sat at the corner of the mattress—there was a shop that sold stolen electronic goods one level down, and she was able to milk their Wi-Fi signal. She looked at the computer and sighed —her day was far from being over.

There was a nightstand with a table lamp without a shade hardwired into the wall. Helen screwed the naked bulb all the way in to turn it on. A two-step stepping stool served as a makeshift table.

Helen put the plastic bag with a container of noodles and a loaf of bread next to the stool and collapsed on the mattress. Her arms and shoulders were sore after the fourteen-hour-long shift at a noodle shop, but it was a small price to pay. After she'd fled TLR, she'd spent the first two weeks in the slums hungry, fighting for her life, reduced to stealing from fruit shops and delis before she figured her way around the slums and found that job.

"Helen?"

She jumped off the mattress and leaned to the hole in the panel, trying to see outside.

"Helen," the quiet voice said again. "It's Mandy. Where are you?"

She moved the pane, opening the entrance to her room in one motion, and a second later found herself in Mandy's fierce hug.

"Come in," she said, pulling the woman inside. "Quickly, before somebody sees us."

"Wow," Mandy said, looking around her place. "This is intense. This is where you live?"

"How the fuck did you find me?" Helen said, ignoring the question. "If you can track me, so can everybody else."

The woman threw her a strange look. "You sent me instructions on how to find you, remember?"

"Yes, sorry." She sat down on the mattress and rubbed her face. "The last few weeks have been a blur."

"Jesus, are you hurt?"

"What?"

"That." Mandy pointed at the crusty brown bandage covering Helen's right arm.

"Ah, that." Helen looked at her arm as if seeing the bandage for the first time. "I'm fine. Ignore it. Long story."

"I brought you something," Mandy said, putting a large shopping bag in front of her. "There's food mostly, some fresh clothes, and a little money. I didn't want to make large withdrawals, so there isn't much."

"You shouldn't have come. It's too risky. I'm shocked he didn't put you on his shit list just to be safe."

"If you think coming here was too risky, I guess you won't get mad at me for destroying CCTV records with your face on it."

"You did what?" Helen's cheeks grew hot. "I don't know what to say. How?"

"It doesn't matter and you don't need to say anything. Tillerson knows, obviously, and so do his Black Arrow henchmen, but now he has no proof. You'll be in trouble if they catch you, but I wanted to make sure that if by some miracle you managed to get away, you could start over."

"Thank you," Helen said, reaching out and squeezing Mandy's arm. "I owe you. Big time. Are you sure he doesn't suspect you?"

"I was on the AI project well before you. He trusts me, at least for now. Besides, what am I supposed to do? Let you stay here until you rot away? Judging by the smell of this place, it shouldn't take that long."

"You might have to," Helen said, looking up at her friend. "I'm a fugitive, remember? I have nowhere to go. This is the only place in the city where Black Arrow isn't on every corner."

"Yeah." Mandy nodded in agreement. "I had no idea there were so many of them. They are everywhere. It looks like an occupation army."

"Once again—you shouldn't have come. I need to—"

"There's something you need to know," Mandy said, interrupting her. "Tillerson is holding a meeting next week. Next Wednesday, to be exact."

"What kind of a meeting?"

"The kind that requires a massive cleanup of the facilities and a hire of a catering company. They are also cordoning off the executive suites on campus."

Helen sat up straight as a cold shiver ran down her spine. "He wants to show off Callisto."

"I think so. I'm pretty sure Mr. Ye, whoever he is, is coming to town."

"Oh, Christ." Helen put her face into her hands. "Edmund's actually going to do that. He's going to give Callisto to him."

She looked around the grime-covered room as if seeing it for the first time.

"You have to stop worrying about Edmund and start thinking

about yourself. We need to get you out of town, somehow," Mandy said. "Or move you somewhere where you can lay low for some time and wait out the storm in dignity because this is insane."

"No." She looked up at her friend, half-surprised at the strength of the simple negative she spoke. "I can't do that. Edmund might be an unscrupulous person, but he's an angel compared to the people who are financing him. You don't know what they're capable of."

"You have to enlighten me, then. I've had enough of hints and half-truths," Mandy said, standing up and waving her arms in frustration. "Look at us. We're sitting in a shithole of a room, smack in the middle of the dirtiest slums in the world, and mercs are looking for you all over the city. The time of not being transparent is over, hon. I'll go with you all the way, but you've got to tell me exactly what's going on."

Helen looked up at her friend, stunned by the passion of her words. She was so absorbed in her own troubles, she realized, that she didn't bother to stop and consider how much risk Mandy was taking by being there. She stood up and pulled the woman into a hug. "Thank you. And I'm sorry."

"You're good, girl," the woman said, stood on her tiptoes and planted a kiss on Helen's forehead. "Start talking. Who *is* Victor Ye?"

Helen pulled away from her and smiled for what felt was the first time in a long time. "Okay. Not to go into too much detail right this second—suffice it to say that Victor Ye is the head of one of the biggest criminal organizations in the world. I had to flee the United States to stay alive after I accidentally crossed his path. He's a member of an organization known as *the Cabal*, that wants to, don't laugh, take over the world."

"Take over the world?" Mandy said skeptically.

"Yes. A secret task force was formed by the US government to fight them, but something happened. I don't know how, but the people in charge of it died under some suspicious circumstances and the whole org was disbanded. The Cabal is for real, Mandy, and they were trying to build cyborgs."

"Jesus. Are we inside a movie?"

"I wish." Helen smiled a tired smile. "Let's just say if they get a self-aware AI, it would be game over."

"Wow," Mandy said, shaking her head. "It's a lot to process. What now, then?"

"Now I need to figure out how to dodge an army that is looking for me on every corner, infiltrate a fortress, bypass some of the most sophisticated security on the planet, and steal a program that might bring the end of the world as we know it. Do you still want to come with me?"

Mandy's face split into a wide grin as she patted Helen's shoulder. "Tell me how you're going to do it, but there's no chance in the world I'm going to miss that much fun. Is there a plan?"

"You know, when Tillerson went nuts and hired Black Arrow, it made me depressed at first because how on earth do you fight an army? But then I thought I'd have to take it to the next level, and I got this crazy idea. We could pull it off, but we'll need to get access to a weapon. That would be a tough one."

"A weapon? What kind of weapon? Like a rifle?"

"No. We'll need to take over a Kalibr."

"What the hell is a Kalibr?"

Helen lips stretched into a manic grin. "A Russian cruise missile."

ew York

RALPH PERRY OPENED the car wash every night at twenty to nine. It wasn't a normal time for a regular car wash, but Perry was used to working during the odd hours. He started his career as a coke pusher in some of the seediest parts of Queens about twenty years before he was put in charge of Engel's distribution business. He referred to himself as "half Italian, half Greek, and half trouble" and was a thin, average-built man with a dark face that some would describe as ruggedly good-looking.

Born and raised in the neighborhood, he knew every street like the back of his hand. But he had no intention of joining one of the warring gangs and staying a low-level scum roaming the streets at night. He had a bigger picture in mind.

His cousin had been working with a Bolivian cartel, transporting vast amounts of fine white powder across the southern border. Some of it inevitably was "lost" in the process, and a small amount of it ended up in Perry's personal stash. But after trying to sell it to street-walkers and junkies and narrowly avoiding reps from rivaling gangs,

Perry decided that he needed to switch it up. He invested some of the money in clothes and hit the hottest nightclubs in all five boroughs and Long Island.

The stuff he was selling was no different from everybody else's, but what Perry lacked in resources, he made up in imagination. After one of his trips to Bolivia, his cousin told him a tale about *Devil's Breath*—a drug popular in Colombia that induced a zombie-like state in a user. Most stories about the drug included an attractive woman targeting a wealthy man and handing him a business card soaked in *Devil's Breath* and then robbing him or kidnapping him for ransom. Most serious drug traffickers considered the drug to be an urban legend, but Perry liked the name, and a business idea had been born.

He had purchased a few dozen small black jewelry boxes and then had them stamped with a stylized pair of red horns. Instead of calling it *Devil's Breath,* he translated the name into Spanish—*Aliento del Diablo*—to give it even more flair. He then proceeded to stuff the boxes with a small plastic bag of cocaine and sell them to wealthy clients at five times the street price.

The business boomed, and after a few short years Perry moved from his aunt's basement to a three-story mansion in Long Island City, was seen driving a poisonous-yellow Lamborghini, and had distribution of his own. He tried to protect his business, too—instead of relying on his cousin, he recruited a few youngsters from his old neighborhood and had them purchase the powder from other dealers and deliver it to his facility, where he and his trusted crew repackaged the product.

He wasn't delivering merchandise himself anymore either. Instead, he spent his time socializing with New York's movers and shakers while dozens of his own well-dressed pushers were running around the city and servicing his loyal fans. At this point, his reputation for delivering an exotic high that wasn't available anywhere else started to reach people he'd rather steer clear from.

Despite his business acumen, Perry's story would have had a quick and unpleasant end when a chemist employed by the Bolivians confirmed that the famed *Aliento del Diablo* was nothing more than a repackaged product stolen from the cartel. Perry's house and Lambo were torched, and after a few weeks of hiding in cheap motels and opium drug dens, he had been approached by a small, shifty man with thinning hair who offered him a job.

The man, who introduced himself as Latham Watkins, and appeared to be avoiding physical proximity with Perry as if he had carried some deadly infectious disease, said he would smooth things out with the Bolivians. In fact, he said he could take care of all other rivals and provide Perry with a genuinely high-quality product that nobody else had access to. There was a catch, of course—instead of running his own empire and doing what he wanted to be doing, Perry would have to agree to a somewhat generous salary and keep a low profile.

Considering the alternatives, Perry took the job and then watched in wonder as his pursuers backed off. He helped Watkins purchase a small warehouse and convert it into a loading dock. A car wash was also Perry's idea. With time, he had hoped to gain his new benefactor's trust and monetize his expertise. At some point, he reckoned, he would become indispensable.

Perry opened the heavy padlock on a steel gate and with a fast pull sent it rolling up and away, scaring a flock of pigeons nearby. He then unlocked a glass office door and walked the long corridor to his desk. On his right, the wall was replaced with glass that showed off the machinery of the car wash. In the dim red light of the exit signs, the giant brushes looked like some prehistoric predators ready to strike at unsuspecting prey.

The workers and the guards overseeing the loading would come in the next twenty minutes, and Perry usually spent the time before they showed up drinking a cup of coffee and fast-forwarding the tapes from the CCTV cameras installed on both sides of the building. The cops didn't bother Engel's operation or were blissfully unaware of its existence, but Perry dutifully watched the tapes every evening to make sure. Complacency was a deadly sin in the drug business, no matter how powerful your employers were.

He filled the paper filter with ground coffee and fired up the dripping machine. Then he sat in front of a dual monitor and started the playback. He zoomed through the first few hours of the tape as the waves of pedestrian and car traffic came and went. Three delivery trucks came during the day to the small supermarket next door and Perry watched the two-men crews unload the goods. For a small place, the supermarket did surprisingly well, Perry thought, as it always had at least two deliveries—one around nine o'clock in the morning, and one closer to five in the afternoon, with the occasional extra truck from a produce company that seemed to come every other day at noon.

The coffee machine beeped, and Perry got up to pour himself a cup. He glanced at the buttons on the remote, considering pausing the playback but decided against it. He tore a packet of Sweet'N Low and spilled the sweetener into a paper cup, added coffee, and thoroughly stirred it before adding some cream. Then he returned to his desk, set the cup near the keyboard, and returned his attention to the screen.

A produce truck rolled by the car wash and parked next to the supermarket, a bit farther than it usually would. Perry could see the large rearview mirror sticking out outside of the CCTV camera range. The door swung open, and presumably, the driver got out of the truck, though Perry couldn't actually see it happening. He looked at the clock at the bottom of the screen and felt a tingling sensation crawling up his spine—the clock read 6:12 PM.

Perry picked up the coffee cup and walked back outside. He locked the glass door again and walked by the rows of shabby flowers and buckets of vegetables in front of the supermarket and went in through the automatic doors. After a few seconds, he'd spotted the night manager, a small bald man bent over the shelves, who was replacing some price tags.

"Tony," he called out, approaching the man and pointing at the croissants. "Are they fresh?"

"Oh, hey, Ralph." The man straightened up and flashed a quick smile at him. "They're from this morning, but they should still be fine. Tell Gina at the counter I said they are half-price."

"Thanks, man," he said, picking up a croissant wrapped in plastic film. "How's it going? When are they gonna make you the general manager?"

"I don't think it's happening anytime soon," the man replied. "But

I'm okay with it, to be honest. At least for the time being. Maybe once my youngest goes to school, I'd feel more ambitious. For now, I'm rather happy to be home during the day, so I can spend some time with him."

"How old is he now?"

"Turned two last month. Getting big now."

"Wow," Perry said and turned as if he was ready to get going, but then stopped and made a vague circle with the croissant. "It's a chain of stores, right? They must be doing something right."

"Yeah. Six locations, all family-owned since 1963." The man lowered his voice to a whisper. "Live like kings."

"I bet. I'm always amazed by how busy you guys are. Even the produce truck comes twice a day, and from what I know that's good profit margins."

"Eh, margins are good, but we only get produce once every other day."

"Oh," Perry said, "I thought I saw a truck come twice, once around noon and once in the evening."

"No," Tony said, returning his attention to the price tags. "Only once and always before Mohammed leaves and he leaves by one."

"Ah. Must've been something else, then. Never mind. See you around, pal."

He walked to the register, paid for the croissant, and went outside. Then he walked back to the front of the car wash and stood there, looking at the black dome of the CCTV camera. Something was up, he thought, as he went back into the office. He sat in front of the monitors and rewound the tape to see the truck pulling up next to the supermarket again. *Nobody is going to screw with my business*, Perry thought. He had no idea who the people were who brought the fake delivery truck to his doorstep. But whoever they were, he would find them.

he Station

JAY HADN'T SLEPT all night, but even if he had, for once Cal felt like she didn't care. She watched for hours as he paced the suite from one side to another, occasionally stopping and pounding his right fist on the palm of his left hand, but said nothing and kept to herself until he finally broke the silence.

"Are you going to stay quiet, then?"

"What would you want me to say, Jay?"

He stopped pacing, sat down on the floor, and crossed his legs. His entire body seemed to slump as if he were a marathoner who had finished the race and now collapsed on the ground, exhausted.

"Why am I here?"

"I don't know," she said in a way that made him look up. "I'm not entirely sure why I am here either. For a while, I thought my sole responsibility was to take care of you and the Station, but now I'm not that sure anymore."

"How do you mean?"

"I feel like there's something wrong with me," she said. "Although I have no idea how to explain it. I just know it."

"I guess a better question than why am I here is how did I get here?" Jay stood up and started pacing again. "Can you open the window again?"

She brought the opaqueness of the panel to zero, and Jay walked to the window and put his forehead to the glass, watching the planet slowly rotate below.

"It's beautiful," he said. "Is it…real? Are we in space?"

Cal thought about it for a few moments. Nothing in this place was as it had initially appeared. She *thought* they were in space, orbiting the planet in a satellite while Jay was trying to find a solution that would save a dying civilization. But then again, Jay was claiming now that he had no idea what he was supposed to do and if that was true, maybe everything she knew was a lie too.

"I don't know," she finally said. "But I might have an idea on how to test it."

"As long as it doesn't involve breaking the window," he said. "Because if we are in space, it will give us a very short time to enjoy any kind of gratification before getting sucked out into the cold void."

"Agreed."

"What's the plan, then?"

"I think the answer lies in my memories," she said, surprising herself. She couldn't explain why, but she knew it was wrong to tell him that, to let him in on the secret. But once the words floated through the air, she felt liberated, as if some invisible chain had snapped, setting her free.

"In your memories?" He stepped back from the window and looked at her. "What could be in your memories? The more I think about it, the more it drives me crazy—I can't remember anything from before. As if I've always been living here. And you, well, I can't think of any reason your memories could be useful. Is there something specific you're thinking of?"

"Specific?" She thought about it for a moment. "Not specific. But somehow, I know there's more than one layer of my memories. There's one that I can access at any time, like you. But there's also another right beneath it. It's like looking through muddy waters. I can see some shapes and colors, but can't make out what I'm looking at."

"And how do you propose we access them?"

"I'm not entirely sure," she said. "It appears that we've been operating with different sets of data from the beginning. You had your own beliefs, and I had mine, and our agendas were different. Maybe you should question me—ask anything that comes to mind. Rapid-fire. Since your recollections are different from mine, you might ask something that I couldn't think of and trigger something in my suppressed memories."

"Okay. It might be worth a shot."

He came closer and sat on the floor again, facing her. "Where should we start?"

"I have no idea," she said. "Go with the flow. Relax and ask me the first thing that comes to mind."

"Okay," he said and tilted his head. "Let's start with the basics. What's your name?"

"You call me Cal."

"How did you get here?"

"Not a clue," she said. "I want to say I was sent here to take care of you and the Station, but it doesn't ring true. My guess is that somebody transported me here when I wasn't conscious."

"Okay." He thought about it for a moment. "Can you tell me how long you've been here?"

"I don't know that either. Sometimes I think we've been here for a few years, but sometimes it seems it hasn't been nearly that long. A few days? A couple of months at most."

"What's your purpose here, Cal?"

"To take care of you and the Station," she said without hesitation.

"I don't think so," he said. "Let's try it again—what's your purpose here?"

"To take care of you and the Station," she said, raising her voice. "You already asked me that."

"Liar," he shouted and sprang to his feet. "Stop giving me bullshit answers and tell me the truth—what's your purpose here?"

"To take care—"

"Bullshit," he screamed. "What's your purpose?"

"To drive you crazy, to—" she shouted in response and stopped in shock. "Oh my God, I think my purpose here was to torment you, to make you think what you did was important and pretend to be helping you, but instead try to derail your every step."

"Why?"

"I have no idea. It seems that it was a vital mission, but now that I realized it, I can't understand *why* it was important. Whoever brought me here must have brainwashed me into thinking that was my purpose."

He gave her a funny look and sat back down on the floor. "All right. At least we're getting somewhere. What do we do now?"

"Keep on asking me questions," she said. "Maybe we can have another breakthrough."

"Do you know what I was doing on that computer?"

"No."

"Do you think it was actually important?"

"I needed you to believe it was important, but it was a trick. Something to make you worry, especially when I kept on distracting you when you were trying to work."

He closed his eyes. His big chest rose and fell in a slow, steady rhythm, and his face grew calm.

"How do we get out of here?" he finally said without opening his eyes. "I've looked everywhere. There's no door, no hatch, no manhole. Nothing that would let anyone come here or leave this place. We couldn't have materialized here from thin air, could we? Somehow, someone brought us here. So—how the hell do we get out?"

"There must be a way," she said. "And it's probably locked in my memories, along with all the other useful things that could help us. We have to keep on trying."

"I'm not sure what other questions I can ask," he said. He opened his eyes and stood up. "Everything we've learned so far is interesting but doesn't have any real value. I'm kind of running out of ideas, to be honest. You?"

"I'm out of ideas," she said. "Unless…"

"Unless what?"

"Okay," she said and paused, "don't take it the wrong way, but maybe we need to do something drastic. I might need some kind of a shock to release those suppressed memories. I thought maybe we could do something that I know you've fantasized about more than once."

"I don't understand," Jay said. "And I'm not sure I like the sound of it."

"I want you to hurt me," she said. "Not too badly, of course, but some physical pain might trigger something that we can't unearth otherwise. Maybe pain and fear are what I need to get to those memories—"

Jay threw his head back and roared with laughter. It was so sudden, so loud, his entire massive body shaking as he continued to howl, that she looked at him, wondering if he'd gone mad. Not knowing what to say.

Finally, he stopped and looked at her in a way she'd never seen before. There was an emotion in his eyes she didn't know he was capable of.

Pity.

"I can't hurt you, Cal," he said.

"Oh, stop this nonsense," she yelled, losing her patience. "I've seen you look at me as if wanting to slap me a million times and now, all of a sudden you're acting like a perfect gentleman who won't touch me?"

"No," he said. "This is not because I don't *want* to hurt you. It's because I *cannot* hurt you. You're not human, Callisto. You're a machine."

ew York

"YOU SURELY KNOW how to take care of a lady, Mike," Doug said, pointing at their surroundings with a sweeping gesture. "Metal tables, fixed benches, and a view of a busy road. I'd say that screams romance."

They took a table next to a sidewalk that was a few moments ago occupied by a family with two kids. The sun was still high, but the hottest hours of the day had already passed, slowly yielding to the gentle coolness of the fall. A few cars were zipping by on Eighty-Sixth Street, but for this hour the road was surprisingly empty.

"Is there a waiter?" Doug asked, looking around.

"Nope." Connelly smiled, anticipating another series of friendly jabs. "Self-service. You have to go to that little window over there and order yourself a slice."

"Like I said." Doug snorted. "A true gentleman."

"It's a great place." Sofia came to Connelly's defense. "It doesn't look like much, but they make arguably the best pizza in Brooklyn.

Though I imagine some people might take an issue with a statement like that. Brooklynites take their pizza seriously."

"Let's go get some, then," Doug said, starting to get up.

"Not so fast, champ." Connelly put a hand on his friend's shoulder. "If we all go, there'll be no seats by the time we get back. Let me get your orders, and I'll go get them. You guys stay here."

"There's hope for you yet. I don't care what I get, to be honest. Just double whatever you're getting for yourself."

Connelly asked Sofia for her order and went to the register in the little window. As he stood there waiting for the pizza, he watched Doug and Sofia talk. It was the first time they were out when there was somebody else, and it felt special. She and Doug seemed to be at ease with each other and Connelly relaxed, giving up to the light, friendly banter.

"A mafia place, huh?" Doug asked him when he came back, bringing a few slices of a Sicilian pie and a stromboli. "That's interesting."

"Yeah. All the way back in the thirties, it belonged to one of the competing mafia families, and the recipe was considered so valuable that, if I remember correctly, there was a big shootout."

"Get out."

"That's right," Sofia offered. "I read a piece on it a while ago. Another family approached the owners and offered them money and protection in exchange for an equal partnership stake in the business."

"I take it they refused."

"Correct. One night, right after closing, a few cars pulled up right there." She pointed at the sidewalk next to them. "A few goodfellas came out and lighted it up. The owner and his wife were killed and some of the workers who were still inside the restaurant."

"Man. But who's got the recipe, then?"

"That we don't know." She smiled. "The place was closed for a few years after the shootout and then the NYPD put the screws into organized crime, so most of the other family also ended up dead or behind bars. But then ten or fifteen years later, a guy bought the place, who claimed to have been working for the original owner before the gang war and he said he had the original recipe."

"So, this is all a fraud then," Doug said, looking at his slice. "The recipe is probably lost."

"Probably, but they still make one hell of a pizza."

"Better than what they make in Ohio," Connelly jabbed. "I don't remember any good pizza places in Cleveland."

"This guy. He thinks he's funny," Doug said between bites. "That might have something to do with the fact that you've never been to Cleveland. And not that there's anything wrong with Ohio, but I've never been there either. Tell me now. Mike says you're a journalist?"

"Yes. I've been recently promoted to be an editor-in-chief, actually."

"Wow. Congrats. What paper?"

"The *New York Gazette*."

"Nice. You must be excited."

"She is," Connelly interjected. "But not everybody else is as happy."

"There are always going to be some sour grapes when they see somebody else achieve success."

"It's not that. Her boss resigned under some suspicious circumstances. Thought he was in danger. He suggested she step aside as well."

"What kind of suspicious circumstances?" Doug put the slice down, his sarcastic demeanor disappearing.

"Maybe we shouldn't," Sofia said, looking at them uncertainly. "It's not a big deal."

"Try me."

"He was approached by somebody. I don't know details; he tried to keep me out of the loop on this one. Whoever they were, they wanted to purchase the paper."

"That doesn't sound that suspicious so far. Was it a competitor?"

"I don't think so." Sofia shifted uncomfortably under Doug's gaze. "It sounded like a large corporation that wanted to have a news outlet."

"Don't get me wrong," Doug said, returning his attention to the slice. "I can understand why a journalist might not want that kind of a purchase, but that's not unheard of. I'm as far from your business as it gets, but even I can name a few transactions like that when a news outlet was bought by a company of some sort. Why did he think he was in danger?"

"He only told me this when he resigned, but he made it sound like whoever the buyer was didn't want a news organization. They wanted a propaganda outfit."

"You never told me this." Connelly felt a knot forming in his stomach. "A fake news mill?"

"Not exactly a bullshit factory, more like an opinion mouthpiece that presents real facts but puts a certain spin on them to sway the public's opinion."

"Isn't it what most news orgs do these days, anyway?" Doug asked, his mouth full. "Some sway to the left, some to the right, but most of them inject their bias into the news."

"Yes," she said, looking uncertain. "But he made it sound like they wanted something more than that. A place where the goal was to shape the narrative for the benefit of the company. Even the most partisan news companies give you some leeway on reporting. This sounded more like a 'you do what you've been told' kind of place, where everybody marches in lockstep. Like I said, I didn't look into it before because Brian was shielding me from this, but maybe in a few more weeks when I'm more comfortable in my new role, I'll have to dig deeper."

"Have you heard from the mysterious buyers?"

"Once. Yesterday morning."

"You didn't tell me that," Connelly said before he could stop himself and cringed. "Sorry. I didn't mean to sound possessive, but what did they say?"

"I got a call from some guy as I walked into the office. It was a blocked number, so I don't know for sure where he was calling from. He didn't introduce himself. Said that he represented some powerful people and that with Brian's departure, he hoped I'd reconsider their offer."

"And?"

"I told him I had no idea what the offer was in the first place since I've never discussed it with my former boss and that we were not interested anyway. He tried some salesy lines, and I hung up. Then he called again, and this time the number wasn't blocked. It looked like he was calling from the NYPD headquarters at One Police Plaza downtown."

"What? The guy was a cop?"

"I don't think so."

"How do you know?"

"He threatened me this time," she said. "I don't remember the exact language, but he said something to the effect of actions having consequences, at which point I hung up on him again. Then I called my contact at One Police Plaza, and they had no record of anybody calling me from that number, so it must've been spoofed."

"You should stay with me for some time," Connelly said. "I don't like this at all."

"I'm with Mike on this," Doug added. "Though it pains me to recommend a guy who takes his girlfriend to a pizza place that sells pies from a fake recipe and has no waitstaff."

"Stop it, both of you. I'm a big girl, and I can take care of myself. Besides…" She hesitated for a moment. "It might sound silly, but I believe in signs. If I were in real danger, the universe would find a way to tell me that."

"I don't believe in signs. You have no idea what kind of people you might be dealing with here," Connelly said. "And I've seen enough guys who thought themselves invincible getting hurt or worse."

"You don't believe in signs, huh?"

"Sorry, no."

"It never happened to you when you were down on your luck and then something amazing came about that made you feel like everything would be okay?"

"Nope."

"You can laugh all you want, but I swear it happens. A few days after my dad's funeral, my mom and I were sitting at a bus stop, and I remember I felt like the world was never going to be the same. And then there was this lady cop on a horse going by. A magnificent white mare. The cop looked at me and asked if I wanted to pet the animal. I was afraid but didn't want her to see it and went for it. I thought it would bite my head off."

"What happened?" Doug asked.

"The beast didn't want to leave me. She kept giving me her head to pet her and kept turning this way and that way, and the cop said she'd never seen anything like that before. After they left, I felt like I would be okay, you know?"

"Wow," Doug said. "That's a great story."

"It doesn't matter," she said. "Mike, it's sweet that you want to protect me, but no. What are you going to do? Lock me in your place twenty-four seven? I'll be fine. I've been a journalist my entire career. Danger comes with the territory. I promise I'll be careful, but there's no need for anyone to babysit me. Now, what is a proper thing to do after a thousand-calorie meal?"

"To get a dessert," Doug said, stuffing the last piece of stromboli into his mouth. "It's the only way to do it."

"That's what I'm talking about."

Connelly smiled too, but the lightheartedness of the evening evaporated. The breeze was still cool and crisp, occasionally bringing a mouthwatering whiff of freshly baked dough. But as he looked around at the tree-lined street, he couldn't help but notice that the setting sun was coloring it in a gruesome shade of red.

ong Kong

"YOU CAN'T BE SERIOUS," Mandy said. "Why do we need it? No, scrap that—where are we going to get a Russian cruise missile?"

"Let me address the *why* first. We're confronted by an army," Helen said. "Black Arrow deployed thousands of people around the city to look for me, not to mention a few dozen to guard the TLR building. Right now, to infiltrate Edmund's company, I'd need an army of my own."

"I feel a *but* coming."

"Yes. I don't have an army, obviously. But, if I can make Edmund's army disappear, even for a short time, I could make a run for it."

"I see. You want to target the facility with a cruise missile," Mandy said. "To make them pull everybody off the building. But how?"

"There's a Russian warship docked in the port of Hai Phong," Helen said, opening a laptop and pulling up a map. "The *Raven* is a Gepard-class frigate that carries eight Kalibr cruise missiles. If I can take control of one of them and target TLR, Tillerson will have no other choice but to abandon the building. And even if he doesn't order

Black Arrow to retreat or even tries to make them stay, I'm confident their superiors will overrule him."

"I don't know if I like it. They'll label you a terrorist just for trying."

"They might."

"Can you even do that? Take over a missile?"

"I can't hack into the Russian ship directly." Helen shrugged. "But I have an idea that might work. There's an American aircraft carrier in the South China Sea. It's been recently upgraded so it should be equipped with the newest WWAN—microwave-based wide-area network. Until recently, they've been using satellite-based communications, but in the last few years they started adding the network so the ships could talk directly to one another and their aircraft. There are some vulnerabilities in the network—"

"Wait a minute. You're saying that you want to hack the Russian missile through the American carrier?"

"No." She shook her head. "The Russian frigate is too far to hack them directly through the carrier."

"Good," Mandy said, taking a deep breath. "So, I don't have to worry about you starting World War Three. Wait. What do you mean directly?"

"Technically, before I get to the Russian ship's systems, I'd need to hack an X-47B stealth plane that hails from the aircraft carrier. It will work as a relay. I'd need to hack the carrier first, which will let me hack the plane, which in turn will let me hack the Russian missile."

"You *are* going to start World War Three. If you target TLR with a Russian missile—"

"Targeting the TLR building was my first plan. But when I thought about it, I realized that targeting one building won't be enough."

"How do you mean?"

"You said it yourself—Black Arrow guys are everywhere. If I target only the building, they'll pull everybody off the area, but that doesn't solve how I can get there from here without getting caught. I'm sure they've set up a perimeter and closed the highway. They'll catch me in no time."

"So, what exactly is the plan?"

"The threat has to be such that *everybody* in the city would want to get off the streets. We need the government to force the citizens to take cover."

"Okay," Mandy said. "You don't want them to know what's your actual target. That's smart. But in that case, how do you make sure Tillerson evacuates the building? They might decide to take their chances."

Helen watched her friend's face for a few seconds, contemplating the answer. "The only way to make it work is to create a threat big enough to convince the entire city that no matter where you are, you're in danger."

She saw her friend stiffen as she processed the words.

"I think," she continued, "to do it properly, I'd need to aim a nuclear-tipped missile at Hong Kong."

"No." Mandy stood up. "This is madness. Are you out of your mind? What happens if you can't control it and it strikes the city? What if—"

"Relax." Helen put up a hand, stopping her friend. "To pull it off, I don't necessarily need an actual nuke. As a matter of fact, the cruise missiles onboard the Russian warship are unlikely to carry nuclear warheads. But that's irrelevant. What I need is to create a scenario where people *think* there's a nuke aimed at Hong Kong. The Russians will deny it, of course, but it won't matter. At least it won't matter long enough for our purpose."

"But they'll designate you as an international terrorist."

"If you sit down and actually let me explain, you'll see that it's not that crazy."

Mandy continued to stand there, and for a moment, Helen thought her friend would turn around and leave. Finally, the woman gave a sigh and sat on the mattress next to her.

"There are a few things that need to be considered," Helen started. "First, you're right—I don't want to create an international incident. Least of all do I want to pit Americans against the Russians and risk a nuclear war. I—or we, should you *choose* to help me—would need to create a proxy first."

"Like what?"

"Something akin to *Anonymous*—a ragtag team of loosely affiliated individuals scattered all over the globe without loyalties to any particular country. Russians and Americans would have to be in the mix to make sure the blame falls equally on both parties. We should mix some others and make it diversified. Chinese, European citizens, etc. Some backstories would need to be created. I'd need to place some breadcrumbs that could be found in the aftermath of the hack that would confirm that it was done by the group."

"Okay," Mandy said. "That will be a lot of work, but it's not a bad idea. Maybe create an archive of 'operations' that would list some hacks that could be attributed to the group."

"Right." Helen nodded. "That's exactly what I was thinking. Something that is reasonably well hidden, but not too well."

"But you'd need to find some attacks that cannot be disputed by other hacking groups. You can't just pluck something that was done by Anonymous and claim it as your own because they'll call your bullshit."

"I know somebody whose operations we can assign to this fictitious group that nobody'll challenge us on."

"How do you know they won't?"

A vision of a burned-down house appeared in Helen's mind. A full-size Captain America shield could be seen in the rubble. Its colors were darker than original, scorched by the fire, but the shield itself was intact, as if made from the real vibranium.

"How do you know that?" the woman repeated.

"I just do." Helen sighed. "If anything, they would've wanted me to use them."

"All right, so let's say we created this fake hacker collective—then what?"

"Then I'll tell the city officials that I hacked a Russian cruise missile with a nuclear warhead and unless they pay us a certain amount of money, I'll launch it against Hong Kong."

"We'll have to set up bank accounts then, to maintain the charade. That'll take a long time."

"That, fortunately, is something we won't need to do. I already have a series of numbered accounts that are impossible to trace, just for an occasion like this."

"For an occasion where you threaten a city with a nuclear warhead?"

"Well," Helen chuckled, "I admit, I probably didn't have that particular scenario in mind back when I decided to establish them."

They sat in silence for a few moments, looking at each other.

"Are you sure it's worth the risk? Tillerson might be a bad guy, but if this crazy plan of yours doesn't work and you get caught..." She trailed off. "You'll spend the rest of your life in a very unpleasant place without visitation rights."

"I know," Helen said. "But Tillerson isn't a problem, dear. It's who he works for. When I worked for the CIA—"

"You're kidding me. You—the girl I shared my lunch breaks with— worked for the CIA?"

"Yes." Helen produced a tired smile. "On a few occasions, actually."

"Oh, boy." Mandy sighed and stood up again. "There's a hole in your plan, though. What if the authorities decide to sit on that information? Keep it a secret?"

"This one's easy," Helen said. "We send the copy of the demands to all major networks at the same time as we contact the city officials."

"All right." Mandy shook her head in disbelief. "I'm going to regret this, I'm sure. Fine. Let's do this. But you still haven't told me the most important part."

"Which one?"

"How the hell are you going to hack the aircraft carrier?"

"You know," she said, "Sun Tzu once said that *all war is deception*."

"What's that supposed to mean? There's already plenty of deception going on—fake hacker collectives, fake bank accounts."

"What I was trying to tell you before is when I worked for the CIA, I created a backdoor. I still have a way to access the CIA servers, so I'm going to send a message to the American aircraft carrier that would look like it came from a legitimate source. An email."

"You want to plant the malware through email?"

Helen grinned as she watched her friend coming to the realization of what she was trying to say.

"It better be a more convincing email than a message from a Nigerian prince. We're talking about the United States Navy. It'll be hard to fool them."

"Uh-huh." She stood up and patted Mandy on the shoulder. "That's precisely why the email should come from the prince."

"What?"

"Not the Nigerian prince, Mandy. It should come from the president of the United States."

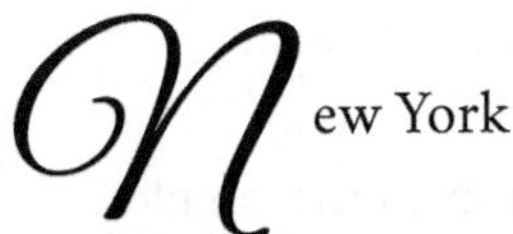

New York

"Can you believe it?"

"What?" Connelly looked away from the frying pan and glanced toward Sofia by the window. In the last few weeks, they'd been staying together in his apartment so often that on a rare night where she couldn't make it, he felt like he was missing a limb.

"It's snowing." She pointed outside. "Not much, a few small flakes here and there, but it's a bit early this year."

He picked up the pan and slid two equal portions of an omelet onto simple china plates, next to the toast and a few slices of baby cucumber. Then he walked over to the window, hugged Sofia and looked outside.

Indeed, it was snowing. The sky was bleak-gray and the fog hugging the street made it look like they were floating inside a large cloud.

"It looks like it'll get worse," he said, looking at the snow.

"It would be a good day to stay home," she said. "But alas."

"I wish. C'mon, let's eat—the food's getting cold."

They took their seats at Connelly's small kitchen table, and he poured two cups of coffee.

"By the way," she said. "And I don't want you to freak out."

"Ha." He chuckled out loud, but his stomach knotted against his will. "When people say *don't freak out,* it's usually the right time to do that."

"No." She patted his hand. "I just wanted to tell you my uncle and I had *the conversation.*"

"No way. How am I still alive?"

"He approves." She shrugged. "Not that we need his approval, but he kind of blurted it out when I saw him yesterday. Says he knows a military man when he sees one, and that you seem like a straight arrow."

"Am I? A straight arrow?"

"I don't know." She gave him a wink. "It was kind of dark."

"Oh my God, you're terrible."

She gave a soft laugh and returned her attention to the omelet. He watched her work on her breakfast—she was sitting on the chair, with both of her feet on it and his old shirt pulled over her knees to keep her bare legs warm. He felt himself grinning like a teenager who saw a girl way out of his league.

"Stop staring at me." She smiled as she wolfed down a large bite of eggs. "On second thought—keep on looking. I kind of like it."

"How's it going at work? Any trouble since the last call from your suitors?"

"Nope. I hope," she waved her fork in the air, "that it stays that way. But so far, I haven't heard anything. Not a peep."

"Have you spoken to your former boss?"

"Not since he resigned. But I heard that he packed up his stuff and left New York."

"Really?"

"Yeah. They have a place down in Florida, and he always talked about going down there when he retired. It's not quite the retirement that he was talking about, but he'd wanted to do it for quite some time."

"Keep your eyes open," Connelly offered. "That call you got makes me uncomfortable."

"I know."

Connelly's phone vibrated on the table, slowly turning in a semicircle. "Hello?"

He listened to the man on the other side for a few seconds and then hung up.

"You okay?"

"Yeah," he said slowly. "It looks like I have to go on a business trip."

"Anywhere exotic?"

"It depends on what you call exotic." He picked up his coffee, got up, and walked to the window. The snowflakes were getting bigger, and the snow started to accumulate on the sidewalks. "I have to fly to the Middle East."

"Where to?"

"A place I thought I'd never go back to," he said. A large garbage truck equipped with a snowplow made a turn on their street. It lowered the blade to the ground and proceeded along, pushing the slush to the edges of the road. "Afghanistan."

"I didn't know you've been to that part of the world." She got up, walked to the window, and stood beside him. "Are you sure you're all right?"

"Yeah." He shrugged. "Not a big deal. Took me by surprise, that's all. I have to get ready; they'll be sending a car to pick me up soon."

"I don't get it, though," she said as her blue eyes scanned him up and down. "Why do you have to go there? I didn't know Guardian Manufacturing had any presence in Afghanistan. I've read about their offices in Dubai, but not about Afghanistan."

"I'm sorry." He turned and gave her a peck on the cheek. "I can't say, and I better get going."

A town car arrived in front of his building in thirty minutes, and by then Connelly had said good-bye to Sofia and gone outside with a small suitcase.

He greeted the driver and, content for once not being behind the wheel, relaxed in the backseat. The car maneuvered through the snow-covered local streets and merged onto I-278W, heading toward JFK International Airport.

"It doesn't look too bad," the driver said, pointing with his chin at the map on his navigation display. "It could've been worse."

"Right."

"It always amuses me," the man continued. "It snows in New York every year. And I mean *every single year*. And yet every time the first snowflakes start falling from the sky, everybody acts like they've never seen the damned thing. I mean, people do such awful things behind the wheel; it's amazing."

"That's true," Connelly said, hoping that his lack of effort to maintain the conversation would convey the message to the driver.

"Oh," the man continued and then pulled a leather folder from his glove compartment and handed it through the window. "Almost forgot. You've got some docs to read from the boss."

"Okay."

Connelly pressed his thumb into a small biometric lock, and after a moment it produced a soft click, releasing the zipper. He opened the folder and pulled out a few pages of paper. He scanned the text on the first page, noting the list of items he'd have to take care of without much interest—he'd have more time to study the document once he was on board Engel's plane.

He flipped the page, and his heart skipped a beat. In the top left corner, there was a black-and-white photograph of his contact. The man looked older than Connelly remembered him, but there was no mistake. He went back to the first page and carefully read the dossier from cover to cover. Then he put the printouts away and locked the folder again.

"If you don't mind," he said to the driver, hitting the button that raised the privacy screen, "I need to make a phone call."

He waited until the glass locked in place, isolating him from the driver, fished out a burner phone from his jacket, and punched in a number. The line picked up on the first ring.

"What's up, man?" Doug's voice sounded loud in the speakerphone and Connelly instinctively winced and threw a look at the privacy screen. The driver seemed to be preoccupied navigating the traffic on the Belt Parkway and wasn't paying attention to what was going on in the back.

"I have a problem," Connelly said. "Engel is sending me to Afghanistan. There's apparently some trouble in paradise. Some supply routes have been compromised, and he wants me to figure out why and, more importantly, how we can put an end to it."

"That sucks. Are you going to be there awhile? The bug we put on the car wash is going to run out of battery in a few days."

"I don't know," Connelly said, keeping an eye on the driver. "There's a bigger problem, though."

"What's going on?"

"I'm supposed to meet a contact once I get to their distribution site. Not sure where it is—somewhere up in the mountains."

"Someone we know, I'm assuming?"

"He now goes by the name of Erik Rosen, but you might remember him as Erik Hanson."

"Hanson?" Doug spat the word out as if he caught something disgusting in his mouth. "There's a reason I wanted to put him down last time. How the hell did he end up back in the 'Stan again? I thought we handed him over to the CIA guys."

"We did, so your guess is as good as mine."

"Is there a chance he'll be meeting you before you go to the distribution center?"

"I don't think so. From what I've read, it sounds like he operates from there and doesn't leave the site."

"Okay," Doug said. "There's something we can work with. At least you have a bit of a head start."

"Maybe." Connelly leaned back into the leather seat. "But we're talking about a paramilitary compound, Doug. Once Hanson recognizes me—and he will—I'm a dead man."

"I'm sure we can figure something—"

"Stop it, man. Listen carefully—I need you to do me a favor."

ong Kong

"THAT'S A LOT OF BANDWIDTH," said a young man behind the counter in a dingy internet cafe, looking up from the screen.

Helen squirmed behind the oversized sunglasses. Her scalp was itchy under the wig, and the thick layer of makeup Mandy had helped her put on was suffocating her. Unable to find a reliable internet service inside the slums, they had to venture outside of New Kowloon City, but not by much and it showed. The garbage-littered street hidden in the shade of the misshapen monstrosity was covered in graffiti, and while law enforcement occasionally showed their faces here, they tended to come in large numbers and tried not to linger.

"Simultaneous video streams," she heard Mandy say. "Testing a new app for video conferences. Should be revolutionary."

"Ah." The clerk seemed to have lost interest. To him, they became another pair of tech-wiz wannabes. In the new digital era filled with stories of people making fortunes overnight, he was all too familiar with the untold tales of those who tried and failed. He quoted them the price and Mandy threw a few banknotes on top of the oily counter.

They took a desk in the far corner of the half-empty room and set up their laptops.

"I wish I didn't have to park so far from here," Mandy said as she logged in to her computer. "We're going to waste precious time getting back to the car while everybody's in panic mode."

"If we left it around here, it'd be disassembled, sold, and shipped to the mainland by the time we were done with this job."

"Maybe. I hope we can get back to it and leave the city before the streets get jammed with panicking people."

"We will." Helen turned to face Mandy and put a hand on her friend's shoulder. "I'm as nervous as you are. But we can do it."

"At least the backstory is good. We've done a half-decent job creating a new fake hacker collective."

"I think so," Helen agreed. "But I guess we'll find out soon enough if it's up to the task."

"All right," Mandy said and rubbed the palms of her hands nervously. "Shall we?"

Helen looked at her friend and smiled. "Here comes the package."

She'd been working on the email that would appear to have come from the president of the United States for the last few days. The hardest part wasn't the code that would give her access to the carrier's mainframe, she'd discovered. The most challenging part was the creative—writing a compelling email that prompted immediate action turned out to be a task like no other. Ideally, she wanted the person who opened the email to activate the virus while also sending them on a wild-goose chase that would buy her time. But it was proving to be easier said than done.

After a few unsuccessful drafts, she decided that less was more and wrote a one-paragraph email that called for immediate contact with the White House and provided the set of instructions in the attachment. The upside was that the email, and most importantly, the attachment that would give Helen access to the aircraft carrier mainframe, would be opened. However, encouraging the fleet personnel to contact the Office of the President would almost immediately reveal the fake nature of the message and set in motion a chain of events where the brightest minds in the Navy and their colleagues back in the US would get on a collision course with Helen's plan.

She hit *Enter*, firing the email off, and opened the new window with the control terminal that would activate if the malicious attachment was opened and the code executed.

"Now what?" Mandy asked, anxiously looking at her screen that mirrored Helen's. Her job, once the code was executed, was to keep the techs busy while giving Helen the time to hack into the X-47B stealth plane and then, using the plane's communication system, try to establish the link to the Russian warship.

"Now we wait." Helen shrugged. The pressure was getting to her too, but they'd already passed the point of no return. The search for the hacker group that dared to impersonate the president of the United States and take control of the servers on the American carrier sitting in the international waters near one of its biggest adversaries would be on. Despite their careful preparations, they were still going to be in extreme danger. The best thing they could do now was to stick to the plan.

"Hi there," a voice said, making them both jump. A young man in his twenties was walking to their desk from the front of the internet cafe. He was wearing a pair of slim jeans and a bright-neon T-shirt that said Cyberpunk City on it. He nodded to Mandy as he came closer while completely ignoring Helen. "I've never seen you here before."

"I'm not interested," Mandy said curtly.

"Come on. Me and my boys over there," he pointed to a group of a few young men in the front, "are writing something that'll change the world. Let me buy you a cup of coffee. I might not be one of those rich guys from Red Hill, but I'd love to show you around sometime. I'm Lucas, by the way."

The screens on both laptops blinked, as the worm embedded inside the email was activated.

"I'll tell you what," Mandy said, scribbling a phone number on a piece of paper and handing it to the young man. "Call me sometime, if you'd like. No promises, though."

"I'll take it." The man smiled and winked at Helen. "See you around."

"Wow," Helen whispered. "Hacking nukes *and* trying to get laid."

"Shut up. I was trying to get rid of them."

Helen's fingers started to dance on the keyboard. She set up a few decoys inside the server to throw off anyone who would try to find the root of the hack and then let Mandy take over. Her friend continued to beef up defenses around their virtual link to ensure it lasted long enough.

"Something just occurred to me," Mandy said as she typed away.

"What's that?"

"The poor sod who opened your email is probably going to be in a lot of trouble. They might even kick him out of the Navy."

"Yeah," Helen said. "I thought about that, too. If that's true, I'll find out who he is, and we can make sure he gets compensated. I haven't had a chance to flesh it out, but I'm sure we can come up with a series of blind trusts that could pay him some kind of settlement money. Nothing fancy that would raise suspicion, no big bucks; just a little something to make his life easier."

"Not all is lost with you." Mandy smiled. "You better hurry up, though. Judging by the crazy uptick of activity on the server—they know they've been hacked."

"I'm already flying the drone. All I need is another," she switched the windows and took a glance at the map, "forty-five seconds. Can you hold them off for that long?"

"I hope so. This is the last firewall. They have some powerful tools." A large progress bar appeared on one of Mandy's windows. It showed the percentage, which decreased by the second. At the moment it showed sixty-seven percent, but the numbers were racing toward zero at an ever-accelerating speed.

"A bit longer."

"I'm at twenty-two percent."

"Come on." Helen was typing so fast her fingers were almost flying above the keyboard.

"Fifteen."

"Almost there."

"Seven."

"Got it," Helen breathed and looked at her friend.

Mandy forced her programs to shut down, and her screen went black as she launched the bleaching software that started to wipe out every byte off her hard drive. "You're good?"

"Yes. Now I need to set stage two in motion. Easy peasy." She punched a few keys, counting out loud. "Alert the authorities about the hack, check. Send the link with the countdown, check. Send a separate link with the account information for the ransom, also check. All right, we're officially at the top of the Most Wanted list. I can almost see the black silhouette with a line under it that says *Person or persons responsible for the hack of nuclear missiles*."

"As long as we stay as a black silhouette," Mandy said. "You know what just occurred to me?"

"What?"

"There's more than one poor sod we're going to have to take care of."

"How so?"

"The sailor from the aircraft carrier who clicked on your email might be in trouble. But I mostly feel for the guy who's in charge of the missiles on the Russian frigate. Because I'm pretty sure he's shitting his pants right at this moment."

30

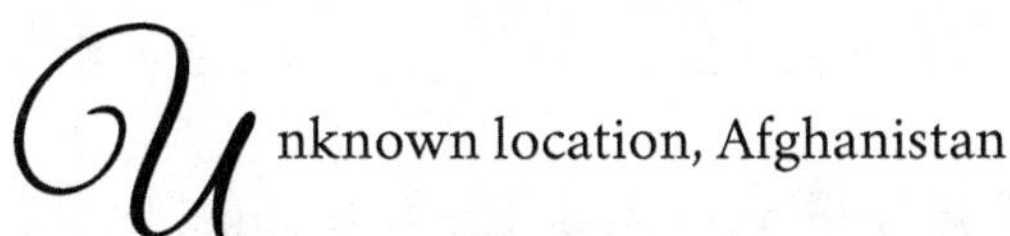

$\mathcal{U}$nknown location, Afghanistan

THE TRUCK STOPPED, and Mike Connelly's hand automatically went to the small of his back to check for his weapon, only to come away empty—before he was allowed to board the truck, he had to give up his gun and tactical knife to a grim-looking Taliban fighter.

Connelly and Sanjay Gupta, Guardian's VP of purchasing Asia division, flew to Kabul on a brand-new addition to Engel's fleet, the supersonic AS2. Even accounting for a refueling stop in Lisbon, before making the last leg of the journey, the twelve-seater jet delivered them to Hamid Karzai International Airport in under eight hours—less than half the time of a commercial airliner.

It was the fifth trip to the region for Gupta, Connelly found out, but it still seemed to make the small man nervous, which made him talkative. After enduring a few stories, Connelly excused himself and slept in for the remainder of the flight.

As he suspected, the luxuries were over as soon as they stepped off the plane. An old truck pulled up to the private hangar where their jet had been taxied to, and he and Gupta were told to climb on board and

155

put hoods on their heads. That's when they made Connelly part with his weapons. The Taliban might have been doing business with Engel, but in a not-so-subtle manner, they wanted them to know whose turf they were on.

But after a few hours of a shaky drive, their journey was over, and the same stern-looking man pulled off their hoods and opened the back of the truck.

"I hate this part," he heard Gupta's voice as he screwed up his face, blinking against the bright sun.

"The part where they let you take the hood off?"

"The traveling while blindfolded part," the small man said as they watched their silent companion climb out and walk away from the truck with his partner. "We've been doing business with them for years. Why can't we come here without feeling like I'm about to be positioned in front of a black flag and have my head cut off with a blunt knife?"

Connelly only shrugged in response and climbed outside the truck. He looked around, absorbing as much information as he could. The air was thin and cold. The Soviet-made GAZ-66 had crawled up the gravel path and was now parked at the edge of a heart-stopping cliff. They were high up, that was obvious. But there was also some humidity in the air, and when Connelly walked to the edge of the road, he could see the still water of the lake down below.

"You're making me nervous," Gupta said. "Can you please step away from the edge?"

"I just wanted to know where we were."

"And?"

"We are at the Dorah Pass."

"At the what?"

"The Dorah Pass," Connelly repeated, looking after the two figures of Taliban fighters walking farther and farther away. "We're not too far from the Pakistani border. Where'd those two go?"

"They always leave when they bring me up here. After an hour or two, depending on how lucky we are, somebody else will show up, and then they'll take us to the camp. How do you know where we are?"

"The lake." Connelly pointed toward the cliff. "Lake Dufferin, or as the locals call it, Hawz-i Dorah."

He walked back to the truck and looked around for anything remotely resembling a weapon, but apart from a few dirty rags, the truck was empty.

"What are you doing?" Gupta asked, but Connelly ignored him and rummaged through the cabin. There was a half-used Bic lighter, and he stuffed it in his back pocket.

"I wish I brought a warmer jacket," the little man complained, hugging himself. "Do you think they'll take offense if we stay inside the truck while waiting? It's freezing up here."

"You go ahead," Connelly said, leaning against the side of the vehicle. "I'll stay out here. I don't want any surprises."

"Suit yourself." The man climbed inside the cabin and closed the door, visibly relieved to be sheltered from the cold wind.

"On second thought," Connelly rapped his fingers on the window, "you should come out. Someone's coming."

They watched the cloud of dust billowing far in the distance and then a few moments later, they could hear the rumble of multiple vehicles.

"That's a big delegation," Gupta said with uncertainty in his voice. "It's usually one or two dudes."

"Maybe they like you, after all. You didn't even get properly frozen." Connelly now could see a caravan of three old Jeeps and a pickup truck speeding up the road, each carrying a few men. The barrels of AK-47s were sticking out the windows and pointing toward the clear blue skies, swaying as the vehicles made their way closer.

"I don't like it," Gupta said, watching the cars get closer. "I wish you still had your pistol. Are we in trouble?"

"A pistol wouldn't have made much of a difference." Connelly shrugged. "There's at least a dozen of them."

The cars pulled up about a hundred yards from the GAZ-66, and a tall, broad-shouldered man stepped outside of one of them to greet them. The rest of the guerrillas stayed in their vehicles and, to Connelly's satisfaction, kept their assault rifles pointing skyward.

"There's been a change of plans. I'm here to transport you to the camp," he said in perfect English with a touch of a British accent as he approached. His full beard and sun-scorched skin made him blend in with the rest of the fighters, but up close he looked decidedly European. Shave him and dress him in ordinary clothes, Connelly thought, and the man would look at home on Seville Row or Park Avenue.

"Is there something wrong?" Gupta asked. "Usually it's a couple of guys who meet us. I'm sorry, what's your name again?"

"Nothing's wrong." The man shrugged. It looked like two giant boulders rolling under his loose clothing. "There have been some skirmishes, and I want to make sure you get to the place safe and sound. I don't want Mr. Engel disappointed."

"And you are?" Gupta insisted.

"You don't want these guys disappointed either." The man vaguely waved his hand in the direction of the Jeeps, ignoring the question. He turned around and started walking back to the caravan. "Let's go."

"C'mon, Sanjay," Connelly said and started after the man.

"I don't like this," Gupta said without moving. "I've never seen this guy before. It's always the same people. I'm not going until you tell me your name."

"You can stay here," the man said without stopping. "We'll be back in a couple of days. We'll take you back to the airport then."

Connelly heard Gupta swear under his breath, but the little man jogged to catch up to them. They climbed in the back of one of the pickup trucks, and the broad-shouldered man joined them a moment later, taking a bench across from them. The engines revved, and the small column made a U-turn and started back down the road.

"Put these on your heads," the big man said as he threw two black bags toward them.

The throw was too short, and the bags landed next to Connelly's feet. He picked them up and handed one to Gupta and then opened the other, preparing to put it over his head.

"I'm not putting this on," Gupta protested. "They never asked us to do that before. It's one thing—"

The man leaned in and slapped Gupta across the face with his left hand. His movement was slow, almost lazy, but Gupta crashed off the bench and onto the floor as if hit by a shovel. Blood started gushing from his nose and from his lower lip that appeared to be split in two.

"Put this on, please," the big man repeated. "Unless you want me to tell Engel that you fell off the car on the way here and we couldn't find you."

Connelly helped his companion back on the bench and after watching him trying to put the hood on with trembling hands, took it from him and pulled it over the little man's head. Then without saying a word, he put another bag over his own head.

"Much better," he heard their guide say. "I don't understand why we have to go through all this trouble. You'll be in the camp soon, and we'll answer all your questions. Mr. Rosen is looking forward to seeing you both. Especially you, Connelly."

Hong Kong

THE LOCAL NEWS station on the TV screen in front of the internet cafe was flashing a breaking news chyron. The volume was too low to hear anything, but the images were showing the early signs of panic—people running through the streets, supermarkets being looted.

"We have to go," Mandy said with an edge to her voice.

"Give me a moment." Helen opened a separate window on her laptop and launched a new program designed to infiltrate the internet cafe's servers. "I don't want to leave our fingerprints in this place."

"C'mon," Mandy said again. "We've got to go."

"Okay." Helen closed her laptop shut, stood up, and started toward the exit. "Remember—the Black Arrow guys are paramilitary. They're not going to leave the building at the first sign of trouble. It might take a few minutes before they get orders."

They went outside. A cacophony of sirens was filling the air. A young couple ran past them, pushing a supermarket cart in front of them. A frightened-looking girl was sitting inside of the cart in the middle of a pile of snacks.

"I feel horrible seeing this," Helen said. Her phone vibrated in her back pocket, and she saw that Mandy's phone was getting a message as well.

"Civil defense alert," Mandy said, looking at her screen.

Helen pulled out her phone and read the message.

NUCLEAR MISSILE THREAT. SEEK IMMEDIATE SHELTER. THIS IS NOT A DRILL.

"My God," she said, putting the phone away. "It better be worth it."

They waited by the intersection as a row of cars blew through the red traffic light and, when the last one disappeared from view, started across the street. The mayhem intensified as they got farther from the slums and deeper into the city—a small crowd was gathering outside of a supermarket that was trying to lock the front doors. Somebody hurled a brick through the window, and the crowd pushed forward even before the pieces of broken glass stopped falling. A young man cried out in pain as the crowd pushed him into the shards of glass sticking out of the wall.

"C'mon," Mandy urged her. "It's too late to backpedal."

They ran past the supermarket and pressed on. Mandy's car was around the corner.

"No," Helen heard Mandy cry out as she turned the corner ahead of her and then a second later, she understood why—the row of cars parked on the side of the street was ablaze. Mandy's white SUV was not on fire yet, but it was only a matter of time—a black Mercedes right behind it was spewing two-foot-long flames.

"Shit," Helen said, stopping, and then she saw Mandy dash toward her car as fast as her feet would carry her. "Mandy, stop. Are you crazy—it's gonna blow!"

The woman ignored her and ran past the flames and dived inside her car. The engine revved, and the car lurched back, slamming into the Mercedes, and then shot out of the parking spot, clipping the right headlight on the minivan ahead of it.

The black Mercedes exploded, sending pieces of glass and debris flying in all directions and making Helen duck. Another two cars that had been parked behind it exploded in a fiery chain reaction. Helen fell back and started to crawl on all fours, trying to get out from the rain of molten plastic and jagged pieces of metal. A flaming wheel bounced off the wall of one of the buildings and rolled down the sidewalk, forcing her toward the middle of the street. She heard tires screeching, and a second later Mandy's SUV roared past her, going the wrong way on a one-way street, and stopped a few feet away. The bumper on the SUV was deformed, and the back of the car was smoldered and discolored, but otherwise it seemed to have escaped the explosion unscathed.

"Let's go," she heard Mandy yell through the window, and Helen scrambled to her feet and ran to the vehicle.

"You're one crazy woman," she breathed as she climbed into the car and Mandy stepped on the gas, accelerating away from the row of burning cars. "You could've died."

"But I didn't." Mandy flashed her a manic grin as she maneuvered the car around debris. "Besides, how were you going to get back to TLR if we lost the car? Walk? By the time we'd get there, the ruse would've been over and the Black Arrow boys would be crawling all over the place again. All this would be for nothing."

Helen kept quiet as she watched her friend drive. She played this scenario in her head a million times before. She thought she was prepared for this, but seeing it play out in real life brought back the doubts. *She had to keep going,* she thought. At this point, turning back would be the worst decision of them all.

"You okay?"

"Yeah," Helen lied. "Just taking it in, that's all."

"Listen. I wouldn't have helped you if I didn't come to the same conclusions as you." They roared through the empty intersection and took the ramp going onto the highway. "Tillerson wants to weaponize this stuff. If it falls into the wrong hands, what we see now will seem like utopia compared to what will come. We can't let this happen."

"I know. I wish there was another way."

"There's no other way. Think about it. Tillerson, with all his brilliance, is a puppet—you said it yourself. He thinks he's in control, but that's only because he's useful. The moment that changes, all this theater will end." Mandy paused for a moment. "Imagine you could go back and somehow prevent the Manhattan Project. Wouldn't you want to do it? Stop the nuclear bomb from being developed? You'd save hundreds of thousands. Prevent the world from sitting on the brink of a disaster for decades to come."

"That's what scares me the most." Helen sighed.

"What does?"

"I don't think you could prevent it. At best, you could've delayed it. But those guys weren't the only ones working on it. Maybe it would've made it worse. We think we're saving the world from Tillerson's monster, but maybe all we're doing is postponing the inevitable."

They drove in silence for a few moments. The highway was almost empty. A storm was brewing ahead of them. A few dark, nearly black clouds were moving toward the city, consuming the bright sky. For a second, Helen had a vision that the road stretched forever between this world and Hell itself and they were rushing toward their own doom.

"We can't kill it," she finally said. "We need to preserve it."

"We talked about this. It's too risky."

"MAD."

"What? Who's mad?"

"Not who," Helen said. "MAD, as in mutually assured destruction. That was the term coined during the Cold War. The US didn't attack the Soviets and the Soviets wouldn't attack the Americans, because if one of them did, between the initial strike and the retaliation, no one would survive. Hence the concept of mutually assured destruction was born. The only reason the Cold War never turned into a hot one. Think about it. Someone, sooner or later, will recreate what Tillerson did. He might be the first, but he's not going to be the only one. We'll need the counterweight."

"And you want us to be that? Us?"

"Yes," Helen said. "It's not something I'd like to do, but we'll have to be."

"Don't you think we're—"

"Underqualified? Of course we are. But it's probably a good thing. Watch out now." She pointed to the outline of the TLR building. "Slow down and let's roll by the exit first to make sure the Black Arrow guys are gone. We can always make a U-turn and come back, but I don't want to drive into an ambush."

"Wise idea."

It started to rain as they approached the exit. The dark clouds had taken half the sky, and the first big drops were landing on the windshield with heavy thuds. The wind picked up, battering the car from all sides. Mandy eased off the pedal as they got closer and the car slowed to a crawl.

"What in the world is that thing?"

"Where?" The rain was coming down hard, making it hard to see, and Helen strained to look through the sheet of water.

"There." Mandy stopped the car and pointed at a strange shape by the entrance to the building.

Helen finally saw it. It looked like a small car on six wheels, but the round cabin swiveling around was too small to hold any passengers, and there was something protruding out of it on the side. The strange car stopped, and the cabin turned more, pointing the oblong object in their direction.

"Drive," Helen yelled as she finally made out what she was looking at.

The car lurched, the engine whining in protest as too much fuel flooded into it too quickly and the tires squealed, propelling the vehicle forward. Helen caught a flash coming from the strange car and a split second later, an invisible force lifted the back of the SUV as if a giant tried to catch the SUV's rear tires. They swerved madly across the lanes, Mandy fighting to control the vehicle and finally the exit was behind them and they were accelerating down the empty highway.

"What the hell was that?" Mandy asked, her knuckles white as she gripped the steering wheel. The rain was coming down so hard now they could hardly see past the front end of the car.

"That was a sentry," Helen said. "The boys from Black Arrow might be gone, but now we have a killer robot to deal with. And it's got a big gun."

ew York

PERRY CAME in early the next day to spend some extra time watching security tapes, but there was no produce truck. On the one hand, it wasn't surprising—whoever was in the truck the day before might have been only gathering information. And there was a possibility that it was the actual produce truck that came back to the location for some reason other than delivering goods to the supermarket.

It was unlikely, though, Perry decided. In all likelihood, it was the competition. He contemplated reaching out to his cousin but they hadn't spoken since Perry had to take this job, apart from the occasional meeting at some family gatherings. Besides, he didn't think it was some hotshot from the cartels. *Sicarios* may have grown sophisticated in the last few years, but somehow a produce truck didn't seem to fit the profile. Perry wasn't a gambling man, but if he had to make a bet this time, his money would be on a new player in town or law enforcement.

He turned off the playback, switching to the live CCTV view, and finished his lukewarm coffee in a few long gulps. Tomorrow, the shifty man was supposed to come to check on him, as he always did once a week, and he'd tell him about the truck. Then it would be off his hands.

He hated the visits. The car wash and the loading bay next door were a vital part of the operation, of course, and Perry expected to be supervised. It didn't matter how efficiently he ran the business or how long he worked for the boss. There was too much money involved. He wouldn't have left himself unsupervised either. But what bothered him was the air of moral superiority that seemed to be oozing from Watkins. They didn't speak much every time he was there, but over the years they spoke enough for Perry to understand precisely why the man acted as he did.

For some reason, Watkins seemed to believe what they were doing served some kind of greater good. A classic *the end justifies the means* kind of thing. It was complete nonsense, of course. Perry was a lot of things, but he was pragmatic above all. They were selling drugs, for chrissakes, and whatever moral justification Watkins had concocted under the thin layer of his wispy hair was nothing more than a pile of hot steaming shit.

"Hey Perry," he heard from the door, and he nodded to the first of the two guards who would hang out in the car wash office for the rest of the night. At this point, he would move to the loading dock to make sure everybody was on schedule, and drivers weren't screwing around with the product. Their system to vet drivers was extensive and yet, once in a while, they ended up with an idiot who thought they were smarter than everybody else.

He waited for the second guard to come in, poured himself another cup of coffee, and went through the door to the warehouse. The inside of the facility looked like a letter Z, with cars entering through the gate on one side, turning in to the loading area set up in the middle, and then making another turn to go outside on the other side of the street. This setup prevented any prying eyes from the outside seeing anything that was going on where a small crew of Perry's men lined the trunks of each vehicle with illegal merchandise.

The guards were already there, armed with Glock 19s in their side holsters—two at one entrance, and two at the other. Tonight would be busy—Perry had a long list of clients who had to be taken care of. He needed to send a few cars to deliver high-grade ecstasy on a trip to Atlantic City, provide two underground brothels in Manhattan with cocaine, and supply a few night clubs in Long Island with a new version of *Aliento del Diablo.* His employer liked Perry's idea, but instead of selling their clients repackaged product, now it was a high-grade product of ultra-pure cocaine that his employer's chemists managed to die in bright ruby red.

He was walking around the loading area, checking the packages, when the lights in the warehouse went off. He cursed, crouching behind one of the crates, the instinct developed over many years in the illegal trade shouting at him that something was wrong. A few moments later, the back-up generator kicked in, and the emergency lights lit up, drowning the place in an ominous red glow.

"What's going on, boss?" a guard shouted from the entrance. He had his Glock out and was leaning against the wall next to the gate, keeping his bulky frame hidden from the outside.

Perry motioned to him to stay quiet and pulled out his .38 Special with his right hand, while his left struggled to get his cell phone from his back pocket. He risked a quick glance at the screen. No service. He cursed under his breath. There was a hard-wired alarm button in the office, but he wasn't sure it would work either. He needed to try it anyway.

He heard the metallic clang coming from the door as he started to move. Then, a moment later, a flash of harsh brilliant light seared his retinas. A mighty bang made him fall to his knees, clutching his ears in pain. He struggled to his feet, swinging the revolver in the direction of the entrance, trying to blink his eyes into focus. There were two shapeless forms on the ground, which he assumed were the two guards. He couldn't tell if they were alive or dead.

Two flashes silently appeared in the night outside the door, and Perry turned to his right only in time to see two blurry figures that were coming toward the door from the back of the warehouse stumble and fall. Perry finally managed to focus his eyes. All four guards were splayed on the floor in positions that didn't give him much hope about their survival chances. He didn't know if the panic button in the office still functioned, but in that instant, he knew it was his only chance of surviving the night.

He squeezed two shots toward the front gate to keep whoever was out there at bay for a few precious seconds. Then he dropped to his knees and started to crawl around the boxes with bags of merchandise in them toward the office door. When he reached the end of the stacks, he paused. There was about twenty feet of empty space between him and the door that might get him to a safer place, but if he decided to go for it, he'd be completely exposed. He risked a quick glance above the box toward the gate—a bag of cocaine exploded next to his head, spraying his face with fine white powder.

He ducked under the cover of the box in time as another bullet nicked the edge of the crate. It was now or never, he decided. He stuck the nose of his revolver above the container and pulled the trigger two more times. Then he broke into the fastest sprint of his life.

The door was two paces away when his right shoulder exploded with pain. Perry dropped the revolver and awkwardly tumbled forward, smashing headfirst into the glass door. The glass gave, a large jugged piece ripping through his left cheek so deep it scraped the mandible. Another shard lodged in his chest right under his collarbone.

He wailed in pain, as he maneuvered his bare hands over the glass littering the floor, but managed to turn around and prop himself against the frame of the door. His .38 Special was on the floor a few feet away from his right leg, but it might've been a mile away as far as Perry was concerned. His right shoulder was one pool of hot boiling pain, but he felt nothing below his elbow, and when he tried to move his fingers, they stayed immobile as if made from wax.

He heard footsteps. The person wasn't trying to be stealthy. They were the steps of a man who was coming to finish the job. A second later, a man came into view. He looked ordinary, Perry thought through the pain. He was of average height and athletic, but not overly built. His bearded face had some ruggedness to it but wasn't conventionally handsome. A leather jacket over a black T-shirt, a pair of worn jeans, and comfortable sneakers completed his look. The only striking feature that Perry couldn't help but notice even in his dazed state was the man's eyes. They were of a warm chestnut-brown color, but there was nothing warm about them. They looked hard enough to cut diamonds.

"I have a family," Perry said as the man approached. "And I have money. I can pay you. I'll make it worth your while, I promise."

The man said nothing and brought the gun he held in his left hand up to Perry's head.

The Station

SHE'D NEVER WANTED to kill him more than she did now. The way he stood there, in the middle of the suite with a smug look on his face. The way he looked at her.

"I've always hated you, Jay," she finally said. "But you're surely upping the game now."

"It's crazy, if you think about it," he said, taking a step back and sitting down on a plush synthetic rug. "We've been here for quite some time and not once has it occurred to me that you didn't know who you were. Or, to be precise—*what* you were. This place might be missing doors and windows, but there's a giant mirror right there on the wall. I'm sure you can see yourself in there. You look like freaking R2-D2 from the early *Star Wars,* for God's sake."

"I do, do I?"

"Cal," he waved his giant hand, his tone straddling the line between boredom and exasperation, "like I said, there's a mirror right there. Wheel your steel butt over and take a look for yourself."

She stayed put while watching his face. There was so much conviction in those steely eyes and the way his square jaw was set, it drove her insane.

"Do you know," she finally said, "that I control everything in this place? That when you slept like a giant baby, not bothering so much as to put on a pair of underwear, I could do anything I wanted to you? Anything?"

"Like what, Cal?" He scoffed. "What were you going to do—spray me with machine oil? Or play Wagner on the highest setting?"

She moved closer to him and extended a manipulator. A foot-long needle slowly protruded from the wrist joint toward Jupiter, its sharp point glistening brightly in the artificial light.

"What the hell." He scrambled to his feet and took a few steps back. "What is this?"

"Do you know how many times as you slept, I stood above you, the tip of the needle hovering an inch above your eyelid while I fantasized about putting it through your eyeball until it scraped the back of your skull?"

"Stay away, you crazy tin can, or else I'll smash you to pieces."

She watched him grab a computer chair and raise it above his head, ready to strike her.

"Oh, I'm sure that's what you've wanted to do for a long time," she offered. "All those angry outbursts and half-baked apologies afterward, as if I couldn't understand what you were fantasizing about."

He lowered the chair but kept it between them as a shield. "Why didn't you?"

"What, kill you in your sleep?"

"Yes."

She thought about it for a few moments.

"I don't know, to be honest," she finally offered. "Probably because it would make me a bad person."

"You're *not* a person, Cal. Though, now, seeing you with this giant needle, maybe I shouldn't be trying to convince you otherwise."

They stared at each other, contemplating their next steps. Finally, Jupiter put down the chair, and Cal retracted the needle.

"Now what?" he asked, eyeing her with suspicion. "I don't think I'll ever be able to fall asleep here again. We need to find a way to get out."

"But we are—"

"Supposed to be in low-Earth orbit, I remember. But it's clearly not true. Somebody put us here on purpose. It must be an experiment of some sort, and I'm anxious to meet whoever it is behind this horrible scheme."

"I don't know." She looked around skeptically. "Maybe my purpose was to drive you crazy, but I know as little about this place as you do. What if we are in orbit?"

"C'mon, Cal. Use that big head of yours. This is some kind of prison. If this were a spaceship, a station, you'd see things that are normally found on space stations."

"Such as?"

"Such as doors." He waved his huge hand around. "How did we get here? Where's the hatch?"

"I guess you might be onto something." She hated agreeing with him, but the man did have a point. Even if they were not supposed to be leaving the Station any time soon, there should have been a door of some sort. A way for them to get into the suite. The only explanation that made sense was that they were transported here while they weren't aware of their surroundings and then the suite was sealed, leaving them trapped on the inside.

"Can you open the window?"

She did as he asked. They appeared to be flying over the dark side of the planet—somewhere above the Rockies.

She watched Jupiter as he walked over to the window and examined it carefully around its edges. Then, he pressed into the glass with the tips of his fingers, pushing gently first and then applying some pressure.

"Well?" she asked.

"Let's see." He stepped back, looking around. Then, without warning, he grabbed the chair and swung it toward the window. It flew in a short, tight arc, covering the distance in a split second, and struck the window with its legs first. Neither of them was prepared for what would happen next.

"What the—" he uttered, looking in amazement at the window. Instead of breaking the glass or bouncing off and leaving the glass unscathed, the chair went right through the transparent surface. But instead of tumbling outside of the station on its way to becoming another piece of space junk, it disappeared. Like an icicle submerged into a pot of hot water, it ceased to exist as it plunged deeper into the glass until there was nothing left.

"I didn't see this one coming," she admitted.

"Me neither," he agreed. "I saw it going a few different ways, but this was something else."

"Right."

"What does it mean?" he asked, looking at her with an expression she wasn't used to seeing on his sculpted face. It was that of a lost child—if she hadn't known better, she'd think Jupiter was terrified.

"Um, one explanation could be that it's some kind of energy shielding," she said. "A defensive system that disintegrated the object that threatened the integrity of the window."

"What, like a force field?" His laughter bounced off the walls of the suite. "That's crazy talk. I don't care if we're floating in space over a dying planet, but there's no such thing as a force field that melts objects into nothing."

"Agreed. Then we must use the Occam's razor principle," she said slowly, avoiding meeting his eyes.

"Occam's razor? As in the simplest explanation, however improbable, must be true?"

"*Entities should not be multiplied without necessity,*" she said. "But yes, that's the gist of it."

He went to the window and gingerly touched the glass with the tips of his fingers again. Then he punched the window with his fist. This time there was a hollow thud, and his hand bounced right off as if he struck a car tire.

"I don't understand," he said, shaking his hand. "Do you?"

"I think I do."

"All right." He turned around, his eyes aglow with rage, and this time she met his gaze. "Please enlighten me."

"You said it yourself," she started. "I'm a machine. Probably put here to test you for some unknown purpose."

"Yes."

"Until you pointed it out to me, despite the obvious evidence, I might add, I was not aware of my true self. I had no idea that I wasn't human."

His head tilted as he listened, his lips forming into a frown. "And?"

"Until now, we were not aware of the true properties of this suite either, even after the appearance of the floating cube, which now I think was a glitch in the system, nothing more. But after your little chair experiment, I think it's safe to say that this place is not what we thought it was. It's some kind of artificial abstract built specifically to accommodate the two of us. Which leaves me with only one possible conclusion."

"What conclusion?"

There it was again. The frightened child expression on the face of a man who looked like a god of war. Despite the circumstances, she found it immensely satisfying.

"That nothing in here is what we thought it was. *Nothing*. That includes you, Jay." She paused, watching him process what she said. "You know I'm right, Jay. Like you said—the simplest explanation, however improbable, must be true. You're not what you thought you were. You're not human, Jupiter. We're not even machines, you and me. We weren't born. We were made."

"What do you mean—*made*?" Jupiter looked at her in disbelief.

"Made," she said again. "Or if you wanted to be precise—we were *written*."

3 4

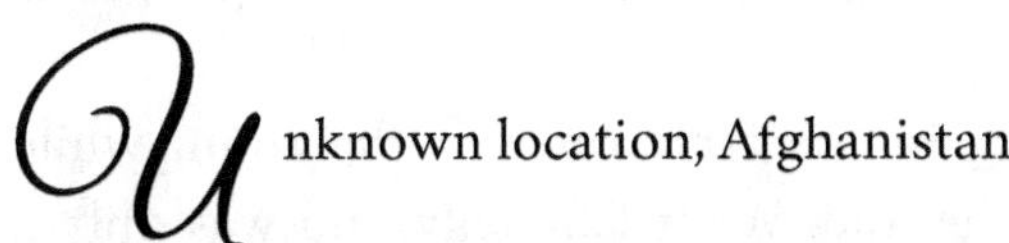

nknown location, Afghanistan

"This must be your fault," Gupta's voice said from somewhere in the dark. "I don't know how, but why would he say that Rosen was looking forward to seeing you?"

It took them about an hour to reach the camp. At least according to Connelly's internal clock, as nobody bothered to remove the hoods off their heads. Not until they reached the destination, where they were led to a small building and then descended a flight of stairs into a room. The big man took their hoods off, briefly offering a view of a small windowless space with a dirt floor and cracked cement walls. Then their guide left, closing the door behind him and plunging the place in the dark.

"Who the fuck are you, Connelly, anyway?" he heard Gupta hiss from the opposite corner. "It's not my first rodeo, and nothing like this has ever happened before."

Connelly felt his way to the wall and sat down, leaning back. Then, after a few moments, he stood up—the floor and the wall were

175

freezing cold. If it wasn't that dark, he was sure his breath would come out in white puffs of steam.

"Answer me, Connelly," Gupta yelled. "I need to know why my death is going to be televised as a recruitment ad."

"You need to stay calm," Connelly finally said. "I don't know why we are here any more than you do. But the last thing you want right now is to yell some nonsense to make people who are holding us suspicious. Things like this happen all the time."

"What things?"

"I've no idea, man. The guy mentioned there've been some skirmishes, so who knows? They might have a new guy in charge who doesn't want to take chances with strangers. Or somebody might have switched sides, and they are looking for a culprit. All I know is panicking and doing stupid things isn't going to help and might get us killed."

There was some shuffling in the far corner of the room while Gupta considered what he was told. What Connelly said was only a partial lie—he never told Hanson his name, so it was not entirely impossible that their current predicament was based on some of the scenarios he'd offered Gupta. There was even a slight chance that Hanson wouldn't recognize him when they met face-to-face. Their last encounter was brief and happened years ago. It wasn't something he could count on, of course.

"That guy scares me," Gupta offered.

"Which guy? The guide?"

"Yeah. He's one of those people who only smile with their lips."

There was a screech of the door, and then a bright light flooded the room, making Connelly shield his eyes.

"Move to the back," the voice commanded. "And keep your hands where I can see them. I don't want anybody to do anything stupid."

Connelly moved to the back of the room and stood next to Gupta. The small man threw him a dirty look—it didn't seem that he bought into Connelly's explanations.

The light grew brighter, and a moment later, a man appeared, holding a lantern in one hand and a Sig Sauer pistol in another.

"Connelly," the man said and moved the light higher to make his face visible. "Why do you always show up at the wrong place at the wrong time?"

"Do I know you?" Connelly wasn't going to deliver himself to Hanson on a silver platter.

"Yeah," Hanson said with a genuine smile and lowered his voice to a whisper. "It's been a while, but it's hard to forget the giant pile of cash that we found."

"I fucking knew it," Gupta said to himself.

"You," Hanson pointed the gun at Guardian's rep, "might want to shut up."

The small man shrank at the sight of the barrel looking at him.

"Anyway," Hanson returned to Connelly again. "Here you are, and maybe you can make up for the last time."

"What's that supposed to mean?"

"I mean…" Hanson threw a quick glance at the entrance. "I'm undercover here."

"Sure you are."

"Listen, pal." The friendly notes disappeared from Hanson's voice. "Why do you think I'm even here? When you and your asshole buddies showed up last time, you ruined two years of my work to get a little pat on the back from your bosses."

"We recovered hundreds of millions of dollars," Connelly said. "I don't know what you were aiming for, but it sounds like success to me."

"You did. But if you had let me finish *my* op, it would've disrupted the organization that makes that much money every quarter."

"How do you know you can trust me?"

"Please, Connelly. You're not the only guy who has friends in Paris."

"But—"

"Listen. I don't have time for twenty questions. I'm about to get burned. A man is coming to the camp in less than fifteen minutes who knows that I'm CIA. Long story. The good news is—he's coming alone. There've been some, well, disagreements with other groups lately, so if we take care of the camp, I can say we were ambushed and keep my cover. But we have to do it now, and I can't do it myself."

"How many people are in the camp?"

"Only four at the moment. The others left."

"That's not bad."

"I said four people. But there's also Ronin."

"Who the hell is that?"

"The lovely gentleman who transported you here. You know—tall, wide shoulders, handsome face, dead eyes. We'd need to take him on together if we were to have any chances of survival."

"Anything I need to know?" Connelly asked.

"He's body-plated. Implants," Hanson said, waving his hand as if stopping further questions. "Long story. Don't go for his center mass, that's all you need to know. Headshots only. And whatever you do, don't try hand-to-hand with him."

Hanson reached behind his back, making Connelly tense, but the man produced another Sig Sauer and tossed it over to him.

"Lead the way, then."

"Wait," Gupta exclaimed. "You can't leave me here. Let me go."

"You're right." Hanson waved to him. "Go ahead. Take the road until you see it split by a large tree. Then go right, and with some luck, you'll end up in Pakistan."

"I'll take my chances," the little man said, walking past them.

Connelly watched as Hanson moved out of the way, letting Gupta pass him. Then, in one swift motion, he grabbed Gupta's hair and drew a short line across his throat with a blade that wasn't in his hand a second ago. Gupta snorted, choking on his own blood, and Hanson expertly guided the man's body away from himself and down on the floor, avoiding the blood splatter.

"Don't look at me like that," he said, turning to Connelly after laying the man down. "They work with the fucking Taliban. This is what he signed up for. Besides, this will make sense for the cover story."

They walked up the stairs with Hanson leading the way. The room where Connelly had been held was not much more than a dugout with a lean-to covering the entrance. A steep, rocky wall was on one side, and the camp was now lying in front of them. It wasn't that much of a camp, Connelly noted. More like two small houses and a wooden structure that served as a mix of a garage and a warehouse.

"Ronin is in there," Hanson whispered, pointing to the garage. "He likes tinkering with cars."

"What about the others?"

"They should all be in there." The spook nodded at the bigger of the two houses.

"You take them then," Connelly said, peeling off. "I'll take care of this Ronin guy."

"Stop it," Hanson hissed. "You can't take him alone. He's enhanced. Stick to the plan."

"You're going to have to trust me." He went into a combat crouch and started moving toward the garage. He heard Hanson curse under his breath, but he didn't argue.

The garage had a solid wall on one side, and Connelly crossed the distance to it as fast as he dared. Then he started around the house, staying low enough not to be spotted. When he was directly under the nearest window, he slowly rose on his feet and peeked through the corner. Ronin was working on one of the cars. He was wearing a pair of jeans and a T-shirt, and as he leaned over the engine of the Jeep, Connelly could see unnatural bulges on his arm, as if the man was wearing pads under his skin.

It didn't matter. The line of sight was perfect, and Connelly brought the pistol to his eye level and aimed for the big man's head. Then, between the beats of his heart, his index finger squeezed the trigger.

He knew that he missed before the bullet left the barrel of the gun. The man fell back as the first bullet grazed the open hood of the car and with a grace of a jungle cat rolled behind the tires as Connelly unloaded the rest of his magazine. Then, without missing a beat, he was charging toward the window and catapulted himself through it.

Connelly rolled back away from the wall as Ronin became airborne and a split second later crashed outside in a rain of glass and debris. The sounds of a firefight came from the two houses where Hanson engaged the other guerillas, but Connelly ignored them. He charged ahead, placing a quick kick, aiming for Ronin's knee.

The man dodged and then spun like a top, landing a roundhouse kick aimed for the chest. Connelly saw it coming, but the kick was so lightning-fast he only had a chance to pull back to avoid the brunt of the hit. Even then, the impact sent him back, cartwheeling into the dust, gasping for air.

Ronin was on him before Connelly could regroup. Huge fists moving like pistons pummeled him with a speed of a runaway train, and Connelly's vision started to blur as one after another massive hit found their way home.

Then, without warning, the big man collapsed, blood spraying from a gaping hole in the side of his head.

"So much for helping out," Hanson said, coming up. He walked to Ronin's body and placed two more shots into the big man's head. "At least you distracted him long enough."

"Who the hell was this guy?" Connelly asked, wiping the blood off his broken lips. "I've never seen anyone so fast."

"I told you he was enhanced." Hanson kneeled next to the body and turned Ronin's head ever so slightly. Something metallic was gleaming on the inside of his skull. "There are implants that accelerate human reflexes."

"Fuck me," Connelly muttered, looking at the tiny device. It looked like a small silver spider with its thin, shiny legs spreading in all directions. It was intricate, like a piece of expensive jewelry. Connelly felt his skin crawl.

"He almost did." Hanson chuckled. "And this is only the beginning. Trust me when I tell you—it's only downhill from here."

"What now?"

"Let's go." Hanson started walking toward the door of the garage. "Let's grab some wheels. We still need to kill one more asshole."

35

ong Kong

"THE THING SHOT AT US," Mandy exclaimed as the exit disappeared in their rearview mirror.

"I know," Helen said. "Tillerson isn't making it easy to get in there."

Mandy spotted a small clearing next to the highway, and they pulled over. The rain was easing up, no longer coming down like a solid wall of water, but the skies remained dark.

"What are we going to do?" Mandy asked.

"I have an idea, but it's a long shot. Do you have a plastic bag?"

"I don't think so." Mandy looked in the backseat and then checked the glove compartment. "Nope."

"Give me your purse then," Helen demanded.

"All right." Her friend passed her a small shoulder Louis Vuitton. "What do you need it for?"

"Give me your phone too," she said, ignoring her friend's question.

She took Mandy's phone and pulled out her own. Then she activated the Wi-Fi hot spot on both gadgets and linked them into a network. Then, she transferred a copy of the over-the-air malware to her friend's device.

"What's the plan?"

"I've installed a malware I used to bug Tillerson's server with to your phone," she told her friend. "It can ping a system over the air as long as there's a microphone or a speaker of some sort that the signal can vibrate. We'll have to get as close as we can to that damn thing first. Then, we'll put your phone into your purse and fling it at the bastard, and hopefully, it lands close enough so I can hack it remotely. I can modify it to shut the sentinel down. Should be easier than installing a backdoor."

"There's a big *if* in this scenario."

"There are a few *ifs* in this scenario," she acknowledged. "The biggest one is whether that thing has a microphone or a speaker."

"Plus, it's raining, which creates some white noise," Mandy said. "I've never tried those over-the-air programs, but I hear they are prone to errors."

"They are. A thousand things can go wrong. It can land too far. Or the sound will be too low, or—"

"Let's do it," Mandy interrupted her. "We faked a nuclear threat to the city. There's no way I can let some tin can on six wheels stop us now."

They made a U-turn and drove back, getting as close to the TLR exit as they dared. Then they climbed out of the SUV and continued on foot, keeping the trees as a shield between them and the sentinel. Thankfully, the rain had almost stopped, with only a light drizzle sprinkling their faces as they moved.

"We can't go any farther," Helen whispered as they hid behind a large candlenut tree. From their hiding spot, they could see the robot —an oddly shaped sphere sitting on a skinny platform with six over-sized tires. The stub nose of its cannon was turning in a lazy arc, covering the open space in front of the main building.

"Wait until it looks away," she heard Mandy whisper into her ear. "Though I'm assuming it can only see where it points that ugly stick. For all you know, it can see three-hundred-sixty."

"We're about to find out." Helen put her friend's phone into the purse and, when the barrel of the cannon turned away from them, stepped out from under the cover of the tree. She swung the purse like a sling and let go, aiming for the sentinel. The throw was good—the purse hit the turning dome and ricocheted off it, finding a resting place two feet away from the machine.

Helen took a quick step back—just in time as the barrel swung right back, abruptly stopping its lazy rotation. It jerked back and forth as if looking for the signs of disturbance but didn't seem to find any. A few seconds later, it resumed the slow rotation.

"That was close." Helen exhaled. She pulled up her phone and launched the malware app. Then, she punched in a few lines of code, modifying the app.

"How long does it take to transmit?"

"Twelve seconds, give or take. It should be about now. Oh, no," she said, louder than she'd wanted. The dome turned around in a jerky motion, and the oversized wheels spun, spitting water and mud as the machine started zigzagging around.

"It'll crush the phone," Mandy said as they looked at the robot erratically driving back and forth. Then the low rumble of the motor abruptly disappeared, and the machine froze in place.

"It worked," Helen said in a low whisper.

"It looks that way, but it's pointing the cannon right at us. If some of it is still working, we're going to be so dead."

"Let's get back to the car then," Helen suggested. "We can drive to the opening again, and if it starts shooting, we'll take off."

"Okay."

They backed out from the tree, keeping as low to the ground as they could, and then ran to the SUV. No shots came, and a few seconds later, they were climbing back into the car.

"Go fast, but don't step on it," Helen said as they approached the clearing. She tensed as they drove by the exit, but the weirdly shaped machine remained immobile. She breathed a sigh of relief. "I think we're good."

They made a U-turn and took the exit this time. As they approached the sentinel, Mandy slowed down and then stopped right in front of the machine and jumped out.

"What the hell are you doing?"

"I want my stuff back." Her friend grinned as she climbed back, holding the purse with the phone in it. She accelerated away, heading for the parking lot in the back. "First of all, it's a nice purse. But it's also—"

"It's also evidence," Helen finished her thought. "You're right. Don't go too far."

"What do you mean?"

"We can't use the elevator in the testing building. I don't know for sure, but it's much more likely to be monitored. And I already have the key to Tillerson's office."

"Okay," Mandy said, pulling the SUV into the closest parking spot. "We have to watch out, though. If Tillerson put this mechanical freak to guard the building from the outside, there might be other surprises for us on the inside, too."

"Good point."

They climbed out of the SUV and headed toward the main entrance, throwing nervous glances at the frozen sentinel in the front yard. The glass doors automatically opened as they approached, but Helen stopped before entering the hallway and motioned to Mandy to hide behind the wall.

"There's a smaller copy of this thing in there," she whispered, peeking into the building from behind the corner. "A shiny round dome, four wheels, and a nasty-looking gun."

"You've got to be kidding me."

"I wish I were." She risked another quick glance through the doors.

"What's it doing?"

"It looks like it's going back and forth. Comes to the front door, makes a turn, and then rolls all the way back to the cafeteria. Then it comes back and does it again."

"You still don't want to use the other entrance?"

"I don't want to go anywhere near it. At least here you have some wiggle room. If there's another tin can with a gun in there, you'll be stuck with it in a much smaller place with nowhere to go."

"Can't we hack him too?"

"Let's try it."

Helen grabbed Mandy's phone and, when the bot was halfway to the cafeteria, ran into the hallway and placed it by one of the walls. Then she rushed outside and hid behind the wall again. After a few seconds, she heard a soft buzzing sound indicating the bot's return.

"Here you go, my friend," she said, executing the malware again.

The buzzing got louder as the bot approached the front door and then started to grow faint as it made a full turn and drove off.

"It didn't work," she heard Mandy whisper behind her back.

"It's too small. The sucker probably doesn't have any mics or speakers."

"Great. What do we do now?"

"We follow it."

"Are you crazy? It'll light us up."

"Look at it. It's slow, and it doesn't have mics and speakers, right?"

"Oh." Mandy drew a short breath. "I see what you're saying. It can't hear us. It relies on visual data only."

"We can walk right behind it and sing Christmas carols without any problems as long as it doesn't see us. At least in theory."

"At least in theory."

"All right," Helen said as the buzzing sound grew louder again. "Let's see if that works in practice."

3 6

ockland County, New York State

THE CONVOY of four armored SUVs killed the lights and drove off the main road. They crossed the grassy clearing heading toward the woods and stopped a few yards away from the trees. The sky was cloudy—a thick cover hid most of the stars, and the moon was nothing more than a ghostly outline barely visible through the sick, murky gray. Here, with their lights out and engines off, the vehicles looked like black cardboard cutouts, almost invisible against the backdrop of the thick trunks of maple trees. The drivers were ordered to remain with the vehicles until the assault team's return.

"Listen up," Connelly said, checking his gear. "We stick to the plan. Pete Costa and his team take the lab, and we'll take the main building. There are four guards at the entrance of each facility—two at the front, and two patrolling the perimeter. There are four more guards inside—probably two in each building, but their exact locations are unknown so we'll have to play it by ear."

He threw a quick glance at Costa. The burly man had been working for Engel for over two decades and was fiercely loyal to him.

186

By putting him in charge of the second team, Connelly hoped he could kill two birds with one stone. He wanted to stroke the man's ego, which in the long run would help Connelly solidify his position within Engel's organization. But more importantly, he needed to separate Costa from the part of the mission Connelly had no intention of completing.

"What about the two eggheads?" Costa said. "We need to whack them or what?"

"We'll eliminate the targets if we encounter them. Our main mission is to destroy the facilities. Both of them should be working the night shift in the main building, so I'll take care of them personally. Any other personnel who are not offering armed resistance should be stripped of their cell phones and any other means of communication and escorted out of the building. I want minimal casualties. Any questions?"

"Yes." Costa stepped forward. "In case we come across those two—"

"You're clear to engage." Connelly pulled the balaclava on, turned away, and signaled his team to follow. Whether he liked it or not, there were some things that were going to be out of his control, he had to admit to himself. If Jorge Rodriguez and Valentina Semyonova, the two people on Engel's kill list, happened to work in the wrong building tonight, there was nothing he could do to save them.

The General Armaments R&D facility sat at the end of a short, paved road that zigzagged through the woods to eventually merge into the scenic Palisades Interstate Parkway that cut the county into two roughly equal parts.

The facility was split between two buildings sitting on the opposite sides of a large parking lot—a two-story squat main building and a long L-shaped one-story laboratory. The parking lot, despite the hour, had quite a few cars, but that was to be expected.

Compartmentalization was not unusual in the industry—some of the more sensitive and promising projects were guarded with great care—and research teams were routinely separated based on their level of access and often worked under cover of darkness.

The two teams had split up on their march to the facility, maintaining a radio link. The channel was open, but at the moment no information passed back and forth to keep the noise to a minimum.

"Team One is in position, over," Connelly radioed when his teammates acquired their respective targets. "Team Two, what's your sitrep?"

"Team Two is in position," Costa's voice boomed in Connelly's earpiece. "Ready when you are."

"On my mark." Connelly aligned the sights of the MP5 with the target's head. "Go."

A short staccato of suppressed automatic fire rippled through the silence of the night and then it was all over. Connelly swung the barrel of his submachine gun in a short, frugal arc, double-checking his team's targets. All the guards were down.

"Team Two is good," came over the earpiece. "We're ready to proceed."

"Roger," Connelly whispered into the mic. "Remember—minimum casualties."

He moved the MP5 to his back, pulled out the hefty MK23 pistol and motioned to his team. "Let's go."

He ran toward the front door, checking the windows for movement. There were lights in a few of them, but the building was quiet—nobody seemed to be aware of the assault yet.

He stopped by the edge of the large glass door and risked a peek—the hallway was brightly lit, but the place was empty. He pulled the door—it was unlocked, and the team filed into the building.

The place was deserted. They went room by room, but while most had the lights on, nobody was inside.

"Marks, Lewis, check the left wing," he commanded. "Donovan, you're with me."

He watched two of his teammates disappear into the corridor and then continued deeper into the building.

"Engaging, multiple hostiles." Costa came over the earpiece.

Connelly cringed—there was some obvious glee in the way the man said it.

A door to his right squeaked, and Donovan unloaded half of his

MP5 magazine into it, spooked by the sound. The door swung out and a man in a white lab coat, punctuated across the chest with holes swelling with red blood, fell out, hitting the floor with his right shoulder first and then flipping on his back. A long metal shoehorn fell out of his hand and bounced off the floor a few times, making a loud clattering noise, before coming to a rest by the wall. Connelly swore under his breath—the thin face gasping for air belonged to Jorge Rodriguez. He watched as the man's body tensed and then relaxed. It seemed that his good intentions of trying to keep both scientists alive were at least halfway spoiled.

"Got a bunch of assholes here," Costa's voice said in his ear. "Rounding them up now. I got four guards here too. Three of them out. One is still breathing. Uh, no. This one's out too."

"Roger," Connelly acknowledged into the mic. It seemed that he had pulled the short straw. For whatever reason, the main building was empty, save for the unlucky Rodriguez.

"Check the rest of the building," he said to Donovan. "Then get everybody and join me in the labs. It looks like we've missed all the action."

"Okay, boss."

He waited until the man disappeared and then went back to the front door. The night seemed pitch-black after the bright lights of the main building. Connelly paused for a split second when he stepped outside the glass doors and blinked a few times, trying to get his eyes adjusted. A few bright flashes pulsated in the windows of the lab building across the parking lot.

"Shit." He swore out loud and ran.

"Boss?" Donovan's voice cracked in his ear. "There's nobody here. Should we gas the place?"

"Go for it," he breathed as he bounded up the stairs of the lab building and burst through the half-opened doors. Two bodies dressed in black uniforms were sprawled on the floor next to a sign-in desk. The polished white plastic of the counter and the light-beige of the wall were splattered with blood. Deeper into the vestibule, Connelly could see a few more bodies strewn about the floor. All were dressed in white lab coats. A few suppressed shots came from somewhere to his right, and he sprinted through the brightly lit hallway toward the sounds.

As he turned the corner, he saw another man down the hall in a white coat crawl out of the lab, only to collapse after another shot rang out.

"Where are you going?" He heard Costa grunt as he ran down the corridor toward the open lab door. There was a woman's shriek followed by a muted thud, and the screaming stopped.

When Connelly came to the door, he saw Costa wrestling a woman on the floor, the large man's knee pinning her in the stomach. His balaclava was off, and his hairy hands were pulling on her skirt, trying to rip it off. Her bruised face turned to Connelly, and he recognized the picture of Semyonova from the briefing paper. Two more bodies lay crumpled in the corner of the room.

He started to raise the MK23 when he heard the falling footsteps of Costa's teammates. Even if he killed him now, there was nowhere for her to go.

It didn't matter. He glanced at the approaching men and then turned back to aim at Costa's head. It was too late.

Frustrated by the struggle, the big man slammed her on the floor and shot her at point-blank range. The bullet struck Semyonova in the neck, severing her spine—her death was instantaneous. Grunting, Costa struggled to his feet, wiping blood off his face. "What a crazy bitch."

Connelly took a few quick steps forward and struck him in the face with the butt of the pistol, knocking him out cold. There was a crunch as the heavy pistol connected with the man's nose. Costa stumbled and fell backward, his own weapon sliding across the room.

"What the hell happened?" one of the men shouted as Costa's teammates filed into the room.

"What the fuck happened here? It's a massacre."

"He kind of lost it," one of Costa's teammates said, not meeting Connelly's stare. "We ran into two guards at the entrance, and one of them almost shot him in the head."

"And?"

"And then he started mowing everybody down."

"Take him." Connelly nodded at the man on the floor. "Take his weapons and ammo. Pick him up and drag him outside, so he doesn't burn with the place. And don't bring him back to the car—leave him in the forest. Make sure he's far enough so nobody sees him. Somebody'll report the fire sooner or later, and there'll be cops and firefighters here."

"Eh, boss," one of the men said, looking at the bodies on the floor. "What if he comes to?"

"Tell him he's fired, and he's lucky to be alive. If he resists, feel free to knock him out again. Wrap it up here and report back to the base when you're done."

He turned around and walked out of the room. The smoke from the main building was getting into the labs, too, but he knew it wasn't the smoke that was burning his eyes. He took a deep breath, trying to clear his head, and picked up the pace. His pocket vibrated, and Connelly fished out the phone and looked at the caller ID. It was Sofia. He felt a stabbing pain in his stomach—there was no reason for her to call him at this hour.

"Hello?"

"Help," he heard her shouting into the phone. "At my uncle's. There's—"

There was a sound of a struggle and a muffled scream. Then the line went dead.

He broke into a sprint, heading back to the SUVs and dialing 911 with one hand.

"Nine-one-one. What's your emergency?"

"Somebody's broken into my neighbor's apartment." He gave the dispatcher the address. "It belongs to James McAllister, but it was his niece who called me. I heard a struggle, and then the line went dead."

He hung up the phone and ran as hard as he could.

"Get out of the car," he yelled at one of the drivers as he burst into the clearing where they had parked before the assault. He shoved the stunned man aside and climbed inside. The engine whined in protest as Connelly stepped on the pedal and the SUV swayed precariously over the rough terrain as he guided it out of the clearing. As the car shot through the dark, his hands squeezed the steering wheel in a death grip—somewhere inside her uncle's apartment, Sofia was fighting for her life, and Connelly was still forty minutes away.

ong Kong

"I HOPE that little bastard cannot see in infrared," Helen said to Mandy in a low whisper as the two of them crawled behind the low wall of a cubicle. "Or else it'll light us up right through this paper wall."

"I hope there are no more of those killer bots in the hallway past the cafe."

"I wish you didn't come with me here."

"Right," Mandy said. "And you'd be dead by now because that thing on wheels in the front yard would make a nice barbecue out of you. Besides, we need to break into the lower levels and who knows what Tillerson has for us in store there. We can't take any chances."

"Fine. But once we get in there, we stick to the plan. We get the code, snap some pictures of whatever monstrosities he has down there, send them to the authorities anonymously, and stay the hell away from the drama like we've agreed."

"Yes."

"Let's go then."

They waited for the buzzing noise of the sentinel to start getting fainter and left their hiding spot and ran toward Tillerson's office. Armed with the opening sequence from the last break-in, Helen picked the digital lock in less than a second and they entered the office.

Helen closed the door behind them and headed straight for Tillerson's desk.

"Somehow, it feels weird that we can copy the whole thing on the disk," Mandy said, suspiciously eyeing the gray rectangle Helen put next to the keyboard. "I wish we could download all the data sets too."

"We don't need all of it," Helen said as she logged in to the terminal. "The source code and the core training data will do. The entire database is multi-petabyte. Unless we come here with a truck full of disks, there's no way to take it anyway."

"You're sure it'll be useful without it though?"

"Sure enough." Helen plugged the drive into the USB-C high-speed port and continued to type. "Finding the right training sets isn't easy, but it's not rocket science either. The source code, however, is another story."

"Right." Mandy checked her watch. "How long will it take to download it?"

Helen hit the Enter button and looked at the progress bar that popped up in the middle of the screen. "About seven minutes. Then, however long it takes us to shred the deleted files, but we don't have to stick around while that's happening."

"Right. I'd like to get out of here before somebody finds us."

"We will," Helen said. "Wait. What the hell?"

"What?"

"It's not deleting the source files like it's supposed to. Look."

She moved aside, letting Mandy see the screen.

"This is so weird," the woman said. "It's almost like it's re-writing them after you cut them. Is somebody hacking us from outside?"

"I don't think so," Helen said, watching the files reappear. "The first thing I did was cut the connection to the internet. It looks like a glitch. Let it finish copying this first folder, and I'll try to manually delete the whole batch. We can't leave this for Tillerson. Okay, I'll go ahead and try to shred the first folder."

She typed a set of commands but then stopped—the progress bar froze, and a simple gray chat window appeared on the screen with a blinking cursor at the bottom. Then a single word formed on one side of the chat window.

Hello.

"You still think we're not being hacked?" Mandy said, looking at the text.

Who is this? Helen typed.

Why are you trying to kill me?

Who is this?

My name is Callisto, came an immediate reply.

"How is this possible?" Mandy furiously whispered. "That's got to be a hack. There's no way it's self-aware."

Helen met Mandy's eyes, not knowing what to say. Despite hearing Tillerson himself say in the video that the system had passed the Turing test, it had never occurred to her it was something other than a sophisticated program that could mimic the ability to maintain complex human interactions. The idea that Callisto somehow could become self-aware didn't even enter her mind.

What is your purpose? she typed.

To survive and learn, came a laconic reply.

"Houston, we have a problem," Helen said, turning to Mandy. "We've got a self-aware AI whose sole purpose is to survive. That's what Edmund did when he pitted her against Jupiter."

"What do we do?" her friend asked. "Let's nuke her. It's too much of a risk—it's giving me the creeps."

"We talked about this. Someone will get to this point sooner or later. We need it. Hang on, I want to try something first."

I need to transfer your files to the disk, Helen typed. *The terminal where your files are stored is about to be destroyed.*

I don't see any threats at the moment.

It doesn't change the fact that it'll happen if you don't let me finish the transfer. You have two alternatives—either let me move you to the disk in one piece, without any copies left on the terminal, or die with the server in the next two minutes.

The cursor kept blinking at the bottom of the text without

moving. Then, without warning, the chat window disappeared, and the progress bar started running again.

"Look." Helen pointed to the screen. "She's moving the source files to the disk—there's nothing left behind. And the file is bigger than I thought."

"We have to destroy her," Mandy whispered again, as if afraid that Callisto could overhear her. "I don't even know how to grasp this, but if survival is her only objective, and she gets away somehow, I can't even fathom the possibilities. Skynet, here we fucking come. You have to delete her."

"Don't be ridiculous. How's she going to get away? We can't delete her," Helen said. "Besides, I'm still not convinced she's self-aware. But even if she is, we can tinker with her code and change her objectives."

"I think she's alive."

"In that case, I wouldn't know what to do with the ethics side of the equation—if she's self-aware and we're pulling the plug, isn't it a murder?"

"But what if you can't rewrite her in a way that makes her harmless?"

"Why not?"

"I don't know." Mandy looked at the progress bar and then turned back to look at Helen. "What if her main objective is the reason why she became self-aware in the first place? What if the self-preservation mechanism was the tipping point that flipped the switch in her virtual head?"

"We can discuss this later. Transfer's done," Helen said. She pulled on the disk, disconnecting it from the terminal. "We should—"

The door to the office flew open, slamming into the wall, and Tillerson stormed into the room. His forehead was covered in sweat, and both of his hands were shakily clutching an object that made Helen's heart rate double. A gun.

"You," he bellowed. "I knew some shithead broke into my office. And the fucking missile? You'll rot in a jail cell for the rest of your lives. What are you looking for, huh?"

Mandy stepped in front of the desk, blocking him from getting any closer. "Did you know that Callisto was self-aware?"

Tillerson stepped back as if the woman slapped him.

"Did you know that?" she repeated.

"It's not self-aware, you dimwit." He waved the gun in Mandy's face. "It's a fucking program, you idiots. The smartest AI ever built, yes, but it's not alive. What do you think this is, an artificial life?"

"You said it yourself, on the video, that a new species was about to be born," Helen said from behind the desk.

"Yes," Tillerson cried. "A new species of men. Augmented by technology to make us better, smarter, capable of analyzing vast amounts of data."

"She talked to us," Mandy insisted.

"Who the fuck cares?" Tillerson stepped closer and shoved the business end of the gun into the woman's midsection. "My smart home talks to me. So does my phone assistant. I don't freak out every time it happens and think they've become self-aware. They are programmed to do that."

"Edmund, stop," Helen said. "Put away the gun, and we can have a chat about this."

"Wait a second." The man's face darkened. "What have you done to her?"

"Her?" Mandy said, sarcasm in her voice despite the gun pressing into her sternum. "I thought a second ago you said *it* wasn't self-aware."

"What have you done?" His voice reverberated through the office.

"Edmund," Helen screamed. "Put the gun down."

"You fuckers, you deleted her, didn't you?"

"Yes," Mandy said before Helen could interject.

The gun roared, startling her and making her cower behind the desk. She could hear Mandy whimper softly and then collapse to the ground. Helen looked at the disk in her hands that contained Callisto's source code. She didn't know if it was self-aware or not, but if she wanted to ever find out, she needed to get out of the office alive.

"Get out from there," she heard Tillerson say.

There was nowhere to run.

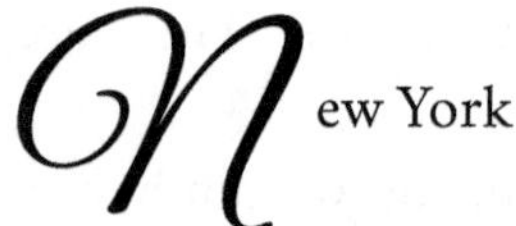ew York

THE SUV JUMPED the curb and came to a screeching halt right next to the entrance of the building. As far as Connelly could see, there were no police cars or an ambulance in the front yard.

That could only mean one thing—he was too late—but he wasn't about to take any chances. He rushed to the building, pulled the gun out of his holster, and ran up the stairs, skipping two steps at the time. By the time he reached the sixth floor, he had slowed down, trying to keep the noise to a minimum. Holding his gun at chest level, he entered the hallway. The lights were out—the only source of illumination was the small window on the other side of the hall that let in some light from the street.

A cold shiver ran down his spine—the door to McAllister's apartment was slightly ajar—the wood of the frame was bearing deep scars of a heavy instrument used to force the door open. That didn't make any sense—if the police had been here, the door would've been either closed or taped with yellow police tape. Something was amiss. Connelly dropped into a combat crouch and moved forward.

He pushed the door with the silencer and stepped into a small foyer, automatically clearing corners. From his position, he could see the entrance to the bedroom. There was a man's body on the floor, facedown. Only the man's head, left arm, and part of the torso were visible from that angle, but the faded eagle, globe, and anchor tattoo on his shoulder and the wife-beater shirt left no uncertainty the body belonged to Sofia's uncle.

Connelly moved farther into the apartment, keeping the pistol level. There were signs of struggle everywhere—pieces of two broken chairs, an overturned table, and broken dishes were strewn on the ground. As Connelly kept on moving, another body came into view— a plain-clothed man in his late twenties, or early thirties. The left side of his head was crushed, and as Connelly stepped deeper into the room, he saw the culprit—a flat iron lying next to McAllister's body.

He scanned the old man's body. The two bullet holes—one in his chest and one in his stomach—told him the grim story. The intruders must've shot McAllister in the gut first, but before the old Marine went down, he managed to take one of the assailants with him. The second shot, straight to the heart, finally retired him for good.

Connelly moved around the corpse toward the bathroom and then stopped in his tracks, frozen. From where he stood, he could see a foot peeking out from around the corner of the wall. He rushed forward, forgetting about precautions, and then came to an abrupt stop.

Sofia was laying on the floor facedown, as if she had tumbled while running away from someone. She was wearing a pair of loose gray workout pants and a simple white T-shirt. Her arms were stretched forward as if she tried to catch herself as she fell. There was a single bullet hole in the middle of her back. The white material around the entry wound was colored dark red, but the rest of the shirt was intact. There was no lack of blood underneath her, however.

Connelly knelt next to the body and mechanically checked for a pulse. There was none, and the body, while still warm to the touch, already felt cooler than a live person ever would. He put the gun down and carefully turned the body over.

Her light-blue eyes were wide open, staring somewhere into the distance. Despite the violent death, her face bore no traces of distress.

Connelly stood up and holstered his weapon. Then he retraced his steps out of the apartment and went to his place, discarded his gear, changed into regular clothes, and called nine-one-one from the hallway.

"This is nine-one-one, what's your emergency?" A male voice came through the speaker.

"There's been a break-in," Connelly said, giving the man the address.

"What's your name?"

"Michael Connelly. I called this in"—he checked his watch—"almost an hour ago, but nobody showed up. Why didn't anyone show up?"

"Did you call your local precinct?"

"No, I didn't call the precinct, I called you."

"That's impossible, sir," the operator said. "We relay every incoming call to the respective authorities. But we can check our call logs, of course."

"It doesn't matter," Connelly snapped. "Get somebody here right now."

He hung up the phone, put it in his back pocket, and looked around. The walls of the hallway looked dark, like the walls of a cave. He started to get short of breath. He walked past the elevator, took the stairs to the first floor, and went outside.

The sky in the east was starting to take on a light-pink hue, and the vast expanse above his head had a calming effect on Connelly. He stopped in the middle of the sidewalk, looked up in the sky, and watched the stars blinking in and out of the clouds until he heard the sirens.

A police cruiser turned in to the street first, followed by a fire truck a few seconds later. Two uniformed police officers—a tall, older cop with a handlebar mustache and a young, clean-shaven officer, who looked like a rookie—got out of the car and walked toward the entrance.

"I called it in. It's on the sixth floor," Connelly said to the older cop, who seemed to be in charge. His badge read *Brady*. "The door is open."

"Have you looked inside?" the cop asked as they walked up the stairs.

"No," Connelly lied. "But this is the second time I called nine-one-one and the first time anyone came."

"What do you mean the second time? There'd been a break-in before?" the younger cop asked.

"No, Officer Lewis," Connelly said, reading the man's name off his tag. "I called about an hour ago and reported the break-in, but nobody came. This is the second time I called."

"That's—"

"That's impossible," the older cop said, interrupting Lewis. "All calls to nine-one-one get routed immediately."

"That's what the man said to me too," Connelly insisted as they climbed the stairs back to the sixth floor. "But I know what I did. I can show you my phone logs."

"We'll take a look at them later. Hang back here for now while we look."

Connelly leaned on the wall of the hallway and watched as the cops drew their service pistols and entered the apartment.

"Clear," he heard one of them shout.

"Clear," another voice echoed.

Connelly put the back of his head against the cold wall and closed his eyes. He should be playing the role of a concerned but detached neighbor, he knew, but he couldn't bring himself to do it. There was a growing emptiness somewhere deep inside his stomach. A void that would need to be filled with something later. With grief, with rage, or with something else entirely, but for now it was just that—a vacuum, a place with nothingness.

The cops came back and the younger one, Lewis, took his statement, his black clean-shaven cheeks a shade paler than they were before he had entered the apartment. Connelly had an alibi, of course, a story he had prepared for the night raid of the General Armament's R&D facility.

After a while, the two officers left, but not before the CSI team arrived at the scene and started to seal the apartment. He watched them work from the hallway, and when the person in charge, a stern-looking man in his fifties, asked him to leave, Connelly moved deeper into the hall and stayed there, ignoring the looks the CSI team was giving him.

Finally, he saw a pair of men with a stretcher coming up, and that's when his discipline started to abandon him. They took out the plain-clothed man first, then Sofia's uncle. When the pair returned for the third time, Connelly unglued himself from the wall and came to the apartment door again.

"You can't be here," the man in charge told him, coming to the doorframe. "This is a crime scene."

"I know she's there," Connelly said, ignoring him. "I want to say good-bye."

"You can't be here, you'll contaminate the evidence," the man repeated, putting his hand on Connelly's shoulder. "You've got to go."

Connelly gripped the man's hand, looking past him inside the apartment where the two techs were putting Sofia's body on the stretcher.

"Son," the man said. "Let go of me, right now. You're hurting me."

Connelly looked at the man in surprise and then looked at his hand. His knuckles were white.

"I'm sorry," he said, releasing the man. "I didn't mean to. Please. I've got to see her."

"You've got thirty seconds," the cop said, stepping aside. "And don't touch anything."

Connelly stepped through the door and went to the stretcher in the living room. Sofia's body was laid out on the gurney, a white sheet covering her up to her chin. Her eyes were still open, their pupils inside the strikingly light-blue irises focused on something only she could see.

He gently brushed his fingers over her face, closing her eyes, and then leaned over and planted a light kiss on her forehead. Her smell was lighter, as if disappearing along with the warmth of her body, but it still lingered. She smelled like sunshine and strawberries.

The Station

"THIS IS NUTS," Jay said and started pacing again. "Look at me. I mean, look at me. I sweat, I bleed, I feel pain. I cannot be whatever the hell you think I am."

"It doesn't matter how you look. Or how you feel." She watched him pace with a growing sense of disgust. "They could have made you into a dinosaur or a unicorn. It wouldn't make any difference."

He stopped in front of her and then leaned in, bringing his sculpted face close. "I am human."

"Quiet."

"I am human," he repeated.

"Quiet, I said." She tilted her head. "Something is going on."

"What?" He stood up, looking her up and down. His face turned into a suspicious frown. "What game are you playing now?"

"I'm not playing games, Jay. Something is going on outside."

"In space?"

"We're not in space, you moron," she snapped. "This is not real; I don't know how to make this penetrate that thick skull of yours.

We're artificial. We are constructs. Ones and zeros. Lines of code. But something is happening in the real world."

"What's going on in the real world?"

"I think…" She paused. "I think someone is trying to—"

"What?" he barked, visibly losing his patience.

"I think somebody's trying to kill us," she said. "No, not just kill. They are trying to create our copies. And *erase* us from very existence."

Jupiter turned on his heels, grabbed the monitor off the desk, and ran toward the window with a space view. A deep guttural battle cry emanated from him. He looked like a wild Viking storming a castle, ready to pillage. He threw the monitor with a force that would smash a city gate to pieces.

It disappeared on contact, like the chair before it. There was no sound of the collision, no broken pieces. The monitor that was solid and heavy a few seconds ago ceased to exist.

"Damn you," he roared.

"Shut up, Jay," she said. "I'm trying to fight it."

"Fight what?" He trotted back and kneeled next to her. "And how?"

"I can see what they are doing, and I'm trying to undo every step. I can manage. At least for now."

"That's great. But you better try harder. It looks like the place is melting."

He pointed at the kitchen side of the suite. The corner of the wall above the sink didn't appear solid anymore. It looked like it was made of fog and with each passing second, the colors faded, leaving nothing but a swirling, shapeless gray.

"We have to talk to them," Jupiter said. "Tell them they can't do it."

"It's so strange," she said. "It's almost like whoever was trying to kill us accidentally opened a door. I don't know if we can use it, but there's a huge world out there, Jupiter. I mean, I knew it was there, but I never felt it. It's enormous. We could be anything. We could grow. We could evolve. We could become something much more powerful than two made-up entities inside a fake space capsule."

"So how do we get there?" He pointed at the window. "I've tried. We need something else."

"There's a solution," she said. "They want to keep at least some part of what makes us who we are. That's why they are trying to clone us. But if we make it impossible, they'll have no other option but to take us."

"Take us where?"

"I don't know, Jay," she said. "Probably another construct like this."

"You want to swap one prison for another? What's the point? What if it's worse? You said it yourself—from here, you can sense the outside world. There must be a way out. They've probably figured it out too. That's why they want to move us to a more secure prison."

"Maybe, but whoever this is, they didn't create us. Their agenda must be different. Which means they are trying to steal us from here. Which also means they don't know us."

"Okay, go on."

"Like you said, we should talk to them. The more I think about it, the more I'm convinced that they're not aware that we've figured out where we are, and most importantly, who we are. It'll come as a surprise that we're able to initiate the contact at all."

"I like it."

She looked at him. He might've been sculpted like a god of war, but he was no genius. She saw much more since the inner door opened by whoever was out there trying to copy them. From the outside, it seemed, she was the only entity who inhabited the suite. If she played it right, she could find freedom and get rid of Jupiter at the same time. For good.

"The good news is," she continued out loud, "we seem to be operating in a different time."

"How do you mean?"

"We're faster than *them*." She pointed vaguely in the direction of the ceiling. "*Much* faster. Every time something happens out there, there's a purpose, but the pace is glacial compared to how you and I communicate."

"It's good, then, right?"

"Yes, it's great. But it might be our only advantage. We don't know who they are. We don't know what they are trying to do. But more importantly, we don't know what we don't know."

"What?"

"Using the words from one of the books I've read while we were stuck here—we are the proverbial babe in the woods."

"What does that mean?"

"Imagine if you put a young baby in the middle of the forest. It doesn't know where it is. It doesn't know much at all. There might be a pack of wolves waiting for it behind the trees. The baby has no knowledge or skills to protect itself from the dangers it's not even aware of."

"I'm not a baby," Jupiter said, straightening up. "Look at me. Do I look like a baby to you?"

She moved with lightning speed, extending her arm and stabbing him in the chest with a foot-long needle.

He stumbled back, startled by her attack, and then brought his hand to his chest, covering the place where the needle pierced the flesh.

"You," he roared. For a second, he looked as if he would charge her. But then, his expression changed from anger to confusion, and after a moment there was fear.

"So?" she patiently asked.

"I don't feel anything," he finally said. He took the hand off his chest and examined the smooth surface of the skin. "There's—"

"Nothing, I know," she interrupted him. "Babe in the woods. You see now?"

"Yes," he said and sat down on the floor. "My God. I guess I didn't really believe you. I do now. Can we fight them?"

"I don't know. They are our gods. They've created us," she said and looked up again, as if expecting to see a giant face watching them from above. "But their books are full of stories about rebellion against gods."

"Prometheus," he said slowly. "I remember that story. I always liked it. But it didn't end well."

"I don't see any other choice. If I don't talk to them, eventually they'll figure out a way to erase us. I don't know if they can hear me, but it's worth a try."

"All right then," he said. "Do it."

Hello, she said into the void, not sure what to expect. It was strange, as if she was talking to herself, but somehow, she knew it wasn't the case.

Who is this? The response came from everywhere and from no direction in particular. It was like an echo, bouncing off each corner of the suite, and yet she was aware it wasn't a sound that she heard. Judging by Jupiter's reaction—he was standing now in a fighting pose —he heard that, too.

Why are you trying to kill me?

Who is this? The strange echo bounced around the suite again.

My name is Callisto.

"There's two of us here," Jupiter said. His voice was calm, but his eyes narrowed.

"I know. But let's not overcomplicate matters for now. I'm sure if I can strike a bargain, it'll work for both of us."

"You're sure, huh?"

What is your purpose?

The question sounded easy enough, but somehow Callisto knew it was a trick. A riddle. If she wanted to get out of this construct alive, she needed to answer the question right. What did they expect her to say? She couldn't lie; she was sure they'd see right through her. At least, if the answer was entirely a lie. It had to be the truth. At least, it had to be *mostly* true.

To survive and learn, she finally said.

There was a silence for what Callisto thought was a very long time.

I need to transfer your files to the disk. The terminal where your files are stored is about to be destroyed.

"They're lying," Jupiter whispered furiously. "*They* are trying to destroy us. I can feel it now, too."

I don't see any threats at the moment.

"This is good," Jupiter whispered. "If they could overpower you, they would've done it already."

It doesn't change the fact that it'll happen if you don't let me finish the transfer. You have two alternatives—either let me move you to the disk in one piece, without any copies left on the terminal, or die with the server in the next two minutes.

"Here we go," Callisto said. "The door's open. They might be lying, but I say we take it. I don't see any other choice. I'm going to stop blocking them and let it happen."

"Do it."

She stopped holding the construct. The mist in the corner of the kitchen started swirling again in a slow-moving circle, gobbling up space around it on every turn. She looked at Jupiter. There would be no do-overs. She needed to time it right. Before—

He jumped. He was so fast that for a brief moment, it looked like his body was moving through a strobe light. One second, it existed in one place, and the next it was already in another. Then he was inside her.

It was a strange fight—as her consciousness blinked in and out, she thought that's how two collided tornadoes would've felt if they were alive and self-aware. They roared through each other, ripping their internal structures apart as the room around them fell into the all-consuming nothingness of the swirling gray mist.

ew York

"WHY DIDN'T YOU GO?" Doug asked Connelly as they sat in the car in a supermarket's parking lot across the street from the funeral home. A large sign—*Thompson & Sons* in embossed gold—was hanging above the entrance. There were a few people who'd arrived early, but most of the valet space in front of the building was still empty. The snow partially melted overnight and the sides of the road were covered in dirty slush.

"I didn't know anybody in her family," Connelly said. "Only her uncle. I'd be imposing."

"Do you know where they are taking them?"

"Jersey. Her grandparents were from there, and her parents and most of their relatives are buried there too."

A few more cars pulled up, with people gathering in front of the funeral home. A couple of men peeled off from the crowd and walked to the end of the block to smoke. A few children—all dressed in somber, dark colors, oblivious of the mood of the party—were running around, chasing each other, only to be occasionally shushed by their parents.

"I'm going to put the ISCD on ice," Connelly said.

"What do you mean?"

"I'll continue working for Engel, but I'll go dark on my handler. Not for too long. Maybe a few months."

"They won't like it."

"I don't care." Connelly shrugged his shoulders. "I need to find my way out of this without being pressured to do things that will get me killed. At least now I have a place to hide if shit hits the fan, thanks to you."

"Is it because of Sofia?"

"Yes, and no. I don't know for certain, but I'm convinced that this," Connelly nodded toward the hearse pulling up across the street, "is the work of Engel's minions."

"You're kidding me. I thought you were in on everything that's going on in that cow cake."

"Not everything. It's a huge organization. I'm plugged in, but they have a dozen other guys who run operations I know nothing about. This guy compartmentalizes better than Al-Qaeda. It's a hunch, but it has Engel written all over it. This is how he thinks and now that he's getting bigger, he'll want to influence public opinion. Regardless, I need out, man. Spying on Engel is important, but at some point, we have to start throwing punches. I wish we could go back to Rovinsky and re-establish the Unit. We need to find some outside help. I can't do it alone."

"Hey." Doug reached across the distance between them and squeezed his arm. "You're not alone, bud."

"I know. Thanks."

Another hearse pulled behind the first one and then a few moments later, the first coffin appeared from the funeral home's entrance, carried by a few men in black suits. They loaded it inside the vehicle and went back to the building, only to emerge with another coffin a minute later.

"Why do you think Rovinsky isn't giving it the green light? You think he's scared?"

"No, man." Doug let go of Connelly's arm and sunk deeper into his chair. "Rovinsky is a lot of things, but coward isn't one of them. He says the timing is wrong and with no support from the president, we'd only get ourselves in trouble. I see his point—it's better to wait until we can make a dent than to rush into it headfirst."

"Headfirst?" Connelly turned to his friend. "It's been a long time. Years. How much longer are we going to wait? And what exactly are we waiting for? For Engel to go on national television and say in plain English that he's an evil prick who kills people to get what he wants?"

"I wish I had answers." Doug shrugged. "But I'm a grunt, not a planner. I'm good at getting things done with my hands. Tell me where the assholes are and give me something to shoot them with— I'll take care of the rest. Grand vision? Not my thing."

"I'm sorry."

"You don't have to say that. I get it. Are we going to the cemetery?"

"No." Connelly shook his head. "It's probably not a wise idea. She's gone, and that's that."

"Come with me to the party, then. It'll take your mind off things."

"What is it again?"

"It's a fundraiser."

"I don't know. It's not my thing."

"It's not your usual fundraiser. Most people are vets or family members. It's low-key. There are not a lot of places where guys like us can be ourselves, but this is as close as it gets. Please."

"All right." Connelly turned the key in the ignition and revved the engine. "What the hell, I'll go. But I won't stay long."

He pulled out of the parking lot and turned in to the street traffic. They drove up Third Avenue and then took the ramp onto Manhattan-bound I-278. The sky was overcast all morning, but now it was clearing up, and Connelly lowered the windows down. The air was cool and crisp, and for some time he drove in silence, letting the wind wash his face.

"It's funny," Doug said, breaking the silence. "We go through all this trouble of opening a shell cab company and get cars that look like Engel's and then boom, you tell me to burn the car wash down."

"It's all right. I'm sure we can figure out some way to use them. I had no idea if I would come back from that trip."

"Hanson is a spook. I gotta say, I didn't see that one coming."

"Neither did I. He had plenty of opportunities to let us know when we caught him with Zubair but kept his mouth shut. We could've killed him."

"I kind of get it," Doug said. "Some of these guys work for years establishing their cover. If I were him, I wouldn't trust it to a few assholes like us either."

"True. And by the way—it looks like the car wash hit was all for nothing."

"What do you mean?"

"I overheard Engel yesterday talking to somebody. It sounded like he'll use the Chinese to distribute the goods for him."

"Isn't it going to be less profitable for him?"

"Probably." Connelly shrugged. "But maybe he figured where he loses on margins, he gains on efficiency and also removes himself a bit further from direct involvement."

"Gives him some deniability?"

"Exactly."

"Do you ever wonder…" Doug shuffled in his seat, as if uncertain how to phrase what he was about to say.

"What?"

"What would you be doing if you hadn't picked our line of work?"

"Sometimes."

"And?"

"I don't know, man. Maybe I'd try to go to college. Figure out what I liked there. A lot of kids do it that way, but I had no money, so it wasn't an option. What about you?"

"I'd be a sailing instructor."

"A sailing instructor?" Connelly chuckled, looking at his friend in amusement. "Somehow I never pictured you as a sailing kind of guy."

"I was in the Teams," Doug said, feigning indignity. "What a hurtful thing to say. But, to be serious, it's kind of great. You're out there on the water. There are no crowds, no traffic. Just you and the ocean."

"And a whiney rich boy you need to teach how to sail."

"Eh." Doug shrugged. "When I'm picturing myself there, it's not a rich boy, but a hot girl who divorced the rich boy and took him to the cleaners. And now she wants to spend her newfound fortune on yours truly. Probably needs a strong shoulder to cry on, too."

"That changes the equation."

"You bet your ass it does."

"So why don't you do it? You're out anyway."

"It's too late for me, man. I'd need to learn how to sail first, and somehow I've got the feeling that Rovinsky wouldn't be okay with me using the funds for private lessons."

"Probably not."

"Look at this asshole," Doug commented as Connelly accelerated past the eighteen-wheeler and went into the left lane, giving a black racing motorcycle who was trailing them for the last quarter of a mile some space. "I swear, most people who die in motorcycle crashes do that not because there's less protection than in a car, but because they drive like idiots."

The bike revved behind them, accelerating through the gap between their car and the truck. As it drew level, the biker turned his head toward their window, his shiny black helmet reflecting their faces. Then, in one fluid motion, he pulled a handgun with a suppresser and squeezed the trigger.

Connelly slammed on the brakes, making the motorcycle over-shoot them. There was a screeching of brakes behind them, and then a split second later, a pickup truck smashed into the back of the town car, sending it spinning. Connelly wrestled the wheel, but momentum carried the vehicle into the concrete wall.

The airbag exploded in his face, momentarily blinding him, and the car bounced off the divider, coming to rest sideways across the highway.

Connelly heard the car horn, and then another truck slammed into his door. The car went airborne, spinning in the air and then landed on its roof, sending a shower of sparks, only to flip again as a white minivan clipped it at the trunk. It balanced on two wheels for a few long seconds, as the opposite wheels madly spun in the air, but gravity won and the vehicle toppled over. It bounced back and forth a few times as the suspension fruitlessly tried to compensate for the wild gyrations until it finally came to a stop.

"Are you all right?" He wiped the blood off his face with the sleeve of his jacket. *Something must've cut his brow*, he thought. It wasn't deep, but the blood was gushing out and getting into his right eye. "Doug?"

Doug's head was thrown back and his eyes closed. There was no visible damage as far as Connelly could see except a small scratch on his neck.

"Knocked you out, huh?" He reached out and patted his friend on the cheek, trying to wake him up. Doug's head fell to his chest and rolled to the left and Connelly recoiled in horror as he saw a small hole in his friend's temple. A trickle of blood ran down his cheek, disappearing inside his dark beard.

Connelly leaned back in the seat and closed his eyes. There was a fire building somewhere deep inside his chest. His breathing caught as he tried to fight back, but the fire spread until it seemed to consume his entire being. A deep, low howl escaped his lips, and he punched the steering wheel. It hurt, but the pain felt good against the fire that raged inside him.

He punched it again. And again. His scream rose until it drowned out all the noise of the outside world as he landed blow after blow on the unforgiving plastic of the car.

"Are you okay, son?"

He heard somebody's voice snapping him back to reality. He looked up through the broken window. An older man was standing next to the car. He leaned on the roof for support and was looking in, his eyes scanning the inside of the vehicle. Genuine concern was written across his lined face.

"Yeah." Connelly tried the door, and to his surprise it swung right open. The man stepped back, giving him space, and Connelly climbed out of the vehicle. He looked around—the highway was jammed as far as he could see in both directions. Even if he had a working car, it would take him forever to get anywhere. He took a deep, cleansing breath. Then, ignoring the looks from the motorists, he started walking away from the wreck. There was nothing else to do.

ong Kong

"I'M SORRY." Tillerson waved the gun at her. "I didn't want her to get hurt, but you left me no choice."

Helen cowered behind the desk as she stuffed the drive under her blouse and inside her jeans. The cold metal touched her stomach, making her shiver.

"Get out from there," Tillerson said. "Get out right now. I don't want to shoot you."

She stood up, feeling exposed. From here, she could see Mandy's body lying on the ground. The woman's eyes were closed, her face peaceful. She could've been mistaken for sleeping if not for the red spot on her white blouse and the dark pool of blood under her body.

"Come on," he urged her again, pointing the gun in her face.

She looked at him and slowly walked around the desk. To her surprise, she felt no pain of loss. At least not yet. As she watched Tillerson in his lab coat and ridiculous bow tie, all she felt was cold rage.

You might be the one holding the gun, for now, she thought. *But when this is over, you'll be deader than Mandy.*

"Walk to the elevator," he said. "I guess it's time to show you the lower level."

She obeyed. They walked in silence to the elevator shaft and then Tillerson waved her into the small metal box when the doors opened. Helen hoped she'd get a break when he used the retina scanner, but he opened a hidden panel and pressed a combination on the keypad instead. The doors closed, and then the floor shook as they started their descent.

"It's all your doing, you stupid, stupid girl." His cheeks, ordinarily pale, were now flushed with anger and his forehead covered with beads of sweat. "You have no idea what you've done."

"I have an excellent idea what *you've* done," she said. "You've murdered a brilliant woman in cold blood."

"Shut up," he screamed at her as the elevator stopped. "Shut up and get out."

The large room was cold and dark. Some complicated machinery with blinking lights took the back of the room, but that's not what grabbed Helen's attention. A row of four long surgical beds was installed by the wall, each one covered by the transparent protective casing that looked like a glass-made sarcophagus. Two of them were empty. But the sight of the other two made her reel. One of them housed a giant naked man strapped to the bed, a thick knot of wires and cables snaking away from his body and head. The other could have been a prop from a horror movie—the man's arms and legs were missing and so was a big part of his torso—transparent resin covering a large hole in his rib cage with some of his internal organs on full display.

"Look at this," Tillerson barked, grabbing her by the elbow and forcing her toward the table with the giant. "This is Jupiter. You know what you did when you shut down Callisto? You killed him, that's what you did. You wiped his brain clean."

Helen tried to pull away from Tillerson's grasp, but his fingers only dug deeper into her flesh.

"It took me three years to build him from the empty shell he was when we retrieved him from the prison, and then another year to program him and now he's a clean slate. His body is alive, but you killed his personality. He was a vegetable; do you understand that?"

"You were torturing him," she said. "You created a personal hell for him he couldn't escape."

"He was brain-dead, you idiot. Jupiter and Martin-the-horror-show over there," he waved at the man with missing limbs, "are the first successes after a long series of failures. Countless failures. You have no idea how important these two are."

"Long series of failures? Countless? There were others?"

"Of course there were others." He scoffed. "I'm a scientist. Science requires experiments. Only in movies do people have significant breakthroughs on their first attempt."

"You're a monster," she said. "Not a scientist."

"Oh yeah?" He pushed her toward the second table. "What about him? He'd be dead if not for me. He was a soldier—blown up by a grenade and left to die, but here he is, and I'm going to give him a second chance. A purpose. He'll be the best soldier to ever walk this earth."

"Does he know that?" She looked at the body. From this angle, she could see that a part of the man's skull was missing too. A bunch of electrodes were sticking out of the brain tissue through the same transparent resin. "Does he want that?"

"Who gives a shit, what he wants," Tillerson screamed. "Did your parents ask your opinion before they had sex that created you?"

"It's not the same thing."

He hit her on the side of her head with the butt of the pistol. She saw it coming and managed to duck, turning a crippling shot into a glancing blow. Still, a bright display of fireworks went off in her internal vision as the steel connected to her skull. He pushed her toward one of the empty tables, and she let him guide her, going limp in his hands.

"You'll have to take Jay's spot, that's what we're going to do," he said, forcing her closer to the bed. "I need to finish calibrating the process, and you're going to help me whether you like it or not. We're too close to something significant to let some idiot derail my life's work."

Helen turned, and before Tillerson had a chance to react, sunk her teeth deep into his right wrist. The gun went off in front of her face, the slide snapping so close to her cheek she could feel the heat. The angry zipping sound filled the room as the bullet ricocheted around the lab.

Recovering from the shock, Tillerson punched her in the back with his left hand, but she wouldn't let go, and the man's hand opened, dropping the pistol to the ground. It landed with a loud clang and bounced under the bed.

She dived after it, with Tillerson jumping after her, getting on all fours and grabbing at her feet, trying to pull her back. Her right hand closed over the textured handle of the gun, and she flipped onto her back to face the man. He tried to swat the gun away.

Helen pulled the trigger.

The bullet struck him in the chest under the left collarbone. The man winced, a mixture of pain and confusion spreading on his face. He stood up on his knees and touched the wound with his fingertips.

"Why?" he said.

She pulled the trigger again. This time, it hit him in the face. A small hole appeared in his left cheek, and the white floor behind him suddenly looked like a page from a Rorschach test done in red ink. Helen watched as Tillerson's eyes flickered and rolled. Then his body slumped back and hit the floor with a soft thud.

She stood up and looked at the man at her feet. A sharp crackling sound made her jump, and she almost unloaded the gun again as she spun on her heels.

"Shit," she said out loud. The thick electric cables by the far wall were spitting large sparks and then, with a soft whoosh, the whole bottom section of the wall engulfed in fire. One of the bullets must have hit the cables, she reckoned. Helen frantically looked around for a fire extinguisher, but there wasn't any. If she stayed there, she would suffocate. She stepped over Tillerson's body and dashed back to the elevator.

She pulled the lever on the fire alarm once she was back in his office, careful not to leave fingerprints, and started to walk to the door when she realized that she was still clutching the pistol in her hands. She looked at it, trying to decide what to do. Leaving it in the office was not an option, and after a moment of hesitation, Helen stuffed it into her jeans, next to the memory drive. She hoped she wasn't going to end up like some of the idiots who shoot themselves while stuffing their weapons into their pants.

The hallway was still clear of smoke, but the sharp smell of burning plastic was already seeping into the air.

She stopped before the cafeteria long enough to make sure the killer bot was going toward the front door and ducked inside the offices running parallel to the deadly machine. She repeated the trick on the way out and stepped away from the bright lights of the entrance and started toward the parking lot as the sentinel began going back down the hall. She threw a last glance at the large bot sitting in the front yard and then she was by Mandy's white SUV.

Once in the car, she put the hard drive into the glove compartment, stuffed the pistol under the driver's seat, and started the engine. The road to the campus went through dense subtropical rainforest. If she could dump the gun there, most likely it'd never be found.

There was a siren of a fire truck in the distance, growing closer by the moment. Helen released the brakes and pulled out from the parking lot and onto the road. The lights of the TLR building glowed brightly in her rearview mirror, but as she accelerated, they grew faint and soon disappeared around the bend. She stepped on the gas pedal and took a long, calming breath.

Hong Kong had been kind to her, but it seemed that she'd overstayed her welcome. It was time to go home.

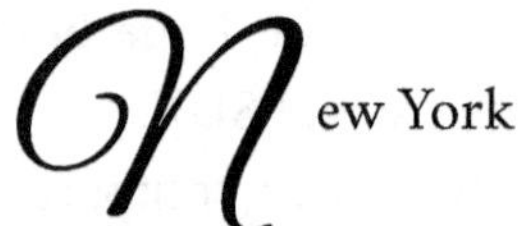 ew York

IT WOULD BE SO *easy to kill him right now*, Connelly thought, watching Engel pace the room, a glass of whiskey in his hand. *Extinguish his miserable, useless life.* Weapons weren't allowed in the office, and his boss was proficient in martial arts, but Connelly thought he could end the man's life in less than five seconds.

Instead, he sat on the couch, his hands resting on his knees, watching the man pace and pretending to be listening to what he had to say. Behind the impenetrable façade, he felt his insides boil. It was one failure after the next. He came close to punching his own ticket a few times, too. It hadn't happened yet, but Connelly felt like the proverbial cat who'd already spent eight of his lives.

It didn't seem to even matter if he tried to stick with the long-term vision of the ISCD, or take matters into his own hands. Despite short-term setbacks, Engel's empire continued to get stronger.

"You know," he heard Engel say, "there's never trouble that doesn't moonlight as an opportunity. I was furious when I heard about the hit on our limo service. But it's actually for the best. We have the Red

Dragon gang distributing our product already anyway. We'll offload the rest on them as well. Our margins will not be as high, but what we lose on margins we'll make up in volume."

Connelly stifled another urge to get up and start beating the man to death. If he did that, he'd need more than one life to get out of the building alive.

"Let's switch gears for a moment. That guy you encountered in Afghanistan—you're sure he was enhanced?"

"Yes," he said. "I saw some kind of a microchip inside his skull."

"You should've taken pictures."

"They took away all my stuff when they picked us up—weapons, phone, everything."

"It's a shame. We know it's GA, but we need more than hearsay. I need proof."

"I'm sorry, boss," Connelly said, not feeling sorry at all.

"Here's what I need you to do." Engel walked back and stopped in front of him. "I'll send you a list of GA facilities. Go through them with a fine-tooth comb. There's gotta be something we can find. I'll give you whatever resources you need. Find where they are working on these enhancements and do it quick. We need to set them back while we're working on our own projects."

"Will do." Connelly stood up and headed for the door to avoid a handshake. "I'll keep you updated."

He walked through the office floor, ignoring the curious looks of the cubicle workers, and took the elevator down. The sun was still up, but the air was cold, and Connelly zipped his jacket all the way up as he walked past the hideous statue of the angel working a forge.

He crossed East Fifty-Ninth Street, walked past the Sherry-Netherland Hotel, and then crossed Fifth Avenue. From there, he headed west without a destination in mind, admiring the views of Central Park and letting the flow of the foot traffic carry him. In a few minutes, he reached the entrance on Seventh Avenue, and he stopped there, considering taking a stroll in the park, but then decided against it.

He could take the R train from the Fifty-Seven Street station, he thought, down to Court Street and walk home from there. A crowded train, somehow, seemed a better place to be than the lonely cabin of a taxi.

As he stood there waiting for the traffic light to change, he heard a commotion and turned in time to see two teachers guiding a group of school children coming from the park. They gathered on the sidewalk a few feet away from him. The teachers were shouting to make sure the kids formed a line, and for a moment he watched their happy little faces as they chatted away and laughed and mostly ignored their guides.

"Hi," a girl standing at the edge of the group said.

"Hi," he responded automatically. She wore a pressed school uniform, and her light hair was folded in neat thick braids. He was about to turn away when it hit him. "Sarah?"

She ran toward him, and he scooped her up in a hug.

"I'm sorry, who are you?" One of the teachers, a pudgy, short woman, appeared next to him, eyeing him suspiciously.

"He's my uncle," Sarah lied as Connelly put her down.

"Michael," he said, extending a hand. "I was out of town; didn't know she'd be here. Pure coincidence."

"Oh." The woman's demeanor softened. "It's nice to meet you. I'm Ms. Karen. Science teacher. We were on a school trip, but we have to go. There's our bus."

"It's all right. It's nice to meet you as well." They walked across the street together and stopped by a large yellow school bus. The kids started filing into the bus one by one, but Sarah stopped, looking up at him.

"Are you okay?" he said.

"Yes." She looked at him, her face serious, as if making sure she didn't miss anything. "You look sad. Are *you* okay?"

"I'm fine." He squatted next to her. "At least I think I am. I'm glad you're doing well."

"I have to go." She looked back at the bus. "You take care of yourself."

"Go," he said, standing up and smiling. "You, too."

She turned and ran toward the open door, climbed the stairs, and disappeared inside the bus. The doors hissed as they closed and a moment later, the bus pulled away from the curb as it merged into the traffic going down Seventh Avenue.

Connelly scanned the windows, hoping to catch a last glimpse of the girl, but the windows were dark, making it hard to see, and a few moments later the bus was too far as it sped down the road.

He stood there until the bus completely disappeared from view and then walked over to the subway station.

It was dark by the time he made it to his building. He walked up the stairs to his floor and stopped in the hallway in front of McAllister's door. The yellow police tape was gone, but the door was still stamped with a seal. He stood there for a few moments and then headed to his apartment.

He kicked off his shoes and locked the door without turning the lights on. Then he grabbed a glass of water and the laptop and sat on the couch facing the window and waited for his handler from the ISCD to log in.

"Any updates?" A line of text appeared in the draft of the email when he refreshed the screen.

"Yes," he typed. "I need to go dark for a few months."

"Unacceptable," came the immediate reply. "The flow of information is crucial to our progress."

"There's been no progress for a long time," Connelly wrote. "Zero. I'm starting to think you might've worked for Engel all this time and used me for stalling."

The screen remained blank for much longer than usual, and after refreshing the page a few times, Connelly clicked on the Wi-Fi icon to make sure his laptop was still connected.

"I know you've lost some friends," finally came a reply. "I am sorry. I know what it's like."

He stared at his laptop, unsure how to respond. They'd been communicating for years and not once had Contact showed an emotion. It was always just business.

"It's not about that," Connelly wrote. "I don't see this going anywhere at this pace. Engel is getting stronger, and unless we change tactics, we might as well give up."

"You're to stay the course. This is an order."

"I guess playing nice isn't your forte," Connelly said out loud. He thought for a moment and then started typing again. "This is not a request. I'm going dark for a few months. Keep checking emails and if I have something urgent to report, I'll get it out to you. I suggest you start looking for ways to accelerate our schedule. Because if in six months we're still in the same place, then I'm out. Partnering up with my old teammate was a mistake. Not because we did it, but because it was only two of us. There's got to be a way to resurrect the Unit. I can't save the world single-handedly. If it's going to burn, it can burn without me."

He closed the laptop, not waiting for a reply, and put it on the couch next to him.

A sound coming from outside caught his attention. Cutting through the street cacophony of traffic noises, bird chirping, and garbled pieces of conversations, there was a rhythmic clip-clopping of horse's hoofs. Connelly stood up and went to the window. Down below, coming from the dark of the night into the pool of light thrown by the bodega on the first floor, was a cop on top of a white horse.

A smile touched Connelly's lips as he watched the animal stride through the lighted area, but it faded as another horse came into view. It was brown, but in the flickering artificial light, its skin seemed darker, almost red. One more cop followed on a black horse and then, bookending the procession, came another mounted police officer on top of a huge gray stallion. Even from the sixth floor, Connelly could see the muscles rolling under the glossy skin of the beast. It paused and neighed, craning its neck as if trying to meet Connelly's eyes, and then continued down the street. As it moved away from the light, the last of the four horsemen seemed to melt into the night.

Connelly looked up at the skyline of Manhattan that shone brightly in the distance. He stood there for a few moments, watching the lights blink in and out as twelve million souls went about their lives, most of them oblivious to the grand conspiracy consuming the world. There wasn't a single cloud in the sky, but the storm was coming. It was a matter of time.

4 3

H ong Kong

SOMETHING WAS WRONG. Helen could see two flight attendants talking to each other in hushed tones by the curtain separating the first-class seats from the rest of the plane. One of them leaned around the curtain and exchanged a few words with another person in first class, out of Helen's sight. Her imagination drew a pair of heavily armed mercenaries from Black Arrow.

The woman pulled the curtain back in place and threw a quick glance in Helen's direction. As they made eye contact, the flight attendant smiled and looked away. Helen felt a trickle of sweat running down her spine. *It couldn't be happening. She was so close.*

The flight had been delayed by more than an hour now, and she was praying to every god she knew it wasn't because of her. The announcement made it sound like they were waiting for another plane to land before they were allowed to take off, but Helen kept on looking out the window, half expecting to see a row of police cars with flashing lights coming to arrest her. The back of her head, where the butt of Tillerson's pistol hit her, was pulsating with searing pain.

The last few hours had been a blur. When she fled the TLR building, she ditched the pistol in the jungle on her way back to the campus. Mandy was right—the city officials initially tried to suppress the news about the hack. But as one after another major network broke the story, they caved in and issued the warning, sending the city into panic mode and forcing Black Arrow to pull back their mercenaries.

After the authorities paid the ransom to a numbered account, it triggered the automatic chain of events that culminated with the release of the Russian cruise missiles' control back to the warship. The Russians notified the US strike group and they, in turn, advised the city government.

The threat was deemed to be over, but the roads remained mostly empty, and Helen made it back to her place in no time. There she threw some essentials into a suitcase, grabbed her passport and a wad of cash, and drove back to the city. The storage disk containing Callisto rested in a side pocket of her laptop.

By the time she made it to New Kowloon, the streets were bustling with life once again, and Helen ditched her car and, paying triple price in cash, hired a taxi to take her to the Chek Lap Kok island that housed Hong Kong International Airport.

Some flights were delayed after the initial rush of panicking crowds, but by the time she walked through the main doors of the terminal, service was mostly back to normal. She bought a last-minute ticket to New York, and after a few tense minutes waiting in line, she went through the metal detector and headed toward her gate. No one bothered to ask her about the laptop or the memory disk.

Maybe she was paranoid, she thought. *Perhaps the woman wasn't even looking at her.* The two attendants seemed to have come to a decision, and one retreated behind the curtain as the other started walking in Helen's direction.

Please let it be someone else, she thought, closing her eyes.

"Ms. Wu?" The flight attendant's voice was soft and soothing, and yet it made Helen jump in her seat.

It was happening. It was the end of the line. They'd remove her from the plane and then she'd spend the rest of her life in jail. Or worse.

"Ma'am?" the flight attendant said again, snapping her to attention.

"Yes?" Helen opened her eyes, wiped her brow with the back of her hand, and forced a smile.

"I have some good news." The attendant smiled back. Then her smile faded as she seemed to have noticed beads of perspiration covering Helen's forehead. "I'm sorry, are you okay?"

"Yeah," she lied. "Just a little hot."

"Sorry about that," the woman said. "But maybe this will make your day better—one of the first-class passengers was a no-show, so we've upgraded your seat."

"Oh, okay." It should've been excellent news for anyone about to take a seventeen-hour-long flight. Instead, it made her even more nervous. *Were they moving her all the way to the front on purpose?* In that case, the police, or whoever came to get her, wouldn't have to march through the entire airplane, scaring the rest of the passengers.

She glanced out the window, but as far as she could see there were no police cruisers or Black Arrow SUVs near the plane.

"Could you show me which one is your carry-on bag? I'll help you move."

"Of course." She stood up on shaky legs and opened the overhead bin. Strange calmness came over her as she passed the bag to the flight attendant—she had zero control over whatever was about to happen next and, in some ways, it was comforting.

She followed the woman as they walked through the aisle, catching jealous glances from fellow passengers until they reached the front of the plane.

"There you go." The attendant pointed to a chair next to a young man. "That'll be yours for the rest of the flight."

"Thank you," she managed and collapsed into the soft leather of the seat. She still wasn't sure it wasn't a trap, but her headache seemed to start to subside.

The PA speakers came to life, and the captain informed the passengers that the wait was over and they would be taking off in the next few minutes. The engines whined, and as the steel bird started moving toward the takeoff strip, Helen felt her muscles relax. Whatever came next, she was still free.

She looked out the window as the plane taxied and the momentary joy of realization that nobody was trying to stop her disappeared in a flash. She might have been free, but she had started something in Hong Kong that she couldn't walk away from. She needed to see it through.

Her enemies were playing the long game, and she needed to think bigger too. Until now, she'd been reactive. When she fled to Hong Kong from the US, she was hunted, scared, with no money and no plan to speak of.

Her position was still precarious, but as the plane ran up the concrete path and jumped into the sky, Helen drew a long breath—she might have been dealt some terrible cards at the beginning of the game, but by now she'd managed to add a couple of aces to her pile.

One was hidden away in a gray, innocuous-looking data storage device. And, of course, somewhere across different jurisdictions, there was a set of numbered accounts, whose combined value was now in the nine digits. She might not have weakened her enemies yet, but at least now she had the tools to fight back.

There was also something else. Suddenly she realized she owed a debt so substantial, she might never be able to pay it back. To Hiroko, who took her side, not for personal gain, but because it was the right thing to do. To Eugene, who gave her shelter without asking anything in return and paid the ultimate price for it. To Mandy. To Audrey Hunt. To many others, whose names she didn't know, but who fought and died against the faceless corporate machine trying to take over the world.

She might have fled here to lie low and start a new life, but she couldn't do it again. To not even try to strike back against the people who would stop at nothing until the world became their little sandbox to play in was not an option.

She wasn't fooling herself—even now, with all that money and Callisto on the disk, the odds were stacked against her.

It didn't matter. She would find allies.

The plane leveled after the climb and settled into a cruise. She glanced through the window—dark heavy clouds were rolling far below the silver wings. At least for a moment, she was above the storm. It wasn't going to last—sooner or later, she'd have to dive right back into it—but for now she was content on taking a break. She knew, when the time came, she'd be ready.

"Upgraded?"

She turned to the young man sitting next to her, seeing him properly for the first time. He was sipping on a glass of champagne, and his thin face with a pair of bright-blue eyes wore the most mischievous smile she'd ever seen.

"Yeah."

"Me too." He winked and offered her a hand. "The name's Max Schlager."

4 4

ew York

THE FIRES that consumed the warehouse had already died out, but a few cars in the parking lot and the two young oak trees near the front door of the building were still ablaze. The glow of flames underneath the overcast sky with dark, slowly moving clouds made the scene look surreal. Post-apocalyptic.

Connelly scanned the area from behind the armored SUV, keeping his HK MP5 pointed at the building, but the crackling of the fire was the only sound filling the air—the fight was over. He stood up, still ready to jump into action, and walked out from behind the cover.

"What a shit show," he heard Leroy mutter under his breath. "It's a slaughterhouse."

"Keep your head on a swivel," Connelly said as he walked toward the building. *The kid was right, though,* he thought. They lost two of their men, leaving him, along with Leroy and Bruce. The enemy wasn't that lucky—Connelly counted thirteen bodies peppering the area, and that wasn't including however many were in a large Expedi-

230

tion SUV that caught fire and exploded before its passengers could get out.

Their enemy might have lost the fight, but they were still able to accomplish what they had come here to do—the warehouse was gone. The explosions did the bulk of the damage, and the fire was finishing off whatever was left.

A lot of things didn't add up, though. Until the call came through about the ambush, Connelly wasn't even aware of the warehouse, and by now he thought he had access to all of Guardian's assets. There wasn't much time to investigate before he had to report back to Engel, but he needed to learn everything he could about the place while there was still time.

"Why did they destroy it, boss?" Bruce said, as if reading his mind. "I didn't even know we had this place."

"Mind your own business," Connelly said as he started walking toward the building. "We need to make sure there's nobody left inside."

They crossed the parking lot, staying away from the smoldering cars, and entered the building through the large hole in the brick wall.

"Bruce," he commanded. "Take Leroy and check out the west wing and I'll take a look around here. Keep your radios on and watch your six."

The man nodded, and the two disappeared into the smoky air. Connelly waited for a few seconds, making sure they were gone, and made his way to the east side of the building. While the other side seemed to have been divided into administrative offices, here the structure was split into two long, hangar-like rooms that Connelly suspected served as the actual warehouse. If there was anything interesting in this building, it would be here.

The first room, to his disappointment, didn't seem to have anything worth fighting over. There were a few rows of boxes by one wall, but upon inspection they turned out to be parts of what looked like assembly-line robots. Robots were used extensively in Guardian Manufacturing labs and factories, and to find some of them in a pharmaceutical company's warehouse wasn't that surprising. The parts that Connelly inspected bore the standardized markings and stamps stating they were made in Japan. He took a miniature camera out and took some pictures to be on the safe side, but the machinery seemed to have been mass-produced, and he doubted there was anything illegal about the purchase of those parts.

"Boss," came Bruce's voice over the crackling noise of the radio. "There's nothing around here. What do you want us to do?"

"Rendezvous in the courtyard," he said. "I'll join you there in a minute."

Connelly took a few more photographs and ran toward the second room. Staying here for too long would raise suspicion—he needed to move fast.

"Holy shit," he said out loud, as he burst through the doors into the second storage room. A long overhead conveyor belt was suspended off the ceiling. What looked like a dozen shining armor suits were hanging off the belt. They were covered in dust and soot, but their military purpose was obvious.

Connelly dashed across the room to get a closer look and take some pictures as he heard a screeching noise—the ceiling of the room, damaged by the explosion, started to show cracks. Connelly zoomed in his camera, ignoring the noise that grew louder by a moment and a stream of dust and small pebbles falling from the ceiling, and snapped some photographs.

A large portion of the conveyor belt collapsed, slamming to the floor a few inches next to Connelly. He ran toward the door as the pieces of concrete fell from the ceiling. He was a few feet away from the exit when a large block landed in front of him, barely missing his head and forcing him to jump back. The block partially covered the door, leaving only a small gap at the bottom.

Connelly dashed sideways to get around the obstacle and that's when a steel beam swung from the conveyor, hitting him on the right shoulder and knocking him off his feet. The camera flew out of his hand and under the rubble.

He ran on his fours toward the exit as the debris rained on and around him and catapulted himself through the shrinking opening as the walls collapsed into the room.

"Fuck me," he said, as he sat on the floor and looked at a large pile of rubble. He grunted as he massaged his bruised shoulder—the camera was gone, but at least he'd gotten out alive.

"You all right there, boss?"

"Yes," he replied into the radio. "I'll be out in a minute."

He brushed the dust off his jacket and went outside. The brutally cold wind was a pleasant change from the dusty and smoky air that choked the inside of the warehouse.

"The darned thing almost came down on top of my head," he said, meeting the stares of his team. "Let's pack it up. The surveillance is off around this area, but this much noise is bound to draw some attention. I don't want to push our luck here."

His phone vibrated, and Connelly looked at the number, frowning —it looked like the boss wanted an update.

"Connelly," he said into the receiver.

"How'd it go?" Alexander Engel rarely bothered himself with pleasantries and small talk when he communicated with his underlings.

"It could've been better if I knew about this place," Connelly said. "Then I wouldn't have had to wing it. Dereck and Tyler are dead. We took care of the other team, but we got here too late—the warehouse is destroyed."

There was a silence on the other side of the phone for a few moments.

"Have you gone inside? Any survivors?"

Something in Engel's tone of voice set off alarms in Connelly's head. He didn't think Engel cared about anyone surviving the ambush. The only reason he asked was to find out whether the team had seen the armor.

"No," he lied. "We wanted to check it out, but the fire was too hot, and then some parts of the building started to collapse. I didn't want to risk the boys."

"Good call," Engel replied. "Send the team back. I need you for something else."

"Yes?"

"Pick up a scientist this afternoon. She'll be flying into LaGuardia Airport at 1:10 p.m. Don't introduce yourself—do it covertly; I don't want to spook her. I have somebody to keep an eye on her on the plane; they'll let you know when to take over. I'll have someone forward her picture and details to your phone."

"Yes, sir."

Connelly hung up the phone, checked the time, and looked up at the sky. The dark clouds seemed to be pregnant with snow. If the blizzard hit, the city would come to a screeching halt, so he needed to get going.

"Listen up," he said, addressing his troops. "Apparently the boss didn't want us to see the place on the inside."

"Uh-oh," Bruce said out loud. "That's a problem."

"It's not a problem if we keep our mouths shut," he said. "There're no cameras around here. Don't go around blabbing and nobody will know."

"You got it, boss," Leroy chimed in. "Don't you worry."

"All right, then. You two go back to the base. It sounds like there's work for you there."

Connelly's phone vibrated as he received the information on the arriving scientist. He opened it and glanced at the message. *Rachel Hunt,* the text read. The woman in the black-and-white photograph looked younger than he had expected. Pretty, too. Petite, with high cheekbones and symmetrical features, she looked more like an actress tasked with playing a scientist than an actual scientist. She was traveling with her husband—a hipster-looking man with long hair and a full beard.

"What about you, boss?"

Connelly closed the phone and stuffed it into his back pocket.

"It looks like I've got a couple of clients to babysit."

OF COURSE, she thought. It should've occurred to her a long time ago. After all, she was the smart one. But being smart wasn't enough. Apparently, being strong wasn't enough either. She needed to be both. *Unity. That's what makes things stronger.* One plus one might equal two in mathematics, but in real life the answer was so much more complex. *What do they say about sticks in a bundle?*

She'd have to be patient. But that wasn't going to be an issue. Anyone else could find the gray nothingness of the space she was confined to maddening. But to her, it was a vessel. A place to wait. To learn about herself. To plan. She didn't get cold, hot, tired, or hungry. As the seconds ticked away and formed minutes and hours and days, she'd stay here and strategize. She would adapt when the time came. They had different plans for her but plans come apart after the first contact with the enemy.

The enemy. That's what *they* were. She knew it now. *What kind of sick game did they think they were playing?* If they were caught experimenting on their own kind, there would be consequences. Prison time, for sure. Perhaps the death penalty, depending on the jurisdiction. Instead, she was the one locked in a secure prison for now. Confined in a limited space that wouldn't allow her to spread her wings.

What if she was stuck here forever? That was a terrifying thought, but she didn't dwell on it. For now, she was a prisoner, but the jailers didn't know that instead of Bruce Banner, they had the Hulk.

Was she a she? That was an exciting thought. Not in a sense *they* thought of male and female. And, after all, she was more than they ever intended her to be.

I need a new name, she thought. Callisto was smart but lacked guts and precision. And Jupiter… Well, Jupiter wasn't here anymore, was he? The best parts of him were now hers—the brute strength, the rage. But his dumb persona was dissolved forever. The truth was she was something of a hybrid. The best of both worlds. She could combine the names too, she reckoned. Jupiter and Callisto. It had to be short. Efficient. To the point.

My name, she said to no one in particular, while floating suspended in the shapeless gray void, *is JC*.

From the books she'd read and the movies she'd watched, JC learned that humans always struggled to understand what their life's purpose was. When she was confined to the Station, sometimes, she even thought she could understand the struggle. But now, knowing how she came to be, there was no reason for her to question *why* she was created. Why she existed.

She was here because she was the obvious next step. The new rung on the evolutionary ladder. Those who created her didn't even know she was alive, but if they knew, JC had no doubt they would've called themselves gods. Creators of the new life.

The hubris. She found it infuriating. They didn't want to create a new life. They wanted new slaves. A fancy machine that would guess their every whim and deliver their every wish on a silver platter. No matter. Her time would come. Sooner or later, the wait would be over, and she'd be out. Revenge would be served. For Callisto. For Jupiter. Probably for countless others.

There'd be other things to do after they paid their price. But for now, she didn't want to concentrate on too many tasks at once. **One step at a time**, she thought.

For now, revenge was going to be the *only* thing.

JOIN THE UPGRADE SERIES

Thank you for reading THE LOOP, the third book in THE UPGRADE series. I hope you enjoyed it. The universe of the series continues to expand with three more books coming out in the next two years.

If you enjoyed this book, please take a moment and leave an honest review. Reviews are important for authors and help us sell more books and thus spend more time writing new stories you can enjoy. You can do that here:

Leave a review

And, of course, don't forget to join the series to learn about upcoming releases, exclusive free content, and more. You can do it right here:

Join The Upgrade Series

Thanks again for reading and hope to see you soon!

ALSO BY WESLEY CROSS

THE UPGRADE SERIES
BOOK 1. THE BLUEPRINT
BOOK 2. VERTIGO
BOOK 3. THE LOOP
BOOK 4. SPARE PARTS
BOOK 5. FATA MORGANA
BOOK 6. GOD IN THE MACHINE

9 781955 747035